# THE GIVING STAR

## SWAY OF THE STARS BOOK 3

## FRANCES DALL'ALBA

Poinsettia
Publishing

# Also By Frances Dall'Alba

<u>Australian At Heart Series</u>
Little Blue Box - Book 1
The Stone In The Road - Book 2
The Silk Scarf - Book 3
Rustic Denim Love – Book 4

<u>Sway Of The Stars Series</u>
The Shooting Star – Book 1
The Glittering Star – Book 2
The Giving Star – Book 3
The Priceless Star – Book 4

<u>Standalone Books</u>
Eight Seconds
Jack& Eva

THE GIVING STAR



ISBN: 978-0-6451162-8-1

*To those who unearth the past, one bone at a time.*
*Our world is a better place for that knowledge.*

# Chapter 1

S ally Barkworth snuggled the ragdoll cat under her chin, giving it a loving hug. "You poor thing," she whispered, "stuck here for months without your family." She'd bathed the cat that morning and inhaled its fresh, clean animal scent.

She would miss this place and all its fury animals she found hard to part with.

Dean, eyes brimming with tears, walked up to her and reached out for the cat. "I wish they weren't coming for him, Sal."

Sally passed the cat over and missed the warmth against her chest.

"I know he should be with his family." Dean nuzzled his face into the cat's fur. "Loved and cared for, but I don't know how I'm going to part with him."

"I know, Dean. I'm sorry this has happened to you. You must understand this family has been missing their pet for four months now and our information on file would've confused anyone if they'd rung checking for him."

Sally's heart contracted as she watched Dean talk with the ragdoll. She would miss this soft-hearted young man with his scruffy reddish hair and a splattering of freckles over his face and arms. They'd become a team, volunteering together on the weekends at the local council animal pound.

His attachment to this cat was going to test him to the max, though. When its owner arrived, she wasn't so sure how Dean would react.

He'd succumbed to the adorable cat's gentle personality, with its soft greyish-white fur and mottled brown face.

With the cat secure in Dean's arms, he cooed in its ear as a thin trickle of tears dripped down his cheeks and into the cat's fur. Although the cat didn't seem bothered by it, Sally worried about Dean, who was navigating adulthood after a traumatic childhood.

While Dean interacted with the placid cat, Sally finally released a sigh of relief. In sheer desperation, because no one had claimed this well-cared-for pet, Sally inspected it herself and was horrified to discover they'd tagged it as a female when it was quite obviously a male. Further inspection revealed a hidden microchip with enough contact details to locate the owner.

Not that the phone number dialled countless times for days was answered. Nor were the calls returned after leaving messages. Sally was desperate. She'd made it her last mission before leaving Malanda to find this cat's family, so why didn't they answer the damn phone?

Finally, yesterday, a message came through. Someone by the name of Ben apologised for taking so long to reply but had been out of phone reception, mustering on his family's property out west.

Sally frowned, confused about how the cat would've ended up in Malanda if it didn't live in the area. She shook her head and let it slide. More mystery surrounded this cat than an Agatha Christie book.

"I'm going to miss you, too, Sal."

"Oh, Dean, I'll miss you so much. How about you put the cat back, and we'll have our afternoon tea? I brought some chocolate muffins with me today."

Dean smiled, striding away towards the animal enclosures. Dean was someone who always appreciated her baking. At the grand old age of thirty-one, Sally sometimes felt like his mother. A young man of twenty-three should be at his peak, but Dean was taking a little more time to catch up with the rest of the world. Locked inside, though, was a thoughtful and kind person. Sally wished the best for him.

As a teacher, Sally was good with troubled kids. She had a knack for it. Not all kids were bad. Most just needed a change of scenery and something good to focus on.

Her skills were about to be tested, though. Richmond in outback Western Queensland was where she was heading. A small place, but she hoped it offered a huge opportunity for troubled kids.

She crossed her fingers as she walked towards the small kitchenette. If her outback plans allowed, she wouldn't hesitate to invite Dean to assist with the life skills program. She could use someone like him, with his infinite patience and the ability to connect with the rejected, hurt and unloved. Human or animal.

With the kettle on, Sally leant against the sink, waiting for the water to boil, taking a moment to assess her life. The reasons she'd instigated change. Friends, cousins, all those about her age were moving on. Creating families and having children. Somehow, she'd been left behind.

So, why move to a small outback community where the population was less than a thousand? If she'd had no success in finding a soulmate in a community of thousands, how was she going to find anyone when the pool was so much smaller?

*Ugh!* She raked a hand through her shoulder-length blonde hair. *Stop it!* Having a family wasn't crucial to her happiness. This outback project would allow her to be a mother in so many other ways. The troubled kids who would be sent to her needed all the love they could get, and she had plenty to spare.

The kettle whistled and she took down two mugs from the shelf above the sink, placing them on the bench. Removing a spoon out of the top drawer, she jammed it shut a little harder than necessary. The gaping hole in her life had got bigger of late. Her cousin Liz now had a six-month-old daughter. Her best friend, Roberta, was getting married in six months.

More overwhelmed than normal, she'd instigated changes in her life, hoping this passion for helping troubled kids would help push aside the nagging inside her head that wouldn't go away. The regret she carried with her every day.

*You've got this girl!*

She fist-pumped the air to an audience of just herself and took a deep breath. There was still so much to do. School term began in less than two weeks. She needed to be settled and sorted in her new town very soon. Her home in Malanda was packed and ready to lease out, and her excess belongings would be stored on her parents' farm. This had to work. It was the biggest change in her life so far, and there was no turning back.

*Richmond, here I come.*

On autopilot, she reached for the coffee jar.

"Excuse me."

So lost in her thoughts, Sally jumped at the stranger's voice, her hand connecting with one of the mugs. It rolled to its side and teetered on the edge of the bench. In a split-second reaction, she lunged for it, making a heroic attempt to save it from crashing onto the hard concrete floor.

*Saved!*

Except her hand brushed against the second mug. No way was she going to save that one. The crashing sound of the ceramic mug hitting the concrete floor echoed around the small space. Shards splintered in all directions.

"Oh, shite!" She bit her tongue before something else came out. Not professional at all!

"Is everything okay?" Dean peered at her from behind the stranger, puffing like he'd run miles to check on her.

When she looked up, it was the stranger's face she connected with. An unimpressed expression met her, like this was her fault, which it technically was, and could she please hurry up because he had places to go.

To the side of where the stranger stood in the doorway, Dean hovered, partially hidden behind him. "I'm fine, Dean, thank you. I'll bring out the morning tea in a few minutes."

"Is there a broom and dustpan here?" the stranger asked, eyes darting around the kitchenette.

"He's here for the cat," a teary Dean said, before turning away and leaving.

*Damn!* She would need to clean the mess quickly, then deal with Dean and the rollercoaster of emotions he would experience once the cat was gone.

"Over there." She pointed to the corner where a broom was propped and the dustpan and its brush left untidily on the floor beside it. Vivid green eyes latched onto hers as his tall frame moved inside, dwarfing the small sectioned-off room.

She averted her gaze, only managing to look as far as his hips, nicely hugged by denim jeans. She glanced away, reminded again of the mess she'd created. Crouching, she began picking up the largest of the broken pieces when she caught a glimpse of brown R.M. Williams boots poking out from under his jeans.

As she picked up the biggest piece, her eyes distracted by the boots, a sharp twinge snaked along her finger as it grazed the sharp edge. Drops of blood quickly appeared and she dropped it.

"Damn!" she muttered, quickly rising, shaking her hand to calm the stinging.

The man put the broom down, leaning it against the wall, grabbed the roll of paper towel kept handy on the countertop, tore off a sheet and held it out. "Here, use this."

Time stilled in that awkward way as she pressed the paper towel against her cut. She bit her bottom lip, hoping to suppress the sting of pain. If she concentrated on this, and this alone, she could avoid the rush of heat racing up her neck. She was going to make a fool of herself in front of this stranger if she didn't get it together. Now!

Ben? Was this the man who'd sent the message? Dark brown curls rested against his neck. Tall and stocky. Sleeves rolled up to his elbows on his navy Ringers Western shirt. He spoke rugged outback. From the way he dressed to his casual speech, and she wasn't so averse to it. Except he was probably here to collect the cat belonging to his wife and children.

"Is there a first-aid kit somewhere?"

*Oh, for goodness' sake, girl, get it together!*

"Er ... it's Ben, right?"

He nodded, a curl falling across his forehead.

"I'm Sally. Thanks for coming today. My finger is fine. A Band-Aid will fix it, and then we can sort out your cat." Sally went to the top drawer where a sealed container held some first aid supplies and took out a couple of Band-Aids. Once she washed her finger and bound it up, she turned around to find Ben sweeping the last of the mess into the dustpan.

He tilted his head towards the garbage bin in the corner. "Can I dump it in that?"

"Yes, sure. I was making us hot drinks. Would you like one?"

"No thanks, I need to keep going. I'll just take the cat and be gone." He emptied the dustpan, the broken shards clinking as they hit the bottom of the bin.

So, he *was* in a hurry. Unfortunately for him, this was the part she didn't like to bring to their attention, but she had no choice. "We have a little paperwork to complete, and there's an outstanding fee to pay for the costs of taking care of your cat."

The metal dustpan slipped from his fingers, landing with a clang where he'd found it. "How much?" Ben asked, before bending down to click the brush back inside the dustpan and lean it against the wall.

Sally knew the amount, having gone through the paperwork that morning in preparation. She had baulked at the figure. "There's an outstanding fee of one thousand, two hundred dollars."

Ben's head snapped up, his body stiffening as she expected. Anyone would, but these were council rules.

"Even though you only contacted me earlier this week?"

"Look, I'm sorry, but I only volunteer here. When you replied to our message, I put the paperwork together. The council calculates the fee."

"You don't honestly expect me to pay that amount?"

Sally sensed his hackles rising, and with good reason.

"I phoned numerous times over the past months, and each time, I was told our cat wasn't in the pound."

Sally inwardly groaned. She knew this but stood her ground. It wasn't her place to reveal how incompetent they'd been in recording the correct details. As Ben overshadowed her, hands on hips, looking down, Sally took a deep breath. "I'm sorry, Mr ... er—"

"Just Ben, thank you, and can I talk to your supervisor, please?"

Sally straightened her shoulders, hiding her clenched hands behind her back. "I'm in charge today, and I will not be able to release your cat until the fees are paid."

Ben took a step closer and her shoulders stiffened. "I refuse to pay that ridiculous amount." Then he reached over her head for another mug. "I may as well have that drink after all and make myself comfortable because it doesn't look like I'll be leaving any time soon. I refuse to leave without my cat, and I won't be paying those charges."

"Sure, stay as long as you want. You'll have to make it yourself, though." It was bad enough the guy was rugged and good-looking, but he would not intimidate her.

Ben arched an eyebrow. "You know, even if I'd purchased the best cat food on the market, no way would I have spent that amount of money. This is highway robbery."

"I don't have a say in this matter." Sally said, taking a step away from the bench.

"Yes, you do. Get on the phone and ring your supervisor. Then pass it over, and I'll do the talking. This is unbelievable. You hold our cat for one week and then charge that amount of money?"

"We've had your cat for four months." Sally stifled a cringe. It was the truth but not entirely. On autopilot, Sally handed over a teaspoon and opened the small fridge to retrieve the milk. She added milk to the teaspoon of coffee and two sugars he'd put in the mug, giving it a quick stir with another spoon before tilting her head towards the kettle, indicating he could fill his mug.

*So much for getting him to make his own drink.*

*Clink!* The sound of the back gate shutting reverberated around the kitchenette.

She froze.

"Are you okay?"

Ben's words were enough to break the trance. The hairs on the back of her neck rose. She dashed out of the kitchenette into the covered compound where all the cages were kept. "Dean, where are you?" Her heart pounded behind her ribs. Something was amiss. When she didn't get a response, alarm bells clanged louder inside her head.

She ran around to the back section of the compound to check the area where the larger cages were kept. "Dean! Dean!" When there was no reply, she rushed back to the covered area to double-check the ragdoll's cage.

No cat!

No Dean!

*For crying out loud!* Her heart thumped harder as she remained rooted to the spot, hands on her hips and her bottom lip jammed between her teeth. Now what? This was her worst fear. Stuck between a rock and a hard place. Dean's welfare was always at the forefront of her mind, but damn it, she also had a responsibility to return the cat to its rightful owner.

Ben followed her, mug in hand, about to take another sip. "What's wrong?"

How to explain? "Um ... Dean has gone and taken your cat with him."

"What? Are you joking? What sort of place is this?" Ben returned to the kitchen.

"Look"—Sally followed him as far as the doorway—"I have a fair idea of where he's gone."

He emptied his hot drink down the drain, rinsed his cup and left it upturned in the sink. He spun around, fury scrunching his brow. "And where might that be?"

"It's within walking distance." Sally would follow the shortcut track through the forest. Dean lived with his foster parents on the outskirts of the small town. That's where she assumed he would be headed. She drew her shoulders back. "We could walk there faster if you want to come too."

"Geez, this is unbelievable. One cat. That's all I came for, not all this drama. You'd better be calling your supervisor about that ridiculous fee after all this."

"Look, you can wait here if you want and clean an enclosure or two." Her patience was wearing thin. This man could cause trouble for Dean if she didn't hurry and catch up with him. "Give me twenty minutes. I'll be back with your cat. Surely, your wife and children can wait a little longer."

"Wife?"

Sally had been about to run out of the compound when the anguish in that one word halted her steps.

All the oomph deflated from his stance, and he crumbled, leaning back on the small sink. "I don't have a wife." Pain crossed his face for a split second and vanished just as quickly.

Sally gulped. She didn't have time to second guess the story behind her careless slip. "Look ... er ... I'm really sorry. How ... how about ..." Her hands flapped helplessly. "How about you wait here? I won't be long."

"No, I'll come too." The irritated look he'd worn earlier, tight lips and narrowed eyes, was back in place. "And hurry up!"

*Great!* "Okay, follow me." She could deal with his impatience so long as Dean wasn't compromised in any way. Dean only did what was best for the animals, and sometimes, how his brain worked didn't always align with the norm. Probably a result of years of neglect and abuse by his biological mother.

But this situation was out of her control. The cat belonged to this man, and there was nothing she could do to change that. As there had been no signs of animal abuse when it was first brought in, there was nothing for her to do but hand the cat over ... once he paid the fee.

*Bugger!* Maybe she should ring her supervisor and plead leniency in this one case. Ben had so much he could hold against them, and Dean's disappearance didn't help.

How had her last mission to complete in Malanda escalated to this?

# Chapter 2

Ben Angwin kept his eyes on the rough, muddy path, his boots squelching over the smaller print of Sally's boots and another fresh boot print of about the same size as his. Sally was right in assuming this was the track Dean had used.

The animal compound looked to be positioned on the outskirts of town, fringed by moisture-dripping tropical rainforest. With more rain the previous night, oppressive mugginess cloaked his body as he followed, his thick cotton shirt sticking to his back with sweat.

A quick one hundred metres and Sally hadn't exaggerated; the first streets on the edge of the town were already visible. Sunlight streamed from above as they exited the forest. It shone on his mud-caked books as the end of the track was met with a concrete path. Ben stamped his well-worn boots against the lichen-encrusted concrete to loosen the mud.

"Dean lives at the end of this street. We're nearly there," Sally said over her shoulder.

Ben nodded, not sure how to handle this situation. He promised his grandfather four months ago he'd find the cat once belonging to his late grandmother. Never once imagining it would take this long. He had yet to lay eyes on the cat, but its return would help keep the memories of his beloved grandmother alive.

Anything to quell the suspicions about his new step-grandmother who'd seamlessly taken over his grandfather's home and life.

He'd almost given up on ever finding the damn cat until Sally's message came through.

"Wait here a moment," Sally said when they reached the last house on the corner.

The front metal gate squeaked on its hinges as Sally passed through. She walked along the short path and climbed three broad concrete steps before knocking on the door of the neatly kept cladded house.

In a flying rush that day, there was so much to get done before the seven-hour drive back home, and this incident was forcing him to slow down for a moment. The first thing to snag his attention were the pretty colours of the front flower beds filled with bright red salvia, colourful nasturtiums and impatiens, and green shrubbery along the edges.

Ben passed through the gate and latched it closed behind him. The wonderful memories of his short-lived marriage cascaded like a flowing waterfall. One thing Rhylee had always loved was her garden around the station homestead. Despite the harsh outback sun, she spent countless hours nurturing the pretty flowers. She'd loved a lot about living in the outback. Vowed on their wedding day to do the best she could—city bred and all that. Until she no longer could. She began breaking promises; then, the arguing started. Constantly. Until the day she drove off angry.

"Ben?"

His face snapped up, Sally's voice pulling him from his dark thoughts.

"Er ... would you like to come in and meet Dean's foster parents?"

Ben gritted his teeth and scrubbed a hand over his afternoon stubble. *No!* he wanted to shout. He didn't want to meet anyone. He wanted the damn cat so he could return it to his grandfather. Then he wanted to hit the road where his thoughts could go to that mindless place as he drove kilometre after kilometre until he reached home. His sanctuary, now that he no longer lived with his grandfather. Where he was strong enough most days to tackle life again.

Reluctantly, he squared his shoulders. "Okay. Is Dean here?"

"He's holed up in his room with the cat." Sally gave him a wry, hopeful half smile. "Please be kind to him."

Ben halted his footsteps, stumbling a little. Did he come across as an ogre? Is this what happened with Rhylee? What changed her?

Sally continued in a whisper, "He was abused as a child, but he's the kindest and most patient human you'll ever meet. He's in a good place now."

Ben looked into thoughtful sapphire-blue eyes, with the weight of the world reflected in their depths. Why hadn't he noticed them before? Should he put aside his concerns and suspicions for his grandfather, his sorrows and regrets when it came to Rhylee, and open his eyes to those around him?

"Come on, we'll go sit with him. Give him a chance to get used to you first."

Ben followed Sally inside the house as a muscle clenched in his stomach. Hurt a child? He swallowed back the bile threatening to rise.

"Hello, Ben. Sally has explained to us what's happened. Your cat is safe."

Ben nodded, extending his arm towards the kindly middle-aged man and shaking his hand.

"Would you like a cuppa?" A short, rotund woman came from the kitchen, wiping her hands on an apron. She smiled nervously, knotting her fingers together.

"Er ... Mrs?"

"Julie will do, and this is Raymond." She pointed her thumb towards the man.

"Thank you for the offer, but I might give it a miss this time. Will you ... ah ... allow me to go sit with Dean for a moment?"

"Thank you for being so understanding," Julie said. "Dean is very special to us."

"I promise I won't hurt him. Sally has explained a little to me, and I'll be respectful of this."

Julie gave his arm a gentle press. "Thank you. I get a good vibe from you. Follow Sally; she knows the way and will show you to his room."

With a nod from Sally, Ben followed her down a hallway. When all life had seemed worthless, and he was walking an endless hallway to nowhere, it was his grandfather who'd taken him in his arms, brought him back to his home in the forest and nursed him back, one day at a time. One giant python in his room at a time. One striped possum eating a banana on the outside patio at a time. One inquisitive young cassowary strolling into the kitchen when the door was left open at a time.

Healing. Cathartic. It'd taken him three years to clear the fuzz. Three years to cure the ache. Three years where thinking didn't hurt so much.

If only the mystery of this damn cat had sorted itself out months ago!

It had been a drain on his energy. But to abandon his grandfather? Not in this life. Not when a malicious woman had taken over their grandmother's place with an agenda he didn't understand. This woman outwardly showed love. Made it look like she loved his grandfather, but Ben believed it was fake and he wouldn't rest until he worked it out.

⁂

Sally knocked on Dean's bedroom door and turned the handle a smidgen. "Hey, Dean."

"Yeah, Sal."

"Can I come in?"

"I guess."

Ben was only a step behind her when they entered. The room was well lit with a set of three casement windows wide open, the curtains gently billowing in the afternoon breeze. He caught a whiff of the light, slightly spicy fragrance of the crepe myrtles lining the front of the property and inhaled deeply. It was a pleasant scent going some way to help calm him.

When Dean saw him, he shrank further into the corner, clutching the cat tighter. It let out a meow. "What's he doing here?"

"He wanted to meet you." Sally stepped to the side to allow Ben to pass.

Ben wasn't prepared for this, but he appreciated how life could deal you a bad hand. If Dean had been dealt the same deal, then they had something in common.

Ben lowered himself, sitting on the tiled floor. The room wasn't hugely spacious, the queen size bed occupying most of the space. There was a built-in cupboard with the doors partially slid open. There was some untidiness behind the doors but nothing to write home about. The room carried a general sense of order and organisation. The brown swirly bedspread was a little faded and worn but smelt clean.

Ben leant against the bed and stretched his legs out in front of him. Dean was well cared for here, and Ben didn't want to do anything to upset him.

But the cat! Heck, this was the first time he'd laid eyes on him. It was Moby alright. It was hard to miss the mottled brown spot between his ears, and that was about all he could see.

"I'd like you to meet Ben," Sally continued to say in a gentle voice, still hovering in the doorway.

"He won't love this cat like I will," Dean said with a pout

Something of his past hurt unravelled inside of Ben. Dean was insistent with his reasoning for running away. He totally got this. "Can I tell you a story, Dean?"

Dean whimpered, cooing into the cat's ear. As a slow trickle of tears fell down Dean's cheeks, Ben almost gave up and walked out. He clenched his jaw to fortify himself. His grandfather needed Moby back.

"This cat used to belong to my grandmother. She loved it just like you do."

Sally sat down on the bed's end, and the movement of the mattress pressed against his back.

"When she died a few years ago, this cat was the only thing helping my grandfather get through each day. He'd sit in his chair and hold him for hours, like you're doing now. So yeah, this cat loves to be cuddled, and I can see why he's comfortable with you. That's a good thing."

The tension in Dean's grip loosened, and Moby relaxed against Dean's chest.

"Do you know why I care so much about my grandfather?"

Dean gave a tiny shrug, the gesture almost invisible under his oversized T-shirt. He was listening, and that's all that mattered for now.

"I was married once. I was so in love with my wife and life was good." His voice caught in his throat, and he needed to swallow back the reminder of the pain. But this young man had also experienced pain, so he willed himself on. "She was a city girl keen to live in the outback. But I was blind, Dean. Can you believe it? I was so wrapped up in my little bubble, and I didn't see things."

"What sort of things were you supposed to see? This happened to me once." Dean's brows furrowed as he made the connection.

"You see, the outback isn't for everyone, and she soon realised it wasn't for her. I didn't see this at first. We argued a lot. One day, she was so upset that she got into the car and drove off. And—and I never saw her again."

"Where did she go?" Dean asked innocently.

"We'd had some heavy rain, some flash flooding. They found the car with her inside it downstream." This haunted Ben to this day. Was the car swept off the causeway, or did she intentionally drive off? "It was my grandfather who took care of me for many months after my wife died. Now I want to take care of him."

Ben looked across at Sally from where he was sitting. Tears filled her eyes. After Rhylee was found, with a sixteen-week-old foetus he knew nothing of, he'd screamed blue murder into the darkness night after night. When his voice was hoarse and he no longer cared, then the blackness descended for weeks, months. For as long as he remained on this earth, he would never reconcile her actions and the crushing outcome. As usual, he blamed himself.

He latched onto Sally's kind, understanding blue eyes, struggling to look away. Suddenly, he was apologetic for how rude he'd been earlier about the council fee.

Still gaping at her like a crazed lunatic, it wasn't until she sniffled and rose from the bed that he could break the magnetic force holding his gaze to hers.

"I'll wait for you outside," she said, leaving the room.

He gave a slight nod before turning back to Dean and Moby.

"Do you want to know what happened to me?" The young man seemed much more at ease now, although his grip on the cat was still firm.

"If you think you can share it, then yes."

Dean stroked his hand along Moby's back. "I had a cat once. I loved him so much. Every time my mum hit or yelled at me, I'd take my cat and go hide. We were a team. One day, I came home from school, and my mum was crazy mad. I don't know what I did wrong. She ... she—" A sob escaped, followed by a groan. Dean brought Moby closer to his face, muffling the sound.

"Shh, that's okay. You don't have to tell me what she did." Ben gradually slid a little closer. Enough to run his fingers along Moby's neck. Close enough to show Dean he wasn't a threat.

"But I want to. I'm always being told talking about things is better. But yeah, my mum strangled my cat in front of my eyes. That's when I think I went a little crazy."

Ben inhaled a deep breath. Filled his lungs to halt the way his heart wanted to break all over again for this young man. He wanted that mother right here in the room so he could strangle her back. So strong were his instincts towards protecting the innocent. That helpless feeling, no different to when he couldn't save his unborn baby, washed over him. He closed his eyes for a moment, hoping to find a store of strength for Dean's sake.

"Anyway, she's dead now. She was always taking some crap, and one day she took too much." Dean mumbled with remorse.

Ben's heart thumped harder, and at the same time, a sense of relief passed through him. Just what he suspected. Probably a single mother, unable to cope. So, so sad, especially when drugs were involved. There was no coming back for some, and the damage done to the kids caught up in the ugly net was beyond repair. At least she couldn't hurt Dean anymore.

Ben wept inside for this young man. *Oh, God!* Did he leave Moby here with Dean? Did he tell his grandfather the truth? Would his mind completely understand?

Something was happening to his grandfather. Day by day. Way too fast for the giant of a man he once was. The family rejoiced when he'd chosen to marry the woman who'd taken care of his grandmother in her dying days. Ben wasn't so sure. For the months spent in the same house, he'd seen her for who she really was. A woman who had conned her way into their family. He would uncover why she wasn't the saving angel everyone made her out to be if it was the last thing he did.

If he'd learnt anything from Rhylee's death, it was to listen to your gut instincts. Ignoring that Rhylee was going through some sort of depression, when his gut told him something was up, had been wrong. He'd never ignore it again.

"Hey, Moby," Ben whispered, scratching behind his ear.

Unprepared for using the cat's name out loud, Moby meowed loudly and sprung out of Dean's loose hold, jumping onto Ben's lap.

"I've missed you, buddy." Ben cooed to the cat, snuggling it closer to his chest, inhaling the clean scent of his fur. Someone had kept him clean and healthy during his stay in the compound. Was Sally responsible?

What Ben didn't tell Dean was that he and Moby had become a team too, during his dark days. Always there by his side when he'd moved into his grandfather's home to recover. How could he ever take Moby away from the only home he knew?

He'd missed Moby too, more than he cared to admit, but with Dean being so heroic about Moby, a knife twisted inside Ben's chest. What to do? Who would benefit the most from having Moby by their side?

"You know what? I'm okay now. I know you will take care of him. I was scared someone mean would take him away. You don't seem to be mean," Dean said.

It had been a long, long time since Ben had cried until his heart tore in two, but damn it, he was close. "Here, do you want to hold Moby one last time?"

Dean didn't hesitate to take the cat back. He rose from his crouched position, walked out of the room and down the hallway. Within seconds, he was in the sunshine outside his bedroom window.

Ben remained transfixed with doubt. He lifted his knees and wrapped his arms around them, rocking a little. How had his day become this moral agony of what to do?

"Are you okay?"

Ben swung around on his backside before rising. "He's some man."

"I know, right?" Sally smiled, enough for it to penetrate the fortress he'd created around his heart and hit a target. "By the way, I rang my supervisor, and the council will waive the fee."

Ben shuffled his feet, clearing his throat. "Look, about that, I'm sorry I was so rude."

Another smile brightened her face. "I'm not going to lie; I thought the fee was a bit over the top too. But I don't make the rules, and under the circumstances, they've agreed. So, let's not question it any further. I reckon if you give Dean a few more minutes, he'll be good to give you back the cat."

"Thank you for taking such great care of him. He'll be a welcome sight when I bring him back to my grandfather."

"I'm glad we finally found its rightful owner. I'm leaving Malanda soon, and I'd made it my last mission to find that cat's owner come hell or high water." Sally chuckled, leading the way out of the bedroom and outside to where Dean was.

The sound of her laughter warmed his heart. He found a chuckle somewhere to lighten the mood, but the mention of high water was still a trigger. When nothing happened, he followed this with a smile. Maybe he was finally past the worst. Could he possibly look life in the face again?

Out in the sunshine, Dean showed off Moby to his foster parents and didn't hesitate to come forward to pass the cat over. "Thank you again, Ben. Please take good care of him."

"I will, I promise. Do you want to lead the way back to the compound? I'll have him delivered to my grandfather within the next half an hour as he lives just outside of town."

The three trudged back through the rainforest to the compound, Dean carrying Moby. Once the paperwork was signed only Sally followed him out to the car. "It was a pleasure to meet you, Ben. I hope life treats you kindly from now on."

With Sally in the room when he'd spilled his sad story, most people reacted this way to his story, offering comfort in words. Not that he shared it often, but for a change, he was comfortable with it around this woman. He had no idea what this meant. It could mean he was ready to move on, even though some days he doubted it. Made no sense at all when, instead of the usual handshake, he stepped closer and hugged her. Totally wrong thing to do by stepping into her personal space, but maybe all the fuzz hadn't totally cleared. Didn't help when he inhaled a lungful of honey-scented fragrance that sat well with him.

Either way, her smile was the last thing he saw as he drove away with Moby secure in his crate on the back seat. It would be a very long day before he could lay his weary head to rest and sleep a solid sleep. After he reunited Moby with his grandfather, he hoped Sally's blue eyes would remain with him for at least half the drive back to Richmond.

# Chapter 3

*Five Months Later*

Sally waved goodbye to her students as they bolted from the classroom, all twenty-three of her preteen charges excited for the next day of cross-country events. The small outback town of Richmond, halfway between Townsville and Mount Isa, boasted an amazing man-made lake—Lake Fred Tritton. Parents and school bus drivers were told to drop off the students the next morning at the water park side of the lake.

This meant most of the day would be taken up with nonschool events, water activities being high on the agenda. These kids were lucky to have such a facility in what would normally be a dry, dusty outback town. After only four months in the area, Sally knew all about the former mayor and his team of councillors who approved the construction of the man-made lake, using the Fitzroy River when it was in flood to fill it initially and to keep using it to prop up the level when required.

Every now and then, this delightful body of water was enough to remind Sally of home, and a little knot would form inside her chest. So used to naturally created lakes, creeks and waterfalls surrounded in tropical rainforest dripping heavily with moisture, arriving in Richmond to discover this lake had been a big surprise.

Sally did her usual walk around the classroom, turning off the air conditioner, checking the computers and equipment to ensure they were shut down and switching off the lights. This well-equipped school boasted about one hundred students. Her teaching day might have just ended, but preparations for the project were only beginning. She had a busy night, which included finally meeting the man she'd corresponded with for the past few months. His property was the lynchpin in what she hoped would cement the ongoing relationship between the troubled preteens and the program.

With the full support of the school principal and other teaching staff, and financially backed by the government, Sally's tentative idea at her previous school barely a year ago was finally ready to begin.

With an escalating number of kids out of control in modern-day society, the intention was to intervene at an age where it might be early enough to halt the downhill slide of drugs, criminal activities and absence from schools. Sally wanted her contribution to their lives to be life-changing.

Why choose Richmond? Because there was something grander in Richmond. Even more so than the fabulous man-made lake. What she hoped would be the backbone of this project. It had taken a lot of work to get to this point, but here they were, all set to go.

About to lock her classroom, she remembered her KeepCup and turned back around to grab it off her desk.

"Excuse me."

Sally jumped at the intrusion, her KeepCup flying out of her hand and clattering onto one of the student desks.

When she turned around, she was met with as much surprise as she was probably showing. His was gone in an instant, only to be replaced with a lopsided smile.

"Have you broken another mug?"

She remembered those vivid green eyes. If she was honest, they had occasionally crossed her fields of thoughts over the past months, but she never expected to see them again.

"I'll just check." Sally swallowed, concerned as to why this stranger was crossing her path for a second time. He was a long way from Malanda, so this felt off. She wound her way around the desks set up in neat rows, five abreast, until she was at the desk where her KeepCup teetered on its edge.

Strong, tanned hands reached it first. "Sorry, didn't mean to startle you, but I was told by the front office I would find a Ms Barkworth here, their brand-new single teacher. I … um … had no idea it was you."

He gave the cup a quick shake near his ear. "Here you go; I don't think there's any damage to this one."

"Thank you," she managed warily, a hint of annoyance masking the 'single' brand attached to her arrival in Richmond. She took the KeepCup and clutched it to her chest. "You're a long way from Malanda. You're not stalking me, are you?" She remembered the tragic story of how he'd lost his wife, but she wasn't taking any chances. She was alone with a stranger and a long way from family and friends.

With a comical expression, his eyes widened. He stood up straighter and took a step back, shadowing the small desk his hip was leaning against. "Ms *Sally* Barkworth, I'm assuming?"

She nodded. Her heart beat an irregular pattern.

"And you've been corresponding with my dad, a Paul Angwin about the troubled teens program?"

*Oh, shite.* Would she regret her harsh assessment? Better to be safe than sorry. "I have, and you are?"

"Ben Angwin, at your service, apparently," he said in all seriousness. "I'll be coordinating the dinosaur fossicking programs with your teens. I'm your palaeontologist. Well, part-time one, anyway."

It was Sally's turn for her eyes to widen. A sense of shame enshrouded her. She'd misjudged badly, and heat raced up her neck, burning the skin around her ears.

"Also, just to make sure we're on the same page, I'm not stalking you, and regardless of what gossip you hear locally, neither am I looking for a wife."

A whisper of pain flickered across his face for a split second. Gone in an instant, though, and replaced with a scowl.

Sally coughed to clear her throat, still trying to dislodge the hint of annoyance. "Well, I'm glad we got that sorted, now ah … Mr Angwin, I'm—"

"As before, Ben will do."

She inhaled a deep breath before expelling it slowly. "Okay, Ben, my apologies for this. I … wasn't expecting to see you again. Especially out"—her hands flapped nervously in the air—"here. Also, my priority is the success of this project. I need your help professionally. No other basis, thank you."

He dropped the rigid stance and appeared more relaxed. "I accept your apology. Now, shall we start again?"

"Okay, but why are you here? In my classroom? At three pm? I have a meeting with Paul tonight at five pm."

"You do. Except Paul has come down with a horrible cold, and I'm on my way to Malanda to check on Grandad. As Dad only has an email address for you, we agreed it would be easier to drop by the school on my way out of town and have a quick word this afternoon. You will continue to correspond with Dad as usual."

"Oh, okay, that makes sense."

"And we should exchange phone numbers before I forget."

Sally's brows rose. "Can I check your licence, please?"

"Huh, haven't we established who I am?"

"Can I please have a look?" She wasn't backing down, not if it concerned her safety.

With a sigh, Ben pulled his wallet out of the back pocket of his jeans before sitting on the desk. He opened it up, fished out his licence and passed it over. The touch of his warm skin triggered a pulse point on her wrist as she grabbed the piece of plastic, which she did her best to ignore.

Disregarding his scowl, she took a step back, needing space to breathe. This was absurd. She wasn't a desperate woman, and nor was she feeling unsafe. But like all women faced with a gorgeous guy sitting barely a metre away, she went straight to his year of birth and confirmed he was two years older than her.

"Seen enough?" He was tapping his fingers impatiently on the desk.

Before she handed it back, she spied his birthdate, locking it in her memory bank with no idea of why. She snatched the licence back when she remembered she hadn't checked his name. "Oh, wait, I want to check one more thing."

"You were looking at my date of birth, weren't you?"

Again, a rush of heat raced up her neck. She did a quick check of his name, Benjamin Reginald Angwin, and passed the licence back.

It was time to put her concerns aside.

"How much older am I?"

"Two years." She stood tall and proud, looking at his face, which held some kind of smirk. Pint-sized, really, beside his sitting hulk.

"And you're not looking for a husband?" he asked in all seriousness before the rigid lines of his face cracked, the semblance of a half smile beginning to show. "Sorry, small town. The lovely receptionist at the office has known me since birth."

*Bloody hell!* How could she have forgotten about small towns? "Look, Mr Benjamin Reginald Angwin—"

"Oh, please, it's Ben if you don't mind, since from next week, we're going to be in each other's pocket most days." A cheeky smile, with a glint of mischief in his eyes, stretched across his rugged and tanned face.

"Alright, Ben." She took a deep breath, worried about what that sunny smile was doing to her insides. "Just to set the record straight, I'm not looking for a husband. I would, though, appreciate your assistance in helping make this project a success."

"Okay, got it. Now, can you please drop the formal and serious you? We've established that neither of us needs a partner, so let's move on to the details of your project and how you'd like it to work. I'll briefly explain how it will happen from my end. Will a few minutes suit you now?"

His gaze caught hers, and she lost herself momentarily in dark green pools. Stumbling over a tongue that had forgotten how to work, she managed to reply. "It ... it will. Would you like ah ... a coffee?" What would she learn about his late wife through the small-town gossip channels? She walked around more desks to switch on the air conditioner again.

It was none of her business, of course, but—

"I'd love one. It's a long drive to Malanda, and it'll keep me awake."

"Should you be doing the drive in one run?" Sally asked as she motioned for him to follow her to the adjoining staffroom where the kettle and fridge were kept. Her drive out to Richmond had taken a couple of days to cover the six hundred or so kilometres. She never took for granted the long distances between Australian communities and how outback people took it in their stride. To just get in their vehicles and drive, often hours at a time, to get to their destination.

"Don't have a choice. I have to get back to the property and your project setup. Between the family, we take it in turns to check on Grandad, so I probably do it once every two months." Ben pulled out a chair and sat down at the small table in the staff room, resting his Akubra on his knee.

It was a tiny area, and it was impossible for him not to intrude in her personal space. To put the kettle on and organise his hot drink, he was close enough that she could inhale the scent of the outback and outdoors that hung on his clothing. Diesel and dirt stirring a hum along her veins, which surprised her. She barely knew the guy, and he'd made it very clear earlier he was a no-go zone.

"Your first lot of children arrive next week. Yes?"

Sally snapped back to attention, her chest swelling with pride. "They do." She was so proud of her involvement; she mentally crossed her fingers that the project was going to be a success. It had to be a success. Everything was riding on it. It was one way she could fix the guilt of her one regret in life.

"Do you keep in touch with Dean? How's he keeping?"

Sally turned to face this man in the confined space as she waited for the kettle to boil, surprised at the mention of his name. "You remember him?"

"A bit hard not to. His story struck a chord with me. One I doubt I'll ever forget."

Sally gulped. She was misjudging this man way too much. Had she been unfairly harsh in her assessment of him? "He's doing very well. My ultimate dream would be to bring Dean out here to help with the troubled teens. He would be perfect for them."

Ben rubbed his chin, a gesture suggesting he was thinking this over. "Hmm, I think I can see it."

"I do, I really do."

"Dean came across as a very sensitive man. We need more like him."

Sally nodded. "Totally agree. Now, it was a white coffee with two sugars?"

Laughter lines crinkled at the edges of his eyes. "You remember?"

"I do." They both laughed unexpectedly, the sound echoing around the small space. When they stopped, an awkward silence hung in the air, thick and heavy like the humid weather of Malanda, and Sally had no idea how to proceed.

"Would you like me to get the mugs down?" Ben asked when she remained mute. He stood and took a step towards the cupboards. "There's something about mugs and you."

When she didn't answer, he reached over her head for two, placing them on the bench. "Here you go. Better get this show on the road."

"Thank you," she uttered, cringing at her inexperienced reaction to being close to this man. She'd never been a complete wallflower. *Come on, woman, get a move on.*

Her hand shook as she opened the small fridge to take the milk out. Not to mention the way her heart beat faster when she straightened to find him staring at her.

Frantic for something to say, she asked, "How's Moby?"

Ben chuckled. "Cheeky as usual and keeping Grandad on his toes."

They were going to be in each other's company day in and day out. She needed to do better than this. Better than irrelevant small talk and shaking gestures. "Oh, that's great news." With the coffees made she handed him his mug.

"It sure is. We're still none the wiser of how he escaped, but I'm glad he's back home where he belongs."

"Yes, that must be nice. Now, are we ready to swap notes?" She pulled out a second chair and sat down opposite.

"Yep," Ben confirmed with a smile.

Like a personal ray of sunshine shining through a window, his smile trained on her face was turning her to mush. She took a sip of her drink and struggled to swallow it. Good Lord, how was her project going to succeed with this distraction?

# Chapter 4

Ben sat up in bed, raking a hand through his mussed-up curly morning hair. A shiver rushed up his spine as his feet touched the cool timber floor. This house, built on an isolated property on the outskirts of Malanda on the way to Mount Bartle Frere, was purchased by his grandfather four years ago. A place for his grandmother to spend her final months after she refused any more cancer treatment. An unusual home, more outdoors than indoors. The pole home's living area and most of the downstairs blended seamlessly with the close surrounding rainforest as though it were one and the same.

Ben managed a lopsided morning smile. It was nothing out of the ordinary to find his grandfather's sprinkler system going on in the living room, giving the rainforest plants inside a thriving chance to prosper.

The little pond smack bang in the middle of the lounge had long since stopped being a source of amusement for visiting family and friends. Once he got downstairs and sat for breakfast, he could enjoy its trickling flow of water over rocks in a never-ending stream of water. Its calming presence gave his grandmother so much peace before she slipped away, a lasting gift created by his grandfather. It had gone a long way in helping Ben to heal, too. He remembered its comforting power all too well during those dark days following Rhylee's death when he despaired of ever coming out the other side.

Raising his arms in the air, Ben stretched his muscles, ironing out the cricks. Like all his family, they each carried a key to the upstairs spare room accessed from a separate set of stairs leading from the outside. He'd used it late last night, well after midnight, when he'd stumbled up and crashed.

Except for the five minutes spent talking to his mum, who'd called to check he was travelling okay, he'd blasted his playlist the entire way, his ute filled with the sounds of Adam Brant, Lee Kernaghan, Troy Cassar-Daley, Keith Urban and a host of other great Aussie country singers. Even Slim Dusty's 'Duncan' got a showing. Singing with gusto for his ears only, loving to have a beer with Duncan; it was always a favourite with his mates and a great party song after a few beers.

It was a killer of a seven-hour drive, and he had a lot going through his mind, but something compelled him to keep driving, to get there as soon as possible to check on his grandfather. Something was off. Something he couldn't quite put a finger on. He was yet to voice his concerns with the family.

Using his foot, he dragged his duffel bag closer to the bed and took out a cotton T-shirt, pulling it over his head. He did the same with a pair of crumpled board shorts he packed at the last minute. Always handy if he wanted to take a swim at the lake before he left. Not that he usually stayed too long. By the next morning, after a quick breakfast, there would be no choice but to do the return drive back. For the quality time he spent with his grandfather, it was all worth it.

He lifted his phone from where it was on charge and checked for any messages. Another smile tugged at the corners of his mouth when he spotted one from Sally.

Not sure why he was surprised. Once Sally got past the uncertainty of why he was there, she relaxed enough that their notes swap was hassle-free and comfortable. This was a good thing if they were going to be spending a lot of time together in a remote area on the station.

Only after their brief meeting, as he was halfway out of the school kitchen, did he remember to exchange phone numbers. After rattling off his number, he asked if she could send him a message so he had her contact on his phone.

Tapping on it, her 'safe travels' message unexpectedly warmed a spot in his chest, and he was not sure why. There was also a message from his mum to check if he made it safely. He quickly typed a reply, assuring her he had. A stab of guilt heckled with his head. He should have messaged her last night.

He put his phone down and massaged both hands over his face, taking a few deep breaths and another moment to wake up fully. His time after Rhylee's death worried his family aplenty. At the time, he hadn't understood it, but as the months and years passed, his brain returned to some form of normalcy. He appreciated the concern his family had shown. They had his back. Just like he would with his grandfather.

He got up to use the toilet in the nearby ensuite. Eager to see his grandfather, he tidied his bed and then used the other door that led into the house, trundling down the steps leading to the ground floor. A clatter in the kitchen signalled his step-grandmother, Gwen, would be preparing Grandad's breakfast.

As he reached the landing, his grandfather walked in from outside, and a smile lit up his face. "Ben, my boy, I was hoping you'd wake up soon."

"Good morning, Grandad. What's up?" Ben wrapped an arm around his grandfather's shoulder and pulled him in for a cuddle. A nagging worry gnawed at him at how his grandfather's health had visibly declined over the past six months. Thinner face, bony shoulders when they hugged. Why weren't the doctors coming up with a sound reason? He was too young to die, and this deterioration couldn't be chalked up to old age yet.

"I want to show you something I found outside," Grandad said, pulling away from Ben's embrace.

"Breakfast will be ready in five," Gwen called from the kitchen.

"Won't take us long, Gwenny," Grandad called towards the kitchen with a conspiring grin. Ben's heart lurched as he followed his slow gait outside. This man had once been a giant. When he inherited the cattle property from *his* father, he'd taken on a very prosperous business that demanded hard work, commitment, respect and loyalty.

And he'd got it. Because he was a good man who led with compassion, generosity and care, never once concerned about working alongside those he employed.

Grandma's death was a cruel blow coming too early in his life.

Ben followed him to a small patch of forest litter near the back of the pole home, beside a small garden shed where Grandad kept his gardening tools.

"Look, my boy." Grandad pointed to the ground.

Ben bent, peering closer, eventually spotting an echidna burrowing further into the leafy litter. Alert to their voices, the echidna's creamy-black spines rose in defence on its dark brown fur. As they watched in silence, it gradually settled again, its spines lowering and the echidna curling into a tight ball where not even its long, spout-looking nose was visible.

Grandad patted him on the shoulder. "Worth coming out for, wasn't it?"

Ben smiled in the early morning light, where the sun struggled to penetrate through the thick forest wall surrounding the pole home. This animal was so different. Along with the platypus, it was the only other living egg-laying mammal species in the world. "Damn special, Grandad. Thank you."

"Now we better get back inside before we upset Gwenny."

"Thanks for showing me, Grandad." Ben patted his back. "You're always doing this. I can't remember a single rock, tree, animal or dinosaur bone you've shown me that wasn't the most exciting find in the world."

Grandad chuckled as they left the little echidna alone. "I lived for the spare moments I spent with you and your brothers. Away from the many hard hours of work, it always brought me so much joy."

Ben took hold of his arm, steadying him as they followed the path in silence. Back in the day, their homesteads had only been a hundred metres apart. Together with his brothers, they waltzed in and out of both homes daily. Raiding biscuits from Grandma's jars was their given right, received with a hug and a kiss atop their head. Losing his grandmother was tough on all of them, especially his grandfather.

For Ben's entire life, his grandfather was his pillar, his support—especially in his time of need. Ben wanted to be that man now. He sensed his grandfather needed that same support, now more than ever.

⁓

As Ben steered Grandad towards the dining area of the house, Gwen walked out from the adjoining kitchen. "Good morning, Gwen."

"Good morning, Ben. Good Lord, I don't know why you all make the long, dangerous drive as often as you do."

No, she wouldn't understand, but Ben kept his mouth shut and produced a stilted smile as Grandad tutted and Ben pulled out his chair to help him sit.

"You do realise I'm a fully qualified nurse? Your grandfather is lucky I can take care of him."

Ben nodded, having heard it countless times over the past couple of years. After spending those dark days here with them both, Ben could never relax around Gwen. Again, that niggle.

"Are you having your usual, Ben?"

"Sure am, Gwen. I'll get it, thanks. No need for you to fuss over me."

"Okay, I guess fussing over one man is enough. Here you go, dear, your porridge just how you like it." Gwen fretted over Grandad, pouring the milk over his porridge like she did every time Ben was there.

Grandad looked up, giving him a conspiratorial wink. He still had his wits about him and was never one to rock a boat, but—

"Save some of the milk for yourself, Gwen," Grandad suggested.

"That's okay; you can have all of this. There's more in the fridge."

Ben sat mesmerised as she poured all the milk onto Grandad's porridge. To the extent it almost overflowed and teetered on the rim of the bowl. Ben thought it was odd—Gwen was not one to waste unnecessarily. Not that a little waste was an issue. Grandad was a wealthy man in his own right, so money shouldn't be tight in their household.

Ben sauntered towards the kitchen and the walk-in pantry, well versed with where everything was kept. The Weet-Bix was on the second top shelf on the right, and he reached for it. As he did, he tripped on a box near the entry and fleetingly looked down. In the paltry light coming from the single bulb, he used his foot to gently shove what looked like rat bait more firmly into the corner, conscious of either Gwen or Grandad tripping over it. Then he went to the fridge for the milk and placed both on the kitchen bench where he filled a bowl with four Weet-Bix and a generous helping of milk.

Back at the dining room table, Ben settled in for a relaxed breakfast before he gave Grandad a hand with whatever needed doing. "Gwen, just take care with how you use rat bait."

A flicker of alarm crossed her face as she looked across at Ben.

"I don't want to worry you. I get that mice can be an issue in this house, but some of the native mice might eat it too. Remember when that cassowary ate a dead white-tailed rat?"

"Wasn't that a spectacle," Grandad added.

"If a native rat had eaten bait, it could've been detrimental for the cassowary," Ben added for clarification, not wanting to upset Gwen but needing to point out the dangers of using bait.

"I was more worried about the dinosaur bird on our back patio about to saunter into my kitchen," Gwen grumbled with obvious annoyance.

Ben and Grandad chuckled. When the cassowary stepped up onto the patio, it was Gwen's shrieks that had them running madly inside to see what was wrong. Somehow, they shooed it back outside into the rainforest. It wasn't a common occurrence, unlike pythons, possums, tree kangaroos and yes, the savage white-tailed rat that could chew through plastic as thick as a man's wrist, who all made regular visits.

"How was your drive?" Grandad asked before slurping milk from his spoon.

Looking down, Moby was stretching against his leg. "Same as usual, but good," Ben answered, filling his mouth with a spoonful of soft cereal, and taking a moment to enjoy the calming sound of trickling water from the indoor pond. Once that was down his throat, he asked, "What's on the go today?"

"I thought we could do some gardening this morning, then in the afternoon I'd appreciate a hand sanding some of the upstairs window frames. They're overdue for a recoat before mould attacks them again."

Ben nodded, getting through another spoonful of cereal and sneaking in a quick rub of Moby's ear. "I might duck into the local hardware shop in Malanda and buy some live traps this afternoon. You can trap the mice this way. Are you still up to the task of humanely putting them down, Grandad?"

"Other than the usual stomach cramps, I get by. I reckon I should be able to."

Gwen settled at the table with two pieces of toast and her usual cup of tea. "I'm taking care of those cramps, Ben, with heat packs. Your grandfather doesn't complain too much. I've suggested we do a round of tests, but he won't budge. But don't worry, I'll keep checking his vitals every day. If I think there are concerning changes, I'll make sure he goes to the doctor."

"Thanks, Gwen," Ben muttered, except he wasn't so sure if he meant it. She reminded the family many times how good a nurse she was. Was he being ungrateful for Gwen's efforts? He couldn't dislodge the concerns that something wasn't right every single time he came to visit. Call him paranoid, and maybe it was a lasting effect of the entire Rhylee thing, but now he was more attuned to everything. No longer did he ignore it when his gut screamed out loud and clear.

"Puh, you pair do go on. A bit of pain isn't going to kill me. I've had enough scans over the years to last a lifetime. There's nothing sinister happening inside there." He patted his stomach. "Probably just old age."

Ben shook his head. At seventy-five years old, his grandfather wasn't old. Built like an ox and supremely healthy all his life, if nothing was going on inside his body, why was he looking pale and unwell?

"Did I mention, Linc, that Richard is coming down to visit tomorrow?"

Grandad stiffened beside him, or had he imagined it? Ben looked directly at him, hating how Gwen called him by the same shortened version of Lincoln as his grandmother used to. "Everything okay, mate?"

Grandad flapped his hand in the air and continued eating his cereal. "You pair will be the death of me. Finish your breakfast, both of you, so we can get some jobs done."

No acknowledgement of Richard's visit by Grandad stuck in Ben's craw. What was it with Gwen's three adult children? Parasites, in Ben's opinion. No hopers who'd done nothing with their lives. Cash strapped, they were always looking for handouts.

Ben remembered Richard's constant nagging and arguing the few times he called in to visit his mother when Ben was still staying there.

Should he broach the subject with Grandad? He wasn't sure who was taking care of his finances, but the thought of Gwen in total control while Grandad declined had his stomach muscles clenching.

*Christ! Eat your breakfast and stop questioning everything!*

But he couldn't let it go.

# Chapter 5

*I*'*m passing through Richmond tomorrow. Want to take a tour of the facilities on our station property?*

Sally had replied to the message with a hearty 'yes'. Now, she raced around completing her Saturday morning chores before Ben turned up. The thought of spending a whole day with Ben had her heart rate picking up and a silly grin settling permanently on her face. Yep, she was acting desperate with the full knowledge Ben was not looking for a wife. What about a no-strings-attached fling? *Oh my God*, there was even a skip in her step as she fished out her washing from the machine and hung it out to dry in the garage.

Once her washing was pegged up, she took a moment to take a deep breath. *Okay, girlfriend, this isn't* Farmer Wants a Wife. *Repeat this many, many times so you don't make a fool of yourself.*

Their short meeting had gone extremely well. Ben was the relaxed sort and had her laughing at his jokes in no time at all. This out-of-the-blue invitation meant she would see the station property a couple of weeks earlier than planned. That's all. Had nothing to do with the man himself. Right?

She dropped the laundry basket near the washing machine, convinced that visiting a real-life grazing property was creating all the excitement. So busy with the start of the school year, new school, new children, final preparations for the program, her weekends and personal time vanished in a rumbling, tumbling fashion as the weeks sped by.

About the only thing she did fit in was some time at the lake on the weekends. Already well used by the community and visitors, she'd watched others enjoy fishing, skiing and canoeing, while some families used the sandy beaches, shaded playground and barbeque facilities. As for the well-maintained water park, even Sally had taken advantage of its cooling waters after using the paved walking track surrounding the lake to enjoy the occasional jog.

Most children she came across recognised her, and slowly, week by week, she was getting to know more of the townspeople. But out-of-towners? She knew no one.

Sally grabbed her toothbrush and zipped up her overnight bag. She had a change of clothes, toiletries, swimwear as instructed, and a water bottle. Strictly no food was necessary, she was told, as his mum would prepare lunch and dinner. She resembled a kid invited to her first birthday party. *Honestly, Sal, come on, get a grip.* She was going to have to get rid of this jittery mood way before Ben made an appearance. A quick check of the white, round clock ticking away in the kitchen, and she squealed with alarm.

There were only minutes left before he was due to arrive.

The sound of a horn tooting blasted the airwaves. Wrong! There were zero minutes left.

Sally hoisted her overnight bag over her shoulder and opened the front door. She tucked all her excitement into a tightly knitted ball and shoved it aside. Locking the front door of the small, cladded home used exclusively by school teachers, she gave Ben a cheery wave as he waited in his white, dust-covered Isuzu utility.

"Hi, Sally." Ben greeted from the driver's seat as she approached the ute.

"Hi, Ben. Thank you so much for this invitation. Please don't tell me you've just driven back from Malanda."

Ben chuckled. "I've just driven back from Malanda."

"How far is it to the homestead from here?"

"Another hour."

Sally opened the passenger door but remained standing outside the vehicle with one foot in. "How about I drive from here?"

Ben eyed her, a deep frown forming on his forehead.

"What's the problem? I'm perfectly capable of driving."

Ben got out of the ute and stretched his arms above his head. The frown disappeared and was replaced by a cute smile. How did he muster up enough energy to smile after such a long drive? Time to tamper down the patter, regardless of how cute that smile was. She had other concerns, like not being comfortable getting into a vehicle with a fatigued driver.

Ben looked across at her over the top of the ute cab. "I have no idea what your driving is like, but my music might be an issue for you."

"Hmm." Sally pretended to think this through carefully, her index finger tapping the open door. "What am I up for?"

"Only the best Australian country music going around."

"Is that all?"

"Is that all? What do you mean?"

"No Dolly Parton or Shania Twain?"

"There's a bit of Amber Lawrence in there if you search."

"What about cruise control? Does this old thing have it?"

"Jeez. You're not asking for much. Do you want to drive or not?"

Sally gave a hearty laugh, losing control of that tightly knit ball for just a moment. "Okay, cowboy"—she walked around to the driver's side, flicking her hand to indicate he should get out of the way—"my turn. You can close your eyes and rest."

His shoulder brushed against hers as he moved out of the way of the driver's door. It was all it took to cause a hum around her body.

"Um ... I'm wide awake now, just so you know."

She shook her head, prepared to be firm. "My driving is not bad. I'll get you there safely, and I'll even tuck you up into bed myself if I have to."

Ben's eyes widened, his gaze never leaving hers as he trudged around the ute for the passenger side. "Nope, nope, nope." His hands waved haphazardly around his head like he was warding off evil spirits. "You do not get to tuck me in. That's not part of the deal."

Sally froze and frowned.

When he followed this with a semblance of a chuckle, she relaxed like a rubber band stretched, and then released. Thank goodness because, for a split second, Sally feared she'd stepped onto sacred ground concerning his late wife. She quickly pasted on a wobbly smile before he was seated. Now, to be careful around Ben with what she said. There'd been no chance to find out anything about his late wife, and she was headed for territory where his wife had once played an important role.

"Which way?" she asked, her heart hammering, a reminder that one wife had been enough for Ben.

"There's only one road out of town."

"Right! Got it."

There was no reason they should both suddenly laugh together. It wasn't like she'd asked for a joke and expected one back. As she turned the key in the ignition, the four-wheel drive rumbled around her. His laughter didn't sound forced, and neither was hers. This time her smile came easily as she steered the ute towards the road.

"So, tell me a little more about how the program will work in town," Ben asked, settling back in the passenger seat.

"I'll drive past the house," Sally said, indicating right.

As Sally drove down the street, she pointed out the large, rambling house, once owned by a station property and used as a halfway house for their family and station workers who needed to come into Richmond for any reason. She slowed the ute with no intention of stopping. The traffic was non-existent this quiet Saturday, so it was okay to idle slowly past.

A large yard surrounded the house, with a few outbuildings and sheds at the rear of the sizeable property. Large towering acacia trees, commonly known as gidgee trees, were scattered around the house and the yard, providing plenty of shade. Along the front of the property, neatly kept native shrubs provided a hedge-like feature.

With her elbow resting on the open window, Sally looked up to the sky. She would switch on the ute's air conditioning once they left the town, so she took a moment to fill her airways with the dry, pungent air under the startling blue sky. Resembling an arch, she could see pure blue in all directions, a slight haze meeting the line where the sky met the horizon.

"It looks like it would have enough rooms."

"It sure does. The children won't need to share a room."

It always took Sally's breath away as she continued to drive slowly past the property, thrilled about what was in store for these teens. Compared to this place, the teens were coming from an alien world. For her, after only a few months, the entire outback feel left her overawed every time she thought about it. She hoped the teens came to love it like she did.

So used to mist, drizzle, lots of rain and cloud cover, she'd come to appreciate the beauty in the outback so different from her beautiful Malanda, yet so unique and special in its own way. A whiff of eucalypt drifted inside the cab from the trees lining the street, and she soaked up a little more of the heat dazzling from above. Long sleeves and an air-conditioned cab would prevent her skin from roasting, but already, her long, slim limbs were changing with a tinge of natural tan. But still, with blonde hair and fair skin, she would always have to take extra precautions.

"We have a host couple employed to act as parents and counsellors for the teens. They will ensure the children are properly fed and clothed and that they are completing their homework each day. We're still considering whether the kids will attend the school. At this early stage, they'll be homeschooled until we assess them individually. Putting them in mainstream school might not be the best for them initially."

"They'll all be coming from different family situations too. I can only imagine they'll be quite unsure and frightened at first. How old will they be?"

"Exactly! We're taking mostly eleven, twelve, thirteen-year-olds." Ben's understanding of the program surprised Sally. He got it.

"It won't hurt to take things slowly and concentrate on the basics," Ben added, his focus intent on the road ahead.

"Yep! These kids have already missed so much vital education. That's where I come in. The education department has assigned me another teacher, and together, we'll ensure these children receive extra attention and a chance to catch up. It'll be sad to give up my regular class, but it was always the plan once the program was up and running."

Ben nodded, a thoughtful expression on his face, like he was taking it all in. His role was to give the kids a diversion. An alternative interest to enhance their lives and make lasting changes. She couldn't wait to learn about dinosaurs and fossils herself.

"Time to wind up the window and start blasting the aircon, Sally. Then some music?" Ben arched a brow as he picked up his phone.

A quick glimpse before she drove back onto the main highway had them smiling at each other. This was ridiculous. They were strangers. He wasn't after a wife. She wanted this project to be a success. He was imperative to its success. Under no circumstances was she going to do anything stupid to put him offside. This meant taking down any fancy ideas about kissing that mouth, displaying the best smile she'd seen in a long time. "You pick, and you better make it good."

Ben snorted, tapping the phone screen.

Within seconds, the cab filled with the sounds of Shania Twain and her hit song 'Man! I Feel Like A Woman!'. She burst out laughing for no reason. Ben wore a silly grin. It looked promising that they might get along just fine.

She was going to enjoy this drive immensely.

# Chapter 6

Ben prised his eye open before peeking at the clock on his bedside table. He bolted upright, ploughing a hand through his hair. How was it five pm? *Fuck!*

Calming down a fraction, he fell back onto his pillow and crossed his arms behind his head, letting his eyes flutter closed again. The early start and the seven-hour drive always left him exhausted. His mum, Ellen, not taking no for an answer, insisted he take a short kip.

With a knot of guilt in his chest, Ben hadn't argued even though he should've stayed awake for Sally's sake. After all, he invited her out for the tour the next morning. Easily reminded of how his mind turned to shit if he was overtired, he didn't trust himself not to say something dumb. All he needed was half an hour, forty-five minutes max. But three hours?

*What the hell just happened?*

"I'll take care of Sally," Ellen had insisted. "I'll show her around the homestead this afternoon, and then you can drive over to the fossicking camp in the morning."

Ben knew that look, a blend of worry and cheekiness, his mum sometimes gave him. She wasn't the pushy mum. Never made decisions for him, except for this nap. He smiled wryly. But those assessing looks, weighing up the new local teacher—Ben would have to nip it in the bud early. Sally may be a rural chick, but she wasn't an outback one. Two entirely different worlds. He wasn't going anywhere near that again for as long as he lived.

The whirr of the air conditioner dulled most of the noise from outside—vehicles driving past and the sound of voices. These days, it easily lulled him to sleep in the small, self-contained donga on the property where he lived. The station owned half a dozen of these modular transportable buildings. Stark and functional, they afforded a little more privacy and space compared to the casual accommodation used by the jackaroos and jillaroos who didn't mind roughing it.

Ben was happy there for now. There'd been no need for him to remain alone in the homestead house once belonging to his grandparents. Nor did he want to move in with his parents only a hundred metres away. After Rhylee died, he didn't need much. Certainly not any daily reminders.

Ben opened his eyes when his stomach rumbled. Even though he usually cooked his own meals, Ellen insisted on cooking dinner that night. He loved his mother's cooking and was never one to refuse it when offered.

He threw his legs over the side of the bed and attempted to pat down his unruly curls. He'd showered on arrival and had slept in his shirt and jocks. He reached for a clean pair of jeans and put them on, then slipped his feet into a pair of worn joggers.

As he left the donga, he caught a whiff of the freshly watered lawn outside his door. Set apart from the main homestead, there were the collection of dongas, another building housing the casual workers, the communal camp kitchen, showers, toilets, and laundry, all surrounded by beautifully landscaped gardens. Ellen worked tirelessly to make the area refreshing and relaxing. Together with a retired jackaroo now employed as the gardener, they kept the grass green, the shrubs and outback plants alive and thriving, all with water pumped from the nearby Flinders River.

It was a peaceful area complete with an outdoor pit surrounded by easy-to-relax-in chairs—which was dubbed the stargazing lounge. The station workers could gather after dinner in the cool outdoor evenings, have a beer, tell a story, toast a few marshmallows over the fire and look up into the star-studded sky. It never failed to help restore Ben's faith in getting him to the next day. He'd done just that on countless nights, sat quietly at the back of the crowd, enjoyed a beer and looked up.

The smell of diesel and horses hung in the air as Ben strolled towards the main homestead. A couple of young jackaroos waved at him on the way to their vehicles. Usually, he would stop for a chat, but he waved back and continued in the opposite direction. Refreshed and feeling good for a change, he was eager to see what Sally and Ellen were up to. Despite his earlier fatigue, he'd enjoyed Sally's driving. Was quietly impressed with how she handled his ute. He could get used to having her around, but of course, he wouldn't. Because where was the sense in that?

He could invite her over to the stargazing lounge after dinner. Catch a few trillion stars. Sometimes, if you were lucky, you'd score a shooting star just for more kicks. *Shucks!* He really needed to stop this train of thought.

The main homestead was a two-hundred-metre walk from the collection of buildings where his dwelling sat. Halfway there, he averted his gaze from his grandparents' old homestead home. His younger brother, Damon, and his girlfriend, Elyce, recently took up residence there for a short time before they left to backpack around the country. Didn't matter what they did or where they went because Elyce was an outback girl. They understood each other. Now it housed one of the station managers and his wife.

At the back door of the main homestead, he stopped with his hand on the screen door handle. Sally's infectious laughter filled the air. He'd heard it for most of the drive from Richmond. The jokes, the banter, the off-key singing. Neither could claim to sing in tune. His mouth turned up at its edges. Easy. Relaxed. Like being in Sally's company could help him shake off the hellish memories of the last three years.

*Whoa! Back down, cowboy.*

He flicked the lever down and swung the door open, letting it close behind him with a clack. He stalked down the short hallway leading to the kitchen, gulping in the delicious baking smells, taking the two women by surprise. Their chatter and laughter stopped abruptly.

"Why the scowl, honey?" Ellen asked. "If you've been asleep all this time, I would've thought you'd at least have a smile. Here—" She handed him a bigger-than-usual chocolate chip biscuit. "I made it especially for you. Sally put extra choc bits on top. I told her they were your favourite."

Without too much thought, probably from years of practice, Ben didn't hesitate to take it. He bit a sizeable chunk off the biscuit but struggled to swallow. "Thank you," he muttered between chewing and feeling guilty. He hadn't realised he'd come in with a scowl. But something about this new woman was disrupting his organised thoughts. The ones he'd striven to get back into some semblance of order after falling through that black hole of misery. And damn it, he'd been succeeding for a while now. He didn't need any distractions.

"Ben, your mum is a fabulous cook. Do you want to know what else we've made?"

He didn't, but he guessed he wouldn't have any choice but to hear it. Ellen placed a cup of coffee in front of him before gently pushing down his shoulder and getting him to sit at the island bench, where the general hubbub of the household happened. His father Paul came in and Ellen handed over another hot mug and biscuit. He sat beside him on another stool, vastly improved from his flu of the past couple of days.

The chatter continued around him as though he was a statue and not expected to say anything. Not sure how they fit in all that baking, but Ben drank, ate and nodded at the right time. Might have uttered a yes or a no when it was appropriate and snuck in another biscuit when Ellen wasn't looking.

Sally was handwashing some dishes, telling them some stories about her childhood, laughing some, talking more and ... and ... fitting in. A crumb caught in his throat, and he coughed to clear his airways. Rhylee never cooked with Ellen. Had never been this spontaneous in his mother's home. Ever.

"Get Ben to take you to the stargazer's lounge later," Ellen casually suggested as Sally and Paul were quiet for a second, the kitchen looking tidy enough to leave until after dinner.

"No. Wait. What?" Sally spluttered. She flicked her gaze his way, her teeth worrying her bottom lip.

He'd already seen this look once before on her. The first time was when she'd demanded to check his licence. Had his mother been telling her stories about him?

"I'm ... ah ... not sure Ben needs to babysit me. I might have an early night and catch up on some reading after dinner. We have a big day tomorrow."

"Chicken," Ben muttered quietly, hoping his parents didn't hear his taunt.

"Huh?" Sally frowned.

Ben's cheeks heated under his dark tan. There was no chance anyone would notice anything different, but why was he giving her a hard time when he totally agreed they should retain their distance and keep it work only? Holy heck, the stargazer's lounge implied so much more. It was seductive as hell; the atmosphere lulled one into believing anything.

"Hmm, is that beef roast I can smell, Mum?" he added quickly, changing the subject. How had he missed its aromatic scent earlier and not guessed what was for dinner?

"Yes, and that's enough biscuits for you this close to dinner." She said it just like he was ten years old again. "Don't think I didn't notice the second biscuit gone."

Ben groaned. Sally burst out laughing. Like the collapse of a string of dominos, Paul and Ellen joined her, leaving him shaking his head.

Sally scrunched up the tea towel she was holding and raised her arm. He frowned when it came sailing directly at him, perfectly aimed at his head. "Ouch! What was that for?" Ben caught it after it made contact, swinging it around his head, threatening anyone silly enough to come too close with a dangerous flick.

"It needs to go to the laundry," Sally said with a victorious grin. "You can either take it there or show me where it is. Just in case I get lost, you know, get scared and act like a chicken," she added with a wink.

Ben scraped his stool back, tea towel around his neck, and scratched his head. *Sassy minx.* He might be in trouble because he liked how forthright she was. "Follow me. I've never known a chicken to have such a strong right arm. That hurt, just so you know."

"Oh, please," Sally uttered with disdain, following him out of the kitchen.

One glance at his mother and she wore a wistful look. "Mum," he groaned, stretching out the word for a few seconds.

"What?"

"Don't. Just don't." She knew full well what he was warning her off as he flicked the tea towel towards her sleeved arm. Paul shook his head, aware of the shenanigans Ellen was up to. As for Sally, he ignored the confused look on her face, leading her out of the kitchen towards the laundry on the other side of the homestead.

Important next step. Remind his mother he wasn't looking for a wife.

# Chapter 7

"I hope this place you're taking me to is worth all the hype. Your mother mentioned it a few times."

Ben groaned in frustration, or was it embarrassment? "Sorry about that."

With dinner over, they strolled away from the main homestead and towards his donga and the communal pit. He grew up hearing the story of how his parents met at the stargazer's lounge. Back in the day when Ellen was a young jillaroo with her first job here on the station.

"It's fine. I like your mum, but let me go back to my room, and you go to your place." Her voice was hesitant, and he wished he could see her face to read if she really meant it.

"Except she'll hear about it, and I'll never get another chocolate chip biscuit. I don't think I can go there."

Sally chuckled. "Now who's the chicken?"

Ben smiled in the star-studded, moonless night. A lone security light stretched its beam over their path as they neared the outbuildings. "I'd already thought of asking you before Mum suggested it. It's a great spot to chill and meet people. We always have new staff joining our crew. This spot gives them the opportunity to make friends."

Sally slowed her step on the gravel path and stretched her arms out wide, turning on the spot. She raised her face towards the sky, enjoying the spectacle he took for granted every night.

"Sorry, but I love doing this. You have no idea what it's like to have grey skies and drizzle nearly *every* night. I hope my neighbours in Richmond don't think I'm a nutcase. I often go out in my backyard and do this. Stare at the sky and marvel at the magnificence of it all. I just love it."

Ben slowed his steps too, thankful for the dull edges of the light illuminating her beautiful smile. Her smile slipped when she stopped to look at him. "It's hard to forget what you told Dean about your late wife. I guess, like any mum, Ellen is hopeful you'll change your mind. I wasn't blind to her obvious ways of getting you to take me here tonight, but I must admit the entire idea of this lounge is fabulous."

Ben winced, wishing sometimes his mum wouldn't do this. "Was she that obvious?"

When she smiled again, it warmed a spot inside his chest he wasn't expecting. "She's a mum. I don't think anything has changed over the centuries, but I'm sure we'll each find our own rightful path one day."

He nodded slowly, thankful for her understanding. He wished he could find the confidence to move on one day and try his luck again.

His ears pricked. Not from any sound but from lack of it. He looked past Sally towards the lounge. "It's awfully quiet in the pit tonight. Let's keep moving."

It was only another hundred metres, but Ben couldn't see the telltale smoke rising from the pit. There was usually a fire on every night. Piles of kindling and firewood were stacked nearby for this reason. When they rounded the last shed and arrived at the stargazer's lounge, Ben came to a sudden stop. It took him a moment to comprehend the silence; then, he slapped his palm against his forehead when it finally hit. "Duh! You're going to think I set you up. No wonder mum was insistent."

"What's wrong?"

"Nothing, except I just remembered there's a rodeo on the outskirts of Richmond. It's the social event of the month, and that's where everyone will be. They won't get back until late tomorrow. They'll sleep off sore heads ready for work Monday morning."

"And you didn't want to go?"

Ben rubbed his chin and sighed for good measure. "I'm not so good with big crowds anymore." At the small enclosed kitchenette set apart on a concrete slab at the back of the lounge, containing a kettle, mugs, basic hot drinks and a small fridge, Ben added, "But there's no reason we can't enjoy this space. It'll be peaceful, if nothing else. What would you like to drink? Tea, coffee, hot chocolate or Milo."

"I might try a hot chocolate, thanks. I'm going to be honest. When Ellen called it a lounge, I was expecting something closed in. Such an open set-up like this would be useless in Malanda."

Ben smiled as he filled the kettle and readied the mugs. "It's only a problem when it rains. Then we all huddle back here, squash the chairs in closer and tell the worst jokes. No stars to be seen on a wet night anyway."

Sally harrumphed. "Let me guess, that would happen like five times a year?"

"Yep, whereas in Malanda, you'd be lucky to get five clear nights."

"Feels like it sometimes, so this will be a nice change. Do you join the workers here most nights?"

"Yeah, most nights. It helps me unwind and relax. I'm mostly tucked in here at the back, minding my own business."

"Do you ever wish upon a star?"

Ben grimaced. "I gave up doing that moons ago."

Concentrating on his task, he felt like the loneliest person on earth. He blinked in the semidarkness, daring anything to come out. He'd given up crying moons ago, too.

In his periphery, Sally strolled about, weaving in and out of the haphazardly placed long chairs, running her hands along the tops of the battered old leather. At the fire pit, she investigated its charred bottom before looking up at the clear star-studded sky.

"Here you go." Ben handed over her mug, putting his down on an upside-down crate. He hadn't noticed how run down the furniture was getting. He might find the time to repair and re-upholster the worst of them. Some of these long chairs had frames of sturdy hardwoods that would outlive him. The leather-covered cushions, though, needed some attention. "I'll get the fire going. Won't take long as this pit is probably still warm from last night. Make yourself comfortable. If you think you need a blanket, Mum keeps some in that timber box over there."

Ben pointed to a rustic, heavy-duty storage box also in the covered space. They weren't used much in summer, but in the middle of winter, it wasn't unheard of for those out here to huddle beneath their warmth. They were still a month or so away from the heart of winter, but there was a slight chill in the air. Sally put her mug down beside his and went to investigate.

Once the fire was alight, crackling and popping, Ben topped it with a couple more pieces of dried hardwood and moved two long chairs closer together with the upturned crate between them.

Sally spread a blanket over her legs and laid back with a relaxed sigh. "I can see why someone would want to spend every night out here."

"Hmm." Ben spent many hours out here. Thinking, relaxing, worrying about Grandad and solving the world's problems. All but his own. He rested his head back on the long chair beside Sally's and closed his eyes. Best to divert his thoughts. They weren't worth a dime.

Opening them again to the spectacle above him, he reached for his hot drink and took a sip. "So, tell me, why are you so passionate about this project? I have a basic understanding of what you're trying to do. I bet most of Australia hopes you have lots of success, especially with how the youth crime rate has escalated so much in recent years. But I have to say I am curious. How *did* you get started? Are you that person who takes on the hardest challenge on earth and just goes with it?"

"Oh, Ben—" Sally said wistfully.

"Only if you want to tell me. Just drumming up some conversation. We can sit here and look up all night, not say a word. That's fine by me, too."

After about a minute, when Ben thought that's what they would do for the rest of the night, Sally put her mug down again and sat forward with a forlorn look on her face.

"My heart broke. That's what it took for me to make a difference."

Ben dragged his gaze away from the brilliant pricks of light above and turned to look at Sally. Her throat moved in time with the emotion this one question must be creating and a little crack opened inside his chest.

"I didn't mean to bring up something painful."

"No, that's okay. It was the turning point I needed to do something good. To help break the cycle of kids' suffering. Especially when it's so totally out of their control. Some days, I struggle to get out of bed because it hurts so much."

"What happened?" Ben asked cautiously because he could completely relate.

As Sally snuggled back under her blanket, he watched her formulate her thoughts. A silent tremor ran across her lips, but no words came out. His heart picked up pace. What happened to her? Her heart broke? Shit, was she going through some crap no different to what he had? A perfect example of how many layers a person could have, both literally and figuratively.

"It was another wet night in Malanda."

So deep in thought, her words startled him. He latched onto her face and the sad lilt to her mouth, unable to drag his gaze away. It took all his effort to stay rooted in his lounge and not move to comfort her.

"Don't get me wrong, I love the town. I think it's the prettiest town anywhere in the world, but sometimes it drizzles for weeks on end, and you just want it to stop. Anyway—" She grimaced, her head bobbing up and down as though the memories of that night weighed her down. "I came home late from a school meeting. I usually slide my roller door down, but security isn't crucial in my street, so I left it open so I wouldn't have to get out to unlock it in the rain when I returned."

She paused. He understood how a lot of life decisions were made based on the weather.

"I don't have a roller door with a remote control. But that's a first-world problem, isn't it?"

Ben smiled, the flicker of the flames in the pit rising high enough to leave weaving shadows over her half smile.

"One day, I'll do something about it."

"My jobs list is as long as eternity, too," Ben admitted wryly. His days were never long enough. A lifetime would never be enough.

"When I drove home, there was a young boy huddled in the corner of my garage. I'd left a blanket needing washing in the laundry basket, and he had it wrapped around himself, shivering. I recognised him from school, but the look of fear on his small face as the car lights beamed over him—oh boy, his eyes were wide open. You never forget something like that."

"How old was he?"

"He was nine years old." Sally picked up her drink for another sip before putting it down again and met his eyes. "Can you believe it? How does a nine-year-old find himself shivering, cold, hungry and hiding out in someone else's garage?"

It was hard for Ben to look away from the pain and despair in Sally's eyes. If *his* child had survived, he couldn't fathom such a situation either.

"He was so cold he could barely walk. Somehow, I managed not to scare him away. Slowly, slowly, I coaxed him into drinking a hot Milo with a couple of biscuits. I convinced him to have a warm shower, loaning him some of my old gardening clothes while I washed his and dried them in the clothes dryer."

"Did he recognise you as a teacher?"

"He did. He called me Miss Barkworth. Oh, Ben, I was so frightened. I had no idea what to do. I didn't know his family situation, didn't want to send him back outside in the weather, and just wanted to take care of him."

"What happened?" Ben coaxed, the pain in his chest already hurting for this young boy.

"I dragged out a mattress and pillow, setting it up in the lounge. I kept reassuring him he was safe and to try to sleep. When I finally got to bed, I'd never cried so much."

"Did he say much about his family?"

"Nope, nothing. I wasn't trained for this. Had no idea how to prise it out of him or what questions to ask."

"Did you see him again?"

A grimace twisted her face as she stared into the night; it was hard to miss the regret. "The next morning, he begged me not to say anything. He'd tried to stop his dad from hitting his mum and ran away when his dad tried to hit him, that was all." *That was all?*

Sally flung her hands up in the air, and then she sat back before dropping them to grip the chair's armrests. There was enough light to illuminate the shine of her knuckles. She looked up at the sky, closed her eyes and swallowed like she was trying to hold it all in.

"I should have done something that night. Called the police, community services, anyone."

Moments passed, and he gave her some space, quiet seconds filled only with the gentle sounds of nature. He understood the turmoil she'd gone through. Sometimes, being there was enough. Words were unnecessary. Her moral compass had been spun uncontrollably, and her regrets would've piled up over time. He knew all about that, too.

She faced him again, his chest constricting as a thin trickle of tears slid down her cheeks. "I didn't do any of that. He begged me not to ring anyone as they would take him away. Who would look after his mum and little sister? His words, Ben. A nine-year-old talking like an adult."

She released a guttural-sounding groan, piercing him close to where his beating heart resided. He could never be sure because it'd been a long time since he'd given his heart any attention, but it was hard to ignore her pain. It was real.

"I had some grand plan. If I provided him with a safe place, he could come any time. My reasoning was I could provide a safety net a lot quicker than the system."

Ben got up to retrieve a serviette that was kept in the kitchen. He handed it to her, and she wiped her face. "I'm sorry this happened to you and the boy."

"His name was Jacob."

A shadow fell across Sally's face, and her shoulders slumped as sadness washed over her. Ben's chest hammered. *Please, please don't tell me he's no longer alive.*

"Eight months I kept this up. He came when he needed to. I purchased some clothes his size, made up the spare bed and wanted him to feel safe. I fed him heaps because he was always so hungry. If he turned up on the weekends, we did some lessons. Surprisingly, he wasn't too far behind, and he was a keen learner. He … he—"

Ben gave her another moment, letting her cry silently as the tears streamed down her face. This time a little faster. Ben rose to grab more serviettes. Taking her used ones on the way, he threw them into the pit, causing a burst of flames as they ignited.

"He … he was such a good kid, Ben. Anyone would want this kind, thoughtful child as their son." Her wail, long and mournful, floated out into the clear night, vibrating the air around him. "Why couldn't his parents appreciate what they had? Why, damn it! Why did they have to fight and bring violence into this little boy's life?"

Now her shoulders shook with silent, shuddering sobs. When he returned to his long chair, he sat sideways, his feet scuffing at the small rocks between them. Should he comfort her? *Christ!* He was in alien territory again, and it terrified him. His gut was screaming out to do something, but he had no clue how to tread here. To comfort might involve getting close to someone. He'd been through his own purgatory. He wasn't ready to go back, but his heart broke that little bit more for this young boy and how fate had dealt him a horrible hand.

"One day, he stopped showing up, and I didn't see him at school. I know the school office notified the department but I never heard anything. I had already noted his home address on the school records, so I knew where his family lived. I found the courage to go check he was okay, but the house was empty and up for lease. The neighbours told me that the family had left, and good riddance too, they added. Oh, my poor Jacob—"

Her shoulders shook again, this time with a tremor that ran through her whole body. This time, Ben didn't hesitate. Down on his knees, small rocks cut through his jeans as he took her in a hug and crushed her tight.

The potent smell of a burning fire rose around them, sheathing them in its vortex of warmth. For once, Ben was okay with it. She cried against his chest. He let her heave and sob for everything she didn't do for Jacob.

When her tears slowly subsided, she pushed back, giving him a chance to sit down again.

"I'm sorry, Ben, I—I didn't mean to load all that on you." She blew her nose with another serviette. "You're the first person to ask me why I took on this crazy project." She hiccupped and sniffled once more. "So there you have it. Even my closest friends don't know about Jacob. I wasn't game enough to say anything while he was turning up in case the department took him away. I wasn't game enough to tell anyone afterwards, in case they locked me away, but ... but now I'll never know what happened to him. It breaks me every time I think of him. I wonder where he is, how he is, how his mum and sister are faring."

"Sometimes hardship and pain can make you go places you never thought you would."

Sally swiped a sleeve across her face, then pressed her fingers over her forehead, gently massaging, taking deep, calming breaths. When she looked up at him with red, puffy eyes, she whispered, "Why do I get the feeling you know this from experience?"

When he didn't immediately reply, she continued to hold his gaze. With a subtle nod, he conveyed that he'd given her all the information she needed.

"Some days, it feels like you're continually climbing a mountain, hoping there's a downhill part soon. I keep looking for Jacob's face in a crowd. Hoping I'll see him again. Will I remember what he looks like? Hoping against all hope he's okay and alive. That's the tormenting part. I don't know what happened to him. I can't even report anything because what I did was wrong, and—"

"No, it wasn't," Ben cut in. "If Jacob is alive, he'll never forget your kindness and generosity. I promise you."

Sally sat back on the long chair and curled into herself, draping the blanket up around her shoulders. "I hope I made a difference. Some days, it's the only thing keeping me going and why I want to keep making a difference. I so badly want this project to work."

"It will; I see your determination."

When she looked across again, her gaze caught his and a breath caught in the back of his throat. Had he gone too far?

"Thank you." She sat up and blindly grabbed for her mug. Only faint tendrils of hot chocolate floated up from their mugs, the hot drinks rapidly cooling. Ben reached over to help her, but his hand connected with hers instead, pushing it towards the mug. Too late, the mug tipped on its side, rolled over to the edge of the crate, landing on the sharp gravel with a crack. Hot chocolate dripped through the open crate onto the ground.

"Shit!" Sally exclaimed, jumping up in a tangle of legs and blanket.

"Damn!" Ben got up at the same time, lifting the crate as puddles formed around their boots. "It's Mum's favourite mug too." The mug had nicely split into two pieces. This time, there were no shards scattered everywhere. It surprised Ben that it cracked at all as it didn't fall from a great height.

"Oh, what, no way. Oh my God, I'm so sorry." Sally stooped down to collect the two broken pieces of ceramic. "What am I going to do now?"

Ben took them from her and dropped them into the fire pit. "I'm joking, Sally."

"What?" She shouted.

He lacked the guts to keep smiling; instead, he looked away, ashamed. She'd barely finished pouring her heart out, and there he was, dicking around like he was drinking with his brothers.

"I'm sorry, it was a joke. Mum doesn't have a favourite mug out here."

"You, you—" she spluttered, and Ben had no idea how to proceed. She poked him hard in the chest with her pointer finger, part angry, part playful, forcing him to move backwards as he struggled to keep a straight face. *I've just done something so idiotic that it's laughable.* He couldn't remember the last time he'd attempted a joke. This one, he feared, had fallen flat.

With her face a criss-cross of annoyance, he took hold of her chilled hands, wrapping them in his warm ones. "I'm sorry, Sal, really, I am. It just came out. I'm an idiot. Maybe blame it on the fact I was raised with two brothers who were always so much funnier than me ... and because I hate to see anyone sad. Laughter is supposed to be the best medicine. Right?"

She stopped pushing and stood within a hair's breadth, her boots touching his, her arms by her side, her chest rising and falling. The scent of burning fire eclipsed the honey-sweet fragrance he remembered from the first time he'd been this close.

"Forgive me?" He stared into dark royal blue eyes, normally the colour of cornflowers. Tonight, they looked nothing like the flowers his grandmother used to grow with so much hardship in the outback. They weren't the friendliest colour at all. *Fool!*

"You totally had me. It might have only been a split second, but I was already thinking of ways to replace it."

A veil of wood smoke swirled around them, its pungent scent filling his nostrils. The crackle of a log spitting shot fire sparks high above the fire pit, breaking their trance. Ben dropped his forehead, resting it against hers, and took her hands in his. Her warmth was drawing him in like a magnet.

Sally took a step back. She untangled her hands and ran them down her jeans. "Okay," she dragged out the word. "Tomorrow morning at six? Right?"

"Right." He replied robotically, his back straightening one vertebra at a time.

"Thank you for"—she raised a hand, encompassing the lounge—"everything," before moving her hand in a semblance of a finger wave. "Goodnight, Ben," she finished, turning around and walking back to the homestead.

She never did forgive him.

*Walk away while you can. I'm a dead loss.*

It hurt that she walked away, but he let it go. It made no sense why it should upset him. Before she was completely out of sight, she glanced back at him over her shoulder, stumbled slightly and then turned back to the safety of the security sensor light, which had switched back on, guiding her the rest of the way to the main homestead.

Now to get some sleep. How was that going to happen? He dropped onto the long chair and quietly swore. Grabbing the discarded blanket from Sally's chair, he draped it across his chest, settling in for a long night. Better than tossing and turning in his bed. He glued his eyes to the flickering flames, willing himself to relax.

No way would he look up.

No way would he wish upon a star.

# Chapter 8

Sally shook all over as Ben drove the ute over corrugations on the rough track, the jarring jolts rattling her bones.

"Sorry about this." Ben braced his hands firmly on the steering wheel, his body too bouncing around the ute cabin. "It's better to drive quickly over them, if that makes sense."

Sally didn't really know too much about rough driving and trusted Ben knew what he was doing.

"The minor flooding last wet season swept away another layer of topsoil, so this is what happens to our neatly graded roads. We're a little behind in getting them cleaned up again, that's all."

Sally nodded, his explanation making sense. In the air-conditioned cab, the only other sound was the rattle of things in the glove box and a couple of empty Diet Coke cans on the floor around her feet. To prevent her hat from blowing away and distracting Ben, she placed a hand on it.

Ben said it was only a thirty-minute drive to the old homestead they'd set up for the teens, so it couldn't be too much longer. Unlike the drive from Richmond, she didn't prod about having music on, deciding to let Ben choose if he wanted any. The stereo remained silent.

Things weren't the same between them after last night. Had she walked off too soon? For someone who'd lost a wife in a harrowing way, maybe she could be that friend. If she controlled the way her body reacted whenever she was close to him. It certainly didn't want to be classified in the friend category.

Instead, their conversation was stilted from the moment Ben arrived at the main homestead to pick her up. Polite was probably a better word, if you ignored the strong undercurrent between them. She was doing her best to work past it, keeping the conversation light and chirpy and asking lots of questions.

For both their sakes.

She couldn't deny he was easy company, but should she have dumped so much personal stuff on him last night? And what was the big deal with the joke over the mug? Surely, she could handle it without being put out? She was once capable of that.

She gnawed away at a thumbnail, giving Ben some peace to concentrate on this rough patch of road. The story of Jacob would always hold a painful spot in her heart, one she'd kept to herself. Only when she went to bed last night did her heart hammer, keeping her awake longer. It'd taken some controlled breathing to calm down. The shock of telling someone hit home. So why Ben?

Keep it professional! This was her motto from now on. Limit personal information. The memories of Jacob hurt her most days, but she'd learnt to move past it by distracting herself with the establishment of this program. Rehashing it didn't help, even though on a different level, the Jacob burden felt lighter after sharing it. Which she hadn't quite reconciled yet.

She mentally shook her head, grabbing the edge of the seat when a particularly bad patch of corrugations rattled the ute again. She looked out the side window, again surprised by the landscape. Before relocating to Richmond, an image of the outback came with vast empty spaces, red dirt and nothingness. Outback Richmond wasn't quite that way. "Why are there so many trees?"

Ben glanced her way for a moment before turning his attention back to the road. "For starters, the Flinders River is very close by, so vegetation is prolific around the river for a distance on either side. We're not talking the density of tropical rainforest, but lots of other native trees like the acacia, wattle and plenty of eucalypts. Some of these trees are probably better known as ghost gums, stringybarks, ironbark and bloodwoods, for starters. The further you get away from the river, the sparser the vegetation becomes. Once the trees begin to disappear, then there are the grasses. Nutgrass, sedge, and the list goes on."

"I thought you were a palaeontologist, not a botanist."

Ben smiled in her direction before resuming his concentration on the road. "Can't help myself." At least he seemed a lot more relaxed since starting the drive out. Sally swallowed, needing to pat down the way her heart did a jig every time he offered her a semblance of a smile. "How did you decide you wanted to be a palaeontologist?"

"I didn't. The world conspired against me." Again, another charming smile allowed Sally to relax a smidgen and chuckle.

"My degree says I'm a geologist, but out here in Richmond, if you don't stumble across some small fossil at least once a week, you're not looking hard enough."

"Have you found the big one yet?"

"Still looking. Every wet season uncovers something new. Just gotta keep your eyes open." The ute jerked sideways when it hit a deep gully on the road. "Sorry," Ben offered as he steered the ute back to the centre of the track.

Sally rubbed her thigh where it'd hit the door. "This area was once under the ocean, right?"

Ben slowed the vehicle when a gate appeared. "Yep, Richmond might be one of the driest parts of Australia, but back in the dinosaur era, it was forty metres under water and covered by an inland sea called the Eromanga Sea. If it's to be believed, this stretch of water covered Cape York to northern New South Wales, and is full of dinosaur fossils. So, you see?"

"See what?" she teased, knowing full well what he meant.

"I had no choice. I sort of fell into it. I'm employed part time by the University of Queensland. When I'm not mustering and working on the property, I'm studying the history of the earth through fossil bones."

"Really? That is so cool."

Sally was glad they could relax together again. She'd been worried her lack of humour the previous night might have shaken things up between them.

"Actually, it can be slow, tedious work. It involves writing lots of papers where spellcheck thinks I can't spell because it doesn't know half the dinosaur names we use. But—" He stopped the ute and put it in neutral. "I hope someone appreciates my work one day. Anyway, we're here. I'll open the gate."

"I'll do it," Sally offered, opening the door and climbing out before Ben could argue. Surely, she could do that without breaking anything.

The gate was straightforward, much to Sally's relief, and she closed it after Ben drove through. Sally looked around but saw nothing, not even a windmill.

"Hop back in," Ben called through his open window. "It's still another kilometre."

"So, being here isn't really being here," Sally quipped once she was back in with her seatbelt done up.

Again, an easy smile lit up his face, and she bit her bottom lip to keep every pulse in her body in check, all the while trying to remain calm and act businesslike.

"Now you're getting the hang of it. We'll get on just fine, I think."

The tension and awkwardness ever so slowly dissipated. Which was dangerous ground when she couldn't keep her eyes off his suntanned hands on the steering wheel.

She turned away from those glorious hands. With the sleeves of his light blue work shirt rolled up to his elbow, there was enough sinewy muscle, making it easy to picture his arms around her. Hugging her tight. Like last night.

*Ugh! Stop it!*

A light sheen of sweat was making itself comfortable on her forehead, and it couldn't all be blamed on the one minute spent outside the air-conditioned cab opening the gate.

A clump of trees, their dull green leaves rustling in the breeze, and a weathered timber and stone building appeared before them. "Where are we? I'm assuming we're still on your property."

"Yeah, we are. You haven't forgotten that—"

"I haven't forgotten," she cut in, "that properties out here are the size of six European countries."

Ben laughed as he pulled on the handbrake and switched the ignition off. "And you have to cope with the heat and the flies. You haven't forgotten that, have you?"

Sally mimed fanning herself. "I was hoping to."

Ben's chuckle followed her as she got out of the vehicle and walked towards the building.

"Okay, let's go take a look. This place was a secondary homestead. Back in the day, my grandfather kept a second station manager posted here. It saved a lot of driving back and forth from the main homestead. In times of flooding, when it was hard to get through to this section of the property, the station manager was on hand to keep a closer eye on water troughs, fences, and a general lookout for the cattle. These days, with better vehicles and choppers, this role died a death. Its isolation from the main homestead made it unsuitable for everyone. Hard on the women and children especially."

Sally followed beside Ben, being careful not to touch him, taking in the rustic building. With its huge wrap-around verandah, it probably took up more area under the roof than the actual living quarters. The yard surrounding the building was a bit scratchy, with only a tinge of green finding its way into the lawn. More dust than grass, if she was honest. What survived looked to be mostly scruffy weeds, with an unruly hedge made of native shrubs doing a circuit of the homestead. Every couple of metres, there was a blank spot where a shrub hadn't survived the harsh conditions. Nothing a little bit of attention couldn't fix, especially if the river was close and the water situation wasn't dire.

"We've done a good clean on it lately to bring it up to scratch for your teens. They'll still be sleeping in swags. We didn't want to take that experience away from them, and I hope when they leave, they'll look back at this spot with good memories."

"How far is the river?" Sally asked as they climbed the three rough-sawn steps to the verandah.

"Far enough that in a flood, it isn't too big an issue, except for those one-in-five-hundred-year floods. Nothing is safe during one of those. But if you look carefully, you'll see this building is set on a raised patch, which gives it some protection. You probably didn't notice the slight incline as we drove towards it."

Sally shook her head. She hadn't noticed it but was getting the hang of how you had to think in the outback. When those flooding years happened, it could look like an inland ocean. Probably no different to the fabled Eromanga Sea back in the dinosaur era.

Ben unlocked the front door, pushing it open. She followed him in, inhaling the smells of yesteryear, of old hardwoods, and the new fragrances of cleaning products mingled together to twitch her nose. A touch of apple, like she'd just bitten into one. Crisp and clean.

The layout was simple as she did a three-sixty turn. A large shared kitchen and living area and a hallway that led away to the bedrooms, she assumed. Not as much privacy as the teens would get in the Richmond house they'd secured, but more of a camping experience. A massive timber table, which easily sat twelve, dominated the open plan, positioned in the middle of the shared kitchen and living area. Sally hoped it was where the teens would learn the value of family and togetherness and some cooking skills. In the evenings, they would encourage board games, cards and the like. An experience many of these kids had little exposure to.

Ben motioned for her to follow as he walked down the hallway. "You access the toilet and shower from the outside. A little rustic but serves its purpose."

"Nothing to complain about here. I'm actually very impressed. This is amazing and not what I pictured. I can't believe we secured the services of your family." A feeling of relief washed over her. Jittery but excited, she envisaged everything coming together.

"We'll walk down to the river later and take a look. The kids can do a spot of fishing, and it's safe for swimming. We've had no reports of saltwater crocodiles this far up the river. Occasionally, we attract a small freshwater one, though."

The hairs on the nape of her neck stood up, and a shiver trembled over her back. "Crocodiles?"

"Yeah, look, don't stress. We're a long way from the mouth of the river where it meets the salt water. No one could pay me to swim or fish in that water, but here, we've never had any issues."

"I'm glad. We don't want the government to drop our funding because one of the teens is eaten by a crocodile."

"They're safe, don't worry. I think there will be other issues for us to worry about. Some of these kids will be users, smokers, and God knows what else. Out here, we're taking phones, internet and television away from them. The difference between being in Richmond and here is huge."

"Some will resist," Sally added, scanning the bookshelf on the far wall, containing the classics and some newer releases, along with a small collection of board games. Apart from this small surprise the rest of the room was stark and bare.

"It's up to you and me to warn them about the dangers of trying to walk away. It's hot, dry and dangerous out there; that's why we have to keep them busy. The plan is to have them fossicking and too busy to consider leaving. Plus, Flora will be supporting them. She's a widowed grandmother who'll supervise the cooking, cleaning and general health of the children. She's an experienced nurse and counsellor. We think she'll be perfect for the job."

Sally nodded, extremely impressed with the woman's credentials. "I think a full belly and a warm bed can sometimes heal these kids in more ways than we think."

"Then you can treat all their other issues."

"Exactly." Sally nodded. How had she landed a place and a family who shared her views? Old-fashioned thinking, but she was sure sometimes this worked best.

"Flora arrives next week with a truckload of food. Which reminds me"—he pulled his phone out of his back pocket—"I need to set a reminder for early next week to put the fridge on."

Sally looked around again but didn't see any fridge. "There is one?"

"Follow me." Ben led the way to a small dark nook off the kitchen where a solid working bench, the pantry, and a big commercial fridge with double glass doors were kept.

Ben and Paul's meticulous planning impressed Sally. He jumped up and perched on the solid bench beside the fridge and swung his legs like a small child would.

She could already picture a row of brightly coloured food cannisters on that bench, the smell of freshly cut veggies, with an organised Flora in command of the kitchen. The teens working with her, preparing meals, learning how to cook, and the importance of nutrition. Sally's skin tingled. This plan was really going ahead! After months of planning, of trying to achieve something, it looked like all her hard work was paying off.

"So, what do you think?" Ben's voice was filled with a quiet confidence that matched his expression.

She choked back the big ball of emotion jammed in her throat, desperate to hide the build-up of moisture threatening to trickle down her cheeks.

"Are you okay?" Ben jumped down, placing a hand on her shoulder.

She sniffled, biting down on her bottom lip to stop the tears, thankful for his comforting hand. "It's just been a long road to get here. I'm sorry, I don't mean to get all emotional over every little detail, but I think the mention of food was enough to do it to me. Food is the most basic of all needs a child requires, and as I found with Jacob, it was missing."

As he gently massaged her shoulder, she glanced up and caught him watching her—his usually vivid green eyes were darker in the dim light of the shadowed corner. That unique outback scent she was fast associating with him invaded her senses as she stood close to him. Dirt, grease, horse, sun, heat. Even a trace of burning wood from last night's fire was still in his hair.

She swayed, wanting a closer whiff like a person with an addiction. Ben tightened his hold, their breathing loud in the tight space. Then he coughed, clearing his throat as he moved aside. "Would you like to walk down to the river? Get some fresh air?"

Sally's back straightened, and she found her footing. *What are you doing, girl?* "Yes," she spluttered, thankful for the dark alcove which would hide a raging blush she felt climbing up her neck. This was ridiculous behaviour. Hadn't he been very specific he wasn't looking for another wife? Woman? Any relationship? *Don't you dare jeopardise this project,* she reminded herself as she turned away, taking a moment to pull herself together. "Lead the way, Ben."

He glanced over his shoulder, warily watching her. Holding her head up, she drew her shoulders back. She would not make a fool of herself and kill all chances of making this project succeed. With a firm line to her mouth, she resolved to be that strong woman.

After what Ben showed her out here, she needed him for this project more than she needed him in her bed. At this thought, a snorting laugh unexpectedly escaped her lips, and she struggled to reel it back in.

"Everything okay?" Ben slowed his steps until she was beside him. They walked side by side out the front door and into the blistering sun.

"I will be." *Damn right, you will be.* "Is the river far?"

"About four hundred metres with two different tracks. One leads to a shallower section of the river with a sandy edge. Easier for swimming, just so you know. The other track takes you to the deeper section of the river. Probably better for fishing at this one. I haven't been towards the deeper section since the last wet season, so I might check on it to make sure it's passable."

Sally nodded. "Let me grab my backpack and put on a hat."

"Did you bring your swimmers like I suggested?"

"I did," and Sally's skin tingled as she did her best to drag her thoughts from out into the open and down onto the dust, where she could stomp on them.

*There will be no touching in the refreshing water!*

# Chapter 9

"This might be a dumb question, but how do you get power out to this property? I didn't see anything obvious."

"Good question, and something most people don't understand if you haven't lived out this far." Ben took a right turn at the junction, taking the track towards the river where the water was deeper.

The vegetation was still sparse, with mostly grasses and the occasional tree dotted along the washed-out track. To the right was a mound of large boulders jutting out of the ground, like Mother Nature had piled them up in a last-minute rush. Tall, brown, spindly grass grew messily from within the pile of boulders, breaking the flat landscape that tapered downhill in slow degrees towards the river and the denser trees lining it. "There's some solar generated power set up on a grid in the paddock behind the homestead, but it's mostly battery powered. We recently installed a big block of batteries in the backyard. They cost a fortune but should last a good ten years plus a bit." Nothing this woman said or did was dumb. Ben pushed his Akubra back a little so he could appreciate her some more.

Sally nodded as she walked beside him as if she was storing away useful information. "Is there a pump that carries water up to the homestead from the river?"

"There is." Ben tried to hide his smile. Most city folk had no concept of how water arrived at their tap. He relaxed. There was some small-town country in this woman—and common sense! The hardest thing to find sometimes.

"Can we waste some of it?"

Ben frowned. He might have to take back some of his thoughts. When Sally chuckled, he stopped on the dusty track, took off his Akubra and used his sleeve to wipe the sheen of sweat off his brow. "What do you mean? We try not to waste anything out here."

Now she laughed, her smile lighting up her face. Enough to send another rush over his skin as it had of late every time Sally was nearby.

"You should see your expression. You're probably thinking I want to fill that bathtub with water every day and soak in it."

Ben gulped. *Nope! Not going there.* But now he couldn't unsee a deliciously naked Sally in the rustic bathtub, complete with soapy suds. His fingers curled around the edges of his hat, creasing it some more, creating fresh memories for this well-worn hat. He was screwed if he didn't change where his mind was going.

"I was thinking more along the lines of promoting gardening chores to the teens. Some of them may take to it like a natural green thumb. Teaching them to garden can be cathartic. I know I'm no flash gardener myself, but plenty of others use it to relax. I think it would be good for them to see how something grows when you tend to it."

Ben's tense shoulders relaxed. *Gardening, you idiot!* "You can use as much as you reasonably need to keep the lawn green and for any other gardening you wish. We've had a good wet season, so there are no real restrictions."

"Good to know." Sally wandered off, continuing down the track while he feasted his eyes on her backside in snug jeans. At least she dressed like someone in the outback should.

Her *oof* had him jerking his gaze away from her curves, breaking the trance. Too late, she'd tripped and was sprawled over the dust. His attempt to grab her arm in time had him stumbling over his feet before landing with a heavy thud on her lower legs. She yelped, her anguished noise clearing the fuzziness. *What the heck just happened?*

"Are you okay, Sal?" he hastened to say, wriggling off her and sitting on his backside.

She lay on her stomach, moving her arms first and then her legs. "My knee. I must have hit something sharp."

Ben scanned the length of her body until he reached the back of her knees. "Can you turn over?"

"I can move it okay." She flexed and stretched her knee. "Though it feels like I'm going to have a whopper bruise."

Something protruding out of the dirt near her knee caught Ben's line of vision. "Here, Sally, give me your hand. I'll help you up."

With Sally standing and rubbing her knee, Ben dropped to his knees, using his bare hands to move the dirt away from the object. His experienced eye assessed it immediately. That was all it took sometimes. A little more flooding to remove another layer of soil and hey presto! This was a dinosaur bone, without any doubt, and adrenaline began doing its thing. It never changed. Until this one small fragment of bone visible was completely assessed to determine if it was just one bone, or part of a bigger skeleton, the excitement level would continue to ramp. He'd lose sleep over it, for sure.

He rose, turning to check if Sally was okay. *Whoa!* She'd dropped her jeans to her calves and was bent over inspecting her knee. The tie holding her hair up had come loose, and a cascade of blonde hair fell over her face, hiding it. He flexed his fingers. The urge to reach over and run them through that tumbled down hair verged on ridiculous.

"Can I take a look?"

Sally looked up from the wound. The blue of her eyes struck him so hard in his core that he nearly doubled over. He was so damned scared of getting close again to another woman, he could barely breathe.

"Argh," she gasped. Her pale skin around her neck suffused to a bright red, and Ben bit his tongue to keep from moaning.

"Your knee will need a good rub to get the blood flowing." A centuries-old remedy his grandfather had used often. "Sit back down. I'll give it a rub now since it's not bleeding."

He'd uttered this remedy like he'd done it a thousand times before, like it was the most natural thing to do, but heck, why wasn't it feeling like the right time to display his paramedic skills? Who did he think he was? Some medical God?

"I'm sorry, I'm making you uncomfortable, aren't I? I was only going to have a quick peek at my knee while you were turned away and have my jeans back up in a jiffy. I wanted to see if I'd split my skin and whether it was bleeding."

Ben attempted a half smile. "I'll see more of you in your swimmers. Don't stress, I won't stare." Christ! He wanted to ogle every bit of her. "Do you have any cream in your backpack?"

"I have some hand moisturiser. Will that do?"

"Yep. Pull out your towel too, so you can sit on it. The track will be hot against your skin."

This was going to test *him* more than her. Touching her skin wasn't on the list when he'd read through the project criteria with his dad. Also, the need to jump up and down at the discovery of the bone was also there. Too much was coursing through his body.

It was messing with his head if, for one minute, he thought rubbing Sally's knee was a good move. He took the offered moisturiser from her, squeezing a coin-sized blob from the tube onto his palm. She was seated on her backside, on top of her towel, her jeans still around her ankles. She'd jammed her navy-blue bucket hat back on after it had fallen off after her fall.

He crouched down and lifted her leg, turning it slightly for a better look. "Yep, this will be a shiner if we don't hurry up."

"It was certainly a good hit. Not sure how I didn't see that rock sticking out."

She tensed for a second when he applied the cool cream to her heated skin. He began rubbing as gently as possible, hoping she would gradually relax. "It's not a rock."

"Looks like one."

He was close enough to smell that hint of honey he did each time he was near her. Could have sworn he had last night when he'd touched his forehead with hers, even though the fire smoke obscured most of it.

When he'd scared her and she rushed off.

His sleep had been crap, as he suspected it would be. Holding off until after midnight hadn't helped. When the last of the flickering flames died, he trundled off to his donga, only to lay awake until God knew when. He eventually fell asleep, those blue eyes carrying through into his dreams.

He glanced up from her leg to find her watching him, her bottom lip caught between her teeth. Reaching for the moisturiser again, he took another small blob and continued to rub. "You should do this again a few more times today. I promise you it'll keep the bruising to a minimum."

"Will you offer to help me? I know the rubbing is supposed to hurt, but it feels so good."

A whoosh of air left his lungs, part groan, part laugh. "Not sure I should." He looked away, concentrating on her slim leg and the red lump beginning to form on her knee. His rubbing got a tad bit harder, and she winced. "Sorry, that should do for now." He drew away, squatting back on his heels beside her.

She reached down to still his hand. "Ben, I think that came out all wrong. I didn't mean to make it awkward between us."

Ben swallowed, his Adam's apple bobbing in his throat. "I'm fine. The good news is you tripped over a dinosaur bone. All of a sudden, you and your teens might be very busy."

"Really?" She jerked her leg back, attempting to rise. When she couldn't get enough traction because of her trapped legs, she tugged on his arm. "Show me," she demanded.

Ben laughed, liking her enthusiasm. He sprung up, giving her a hand. "Pull those damn jeans up. I'm not showing you anything until you're decent."

She poked her tongue at him while she hoisted her jeans up, her laughter getting swept up in the excitement of the here and now. For him, all the boxes were ticked. Isolated outback track. River close by. With a caring, compassionate, driven woman, and beautiful to boot. How did she come to be in his life? The discovery of a dinosaur bone could keep him busy for months and months, and hopefully with Sally by his side.

*Okay, time to shut down that thought. Now!*

With a sudden movement, she grabbed his hand, pulling him closer to the bone. "Tell me how you know."

He entwined his fingers with hers for a moment and gave a quick squeeze before letting go and crouching near the bone. "Let me show you."

# Chapter 10

B en impatiently tapped his foot against the aged-old verandah post, relief sweeping through him when he spotted the telltale spiral of dust rising from an approaching vehicle.

"You're going to wear those boots out, son."

Leaning against the sturdy black penda post holding up the verandah, Ben turned to Flora standing in the doorway of the old homestead. He casually folded his arms, doing his utmost to appear calm. "This must be Lucy."

"I sure as heck hope so, or you're not going to make it to tomorrow with all this fretting."

*Bugger!* Fool Flora? Yeah, right. He couldn't fool himself. He was anything but calm. "You know how it is, Floss." Ben used the family nickname the three boys had long ago assigned to her. His fingers bit into his arms as the anticipation ramped up, his heart hammering hard. This had the potential to make or break his career, and he was so ready for it. "I need Lucy to check I'm not seeing things. If she agrees, they need to send a team up here; they'll practically be here by breakfast tomorrow."

"Oh, great," Flora responded with a helpless smile. "Not only will I have half a dozen teens to feed and take care of, but I'll also have a team of scientists eating me out of house and home."

Ben smiled, rotating around a smidgen to check the approaching spiral of dust. "Palaeontologists, Floss, and I have a good feeling about this. I just know it. I think I've found something very special, but I don't want to contaminate it until we're set up correctly."

Flora moved out onto the verandah and shielded her eyes as the afternoon sun snuck underneath the verandah roof. "If this is Lucy, she's nearly here," Flora added, following the spiral of dust as it drew closer.

Ben grunted. Two weeks was a long time. He'd set up a fence around the bone, a temporary platform, and drove over every couple of days to check up on it. Like a bone buried for millions of years couldn't get through another couple of days.

"I hear she's quite the girl."

Transfixed by the approaching vehicle and his concerns about the discovery, Ben did a double take when Flora's words sunk in. He spun around to face Flora, who'd taken a step back out of the scorching sun. Frowning, he gave her one of his special slit-eye glares when she boldly looked back at him. He gave her a decent stare-down, mouth straight, teeth grinding together. Until he realised he was never going to win with Flora and relaxed. Instead of firing back with an angry mind-your-own-business retort, he scraped a hand over his rough chin with defeat. "Floss, don't even go there."

"I was chatting with Ellen the other day."

Ben moaned like she'd thrust a knife into his chest. She was completely ignoring his gentle warning. "God help me," he muttered, feeling the despair that his mother and Flora were pitted together in this quest to find him another wife.

Flora chuckled. "It's time you moved on, son. Ellen won't say it to you. Your good father won't either. I'm brutal, but someone has to be. Why would you choose to be unhappy for the rest of your life? I sensed Rhylee had her struggles, but nobody said anything. Maybe outback life wasn't meant for her. I get it, but now it's time to grab life with both hands and run with it. Every day, I wish my old Marty was still here. I really do, because I'm not getting any younger—only lonelier. If I'm given a second chance to share my life, have someone to talk to each day, maybe hold their hand,

I won't waste it. Let's face it, I could still be around another twenty years, the healthy ox that I've always been," Flora added with a laugh.

Ben managed a smile. Being around Flora again would be good for him. Until he got all serious again when he remembered how busy his life was going to get. "Look, Floss, I'm not sure I have time for all that stuff. I have a dinosaur to unearth."

"Well, make time for it. When was Sally arriving with the kids?"

*Sally.* It was bad enough those blue eyes of hers had crept into his sleep. Her gorgeous curves in jeans he kept seeing at the oddest times. That soft knee he'd rubbed the day she tripped. He couldn't unsee it anymore. Even spending a few minutes relaxed and gazing up from the stargazer's lounge, he didn't see a single prick of light, so consumed with her image flitting across his mind.

"They're leaving Richmond after breakfast tomorrow. Mum is prepped to give them smoko, then they'll drive straight here. I think you can assume they'll be here for lunch."

Flora nodded, taking another step back and plonking her small yet sturdy frame down on the rustic chunks of timber screwed across two tree stumps used as seating out the front of the homestead. Flora was a true outback woman. Not scared of hard work, used to the knocks of life. A healthy woman, incredibly strong for someone in her late sixties. Ben could've sworn she'd never carried a strand of grey until she suffered the sudden loss of her precious Marty to a heart attack. A woman with an oversized heart is how Ben liked to think of her.

"What happens when the kids move from the Richmond house to out here?"

Ben removed his Akubra and put it beside him. "Sally and the second teacher set up individual structured lessons while the kids were at the Richmond house. These same teens will now come out here and stay for a month. Then, a second lot of teens will arrive in Richmond. The other teacher will spend a month with them before sending them out here to Sally. They'll continue to swap locations, with the entire program for each child lasting about six months."

"I'm guessing lessons will continue out here too?"

"I believe so. Their extracurricular activities will be fossicking, fishing, swimming, cooking, gardening and learning outback Aussie bush skills. Are you ready for this, Floss?"

"The kitchen is brimming. I can't wait. And I can't wait to see Lucy again. Those babies of hers must be primary school aged by now."

Ben nodded. "Yeah, they're growing up real fast." He did his best to keep in check the pain that always afflicted him whenever he thought of his unborn baby. He was an adopted uncle to Lucy's two children, and he valued this relationship, but sometimes it wasn't enough.

A wisp of dry breeze touched Ben's cheeks as he swallowed back old regret. But it was tampered with the excitement of seeing Lucy again. He breathed in the dry outback air, allowing it to filter to different parts of his body, hoping to disconnect his mind from that past and onto an earlier past when good times had abounded.

He and Lucy became partners in crime when they met at university. Somehow, the two outback kids always fell into each other's pockets when it came to on-the-field work. Both competitive by nature, always trying to outdo the other, their working relationship was one where Ben trusted her opinion explicitly.

Sally was sworn to secrecy while he waited for Lucy to put a halt on her everyday life and leave her husband and young family for a few days. She was making her way from Brisbane, where she now lived, to confirm what he already knew. All this had taken nearly two weeks of planning.

Deep down, he was hoping against all hope he could surprise Sally with this significant find. He really wanted it to be the one. Why? Who knew? There was something about Sally that was loosening the bonds Rhylee's death had clamped around his heart. Flora's advice wasn't so stupid ... if he got over the barrier that Sally was not a true outback woman. His number one condition for crossing that line again.

The two weeks of waiting had nearly killed him.

Lucy was here now, having borrowed one of the spare station utilities, leaving her hired car back at the main homestead. The dust plume dropped once she'd parked and turned off the ignition, but a sprinkle of red powder gently settled over the white vehicle, each particle sparkling in the afternoon sun. Ben shoved his hat on tighter, ambling down the steps to the parched, barely there lawn while she got out of the vehicle.

She'd be tired from travelling, but the first thing Ben saw was her wide, cheery smile. It always did him good to be around Lucy.

"Hey, Flora," she exclaimed once she spotted her. "A little birdie told me I'd find you out here. Looks like they've got you pandering to this annoying nerd, too?" This was said with a hearty laugh, filling the surrounding air, encompassing them all.

Ben smiled. "What took you so long?" He gave her a pat on the shoulder before succumbing to a hard hug, her laughter still ringing out aloud; her chatter, once it got started, would never stop.

Stepping out of his embrace, she kept talking, all the while racing up to the verandah to hug Flora, too. "Gawd, sometimes I forget how far everything is out here. I hope this is all worth it, bro. Rod is already shaking his head and rolling his eyes, knowing he's probably lost me for a few months."

Rodney, Lucy's long-suffering husband, and the good man that he was, missed his wife when her hands-on approach to palaeontology had Lucy absent from their home for months at a time.

"Great to see you, Lucy." Flora enveloped Lucy in her strong arms.

"Same here. I hope we have real dinosaur bones here because this will be like old times. What do you say, Floss?"

"I'll be busy cooking for so many people; I won't have a minute to myself, and those girls of yours?"

"How are Lara and Millie?" Ben interjected.

"Growing up too fast," Lucy responded, "and sour about not being able to come," she directed to Ben and stepped out of Flora's arms. "God help us, Ben. Those two are more outback-orientated than I ever was and they barely leave the city. But they made me promise if this was a real dig, that they could come out and do their schooling and their share of digging."

"What's wrong with that? I miss those two."

"Nothing, I guess, so long as they don't get into any mischief with their Uncle Ben. Now, get moving and show me this bone," Lucy added, leaving the verandah with a spring in her step to join him in the sun.

"Can't guarantee that," Ben piped up, surprised how Lucy's presence always lightened the load. Made life more carefree. Produced more laughter in a short space of time than at any other point in his life. Together, they'd been the worst and then some. But they were a team, and he needed her more than ever if this discovery was as good as he predicted it would be.

"Will you want a cuppa when you get back?" Flora asked.

Lucy stopped midstride and turned back to Flora. "Is that even a question? I hope your lousy boss gave you enough supplies to make some of your divine chocolate cake because I've been craving it since I heard you were going to be here."

Flora gave a hearty laugh, disproportional to the petite-sized woman she was.

Ben shook his head. It was going to be these two women against the world. Would it change when Sally arrived tomorrow? Why was it so important for Sally to get on with these two women? He mentally shrugged, not really understanding why, just that it was.

"I'll have it ready." Flora shooed them off. "Now go find me some dinosaur bones."

# Chapter 11

Adrenaline kicked in the closer the two hired 4WD troop carriers got to the old homestead. Sally sat in the first one with her designated driver, three teens, and lots of gear. Sourced out of Richmond, these vehicles would ferry the teens back and forth between Richmond and the old homestead.

The badly rutted corrugations had her sliding across her seat until the seatbelt bit into her skin. She twisted around to check on the three boys. They beamed enormous smiles at her as they laughed at the rattling vehicle.

Her heart expanded with each vibration. They weren't bad kids, and she was already growing an attachment to each one, which would be hard to sever.

Another jolting shudder had her switching her thoughts to the same drive shared with Ben barely two weeks ago and all it entailed. She rubbed her kneecap, finding it hard to forget how he had insisted it be massaged every couple of hours. Twice he'd rubbed her knee and, true to his word, the bruising had been minimal. The sensitive touch of his fingers on her pale skin, the way her heart beat crazily each time, the uncertain glances between them. It had only been a day trip. An extra special weekend by the time Ben delivered her back to her home in Richmond.

Wonderful memories hard to push back and forget as she allowed a small smile to hover, reminded of the final hug they'd shared before he turned around and drove off. She was doing her best to remain businesslike. To remember he wasn't looking for another wife. She shrugged with another rough rattle of the vehicle. As to how well her intentions were going, she wasn't so sure.

She'd spied another side of Ben that weekend. The palaeontologist. The thrum of excitement he couldn't hide. The swearing to secrecy. They'd messaged twice over the past two weeks, but it had been twenty-four hours since Lucy's arrival, and she'd heard nothing. The waiting was killing her. Was it a find of great significance? Did they know yet? How did this sort of stuff work? Why hadn't he sent through something? Anything?

Sally ground her jaw. It shouldn't concern her, but it did. She wanted this as much for Ben as she wanted it for herself and the program. The unique experience these teens would be involved in was a once-in-a-lifetime opportunity.

But Sally was hyped up for other reasons. The past two weeks were the best in her teaching career ever. One-on-one with a troubled teen, getting them to realise it was possible to succeed, seeing the light shine in their eyes when even a miniscule of progress was made, expanded everything inside her chest.

These kids had missed out on so much already. Lack of a cohesive family unit, some violence and exploitation, and some substance abuse by the parents. A constant two weeks of counselling with the experts and sorting out their educational needs. She would thrive on this for years to come if the government allowed the program to continue. It was a boot camp of sorts but without the extreme exercise.

There was so much more required to help heal these kids. If you took them away from the problems and allowed them to focus on the necessities of life, like health and education, then anything was possible. The parents would also receive counselling in their child's absence.

Nothing was straightforward, though. There were so many children in much greater need, making it harder to get them back on track. Sadly, for some, they would be thrust into the adult world totally unprepared. It would be a vicious cycle of violence, crime and abuse leading up to a continual merry-go-round of jail time, lack of education and no career prospects. They would have to be super strong to stop the cycle.

She had to be satisfied with the teens she could help. Their parents being those exact same kids who'd never received the help they desperately needed.

Finding the right foster homes would be hard work because, in most cases, sending them back to their fractured family or single parent would only bring them back to square one, undoing all their hard work. But was it right to take them from the only family they knew?

Always the dilemma.

Sally never expected it to be easy, but when these kids left this program, she wanted them to know they could reach out at any time. She, specifically, would always be available for them, regardless of the bumps along the way.

She touched the spot where her heart beat against her ribs, reminded of Jacob. Always hoping he was safe somewhere.

When the driver stopped at the gate, Sally piped up, "I'll open it." She got out with renewed determination. In her mind, she'd already christened this program *Jacob's Way,* and it *had* to succeed. The time was ripe, and the community was tired of the growing teen crime problem. These kids needed help *now,* and she was the right person for the job!

Sally waited at the open gate, swatting flies with her spare hand and closing her mouth to prevent getting a mouthful of dust, until the second troop carrier drove through. A sudden whirl of breeze picked up, twirling leaves and dirt around her head. She pushed her sunnies closer against her face, hoping to keep it out of her eyes. With the gate closed, she bolted back inside the air-conditioned cab, her nostrils filled with the unique smell of outback Australia. Dust, earth, eucalypts, slow-moving river water she knew was close by. Now her heart thumped harder. In barely minutes, she would see Ben again. They would be spending months together. She mentally shook her head, reminding herself he wasn't looking for a wife. It was the mantra she forced herself to repeat. But something was happening between them, and she couldn't be the good girl here. Didn't want to be that girl. Who needed to be a wife anyway?

Inwardly groaning, she reprimanded her wayward mind. Too bad it was stuck on how hot Ben was, especially when he came complete with R.M. Williams boots, a well-worn Akubra, just the right Ringers Western shirt to hug those abs made of steel, *and* strong, capable hands gifted with the skills to perform the gentlest of massages.

Thank God the old homestead came into view, and she flicked all those thoughts to the back of her mind. Except three people waited on its front verandah, and one of them was Ben. Her breath snagged. Nothing had changed. Her mind hadn't blown him out of all proportion in her absence. God help her; Ben was the real deal, and she was in trouble.

When the driver stopped and turned the ignition off, the blessed quiet inside the cab blanketed them all, rendering them speechless. This lasted for all of about three seconds, then doors opened, and they noisily clamoured out. The three boys, together with the other three boys in the second vehicle, ambled across the lawn towards the homestead, talking over each other, joking and laughing.

An older woman, who Sally assumed was Flora, wound her way around the boys, giving a shoulder a tap here and there. Another woman, much younger, joined her, patting a boy on the back as she welcomed him and then the others. Sally guessed this was Lucy; Ben had given her some background, and she looked the part. How she talked and how she wore her clothes.

The women left the boys huddled and chatting with backpacks strapped over their shoulders and came across to where she waited. She stayed back a step, more to catch her breath, hoping she wasn't openly staring at Ben who had remained at the bottom of the homestead steps.

"Welcome, Sally. It's a pleasure to finally meet you." Flora took her in her arms and gave her a hug before pulling back and assessing her. "Are you ready for this craziness?" A wide smile spread across her face as they walked across the lawn.

Sally let out the breath she wasn't aware she was holding. "I am, I really am." This program was actually happening, and her heart somersaulted. She was so ready for this.

"Hi, Sally."

Sally turned to the other woman. "You must be Lucy. Lovely to meet you."

"Same here. Boy, are we going to have some fun."

A bubble of excitement spread across Sally's chest. "Does this mean there's good news to share?"

"Hasn't Ben said anything to you yet?" Lucy tutted, glancing back to where Ben was, alone, colossal, everything she'd dreamt of over the past two weeks.

"Lunch is ready," Flora said over the hubbub, "and you pair have a place, too." She directed the designated drivers to the eating area.

"Come on, boys," Lucy encouraged. "I'll give you a hand, Flora," she added, helping to herd the boys and drivers towards the homestead steps. "We'll leave Ben and Sally to catch up for a moment."

Ben came a few steps closer, groaning at Lucy's suggestion. She'd seen it with Ellen. Were all the women in his life ganging up against him? Forcing him to think about moving on? Was he resentful of this?

When it was just her and Ben in the front yard, she came closer, her outback boots crunching on the parched lawn, reminded of her gardening pledge.

Finally braving it, she looked up at him. Fully taking him in and liking every single thing she saw. She swallowed, unsure of what to say. "Hi," she managed with a shrug. "We made it."

His gaze brushed her face, gentle with its touch. Almost relief like that she'd finally arrived. Like the past two weeks hadn't been the slowest in eternity, whereas, in reality, the days had flown by.

But she wouldn't be that swoony chick. Underneath all these new feelings trying to find their way out, something really irked her. She could own it now. Why hadn't he messaged her with Lucy's verdict on the fossil? Heck, wasn't this the most important event to ever take place in his palaeontologist life? The big find they were all hoping to make? *She'd* tripped over the bone. It might still have been a mystery if it wasn't for her clumsiness.

She'd kept her mouth shut as promised. Hoped they were in this together. So, what was the real reason irritation clawed at her vital organs, sending them haywire? Even she wasn't expecting to have this unusual reaction. Was it frustration for being left in the dark for the past twenty-four hours, or was it something else? Because God help her, she was never going to be able to hold off from touching this man. She would burn to a pile of ashes for these ridiculous hopes unless she rose like the phoenix and was brave enough to take the necessary steps.

First, she had to deal with the silence from his end. He couldn't send her *one* message? If he was that lousy, why would she want to bother with a first move?

# Chapter 12

"Sally, hi." The words jammed in his throat, and Ben cleared his airways with a wrangled cough. One splutter did the job, but so not how he planned Sally's arrival. He rubbed the back of his sweaty neck, giving the muscles there a good knead. Anything to smarten himself up.

Sally remained motionless, an intense frown on her face. Maybe the direct sun beating over their heads was getting to her. "Ah, did you want to go inside and have some lunch?"

"Ben, how could you?"

*Huh?*

"Twenty-four whole fucking hours," she whisper-hissed, "Lucy has been here, and you tell me *nothing*?"

Ben's eyebrows shot up, never once envisaging Sally as the sort of woman to swear. Heck, he and Lucy did so daily when they were together, more to release the frustrations of life as a palaeontologist, but Sally—

He couldn't hold back the choked laughter that erupted from his throat. Her scowl deepened, and he cut off the laughter in an instant. "I take it that's a no to lunch and a yes to walking to the site for a look at what I've done?"

"Damn straight it is. And I apologise for swearing, but how dare you keep me waiting this long?"

Oh boy, the way her jeans hugged her curves and followed those legs he remembered too well. Her buttoned-up, long-sleeve pale pink shirt she wore hugging her shapely chest. No flat-breasted woman here. The way she wore her new light beige Akubra over her blond ponytail like she was a born and bred outback chick.

*Fuck!* It would be so easy to forget where he drew the line with women. *I don't want to go there again. You're too much of a temptation. I haven't forgotten the feel of your soft skin. Your eyes are the last thing I see when I close mine.*

"I didn't think you'd be interested."

"Liar!" She planted her fists on her hips.

Ben turned and stalked off with Sally one step behind. He'd been called out, and he knew it. Not something to be proud of. He had gone to tap on her phone number several times but always swiped aside the screen at the last minute. Why? He trusted her to keep the discovery under wraps.

He curled his fingers into a ball and shoved his hands in his pockets. Always that line. Always that promise never to go there again.

"I found the damn bone; I practically own it," she grumbled from a few paces behind him.

She had a point. Something that simple was easily missed, but she'd never own it. Not even the fact they'd found it on his family's property would they be able to lay claim to it.

"Ben, talk to me, damn it! How are we supposed to work together if you can't even get one important message through to me?"

When they were about a hundred metres away from the homestead, Ben spun around, not sure what to say or do. Sally came to an abrupt halt, too, almost colliding with him, frown lines etched on her forehead.

He was all over the place, and this woman was finding the one hole in the wall leading to his heart. It had to stop before he got too carried away, but any matter related to his heart was way over his head, so he went for the easy question to answer. "You can never lay claim to it. The government will take ownership of the find and bring it back to their fancy museum. We'll never see hide nor tail of it again."

"Huh? Why?" Her frown grew deeper.

"What do you mean why?"

"Why can't Richmond lobby the government to build a state-of-the-art museum right here in town and make this place the heart of dinosaur country? Why does everything have to go to the city?"

"Because it takes people, money and volunteers. We lack all three."

"Look at Lake Fred Tritton. Wasn't that achieved by a big push by the local council and the community? How else would it have come about?"

Ben eyed her. She made sense, but never would he have considered such a plan to build a museum in Richmond. Why would the government fund this in such a small town?

"Instead of travellers making it as far as the only service station, fuelling up and bypassing the town, they'd come for a couple of days or weeks, do some dinosaur digging like my project is organising, visit the museum, fill the caravan park, buy food from the supermarket, buy snacks from the cafés."

"Sally, this is big. Huge. I've been too scared to admit to myself how special a find this is. I can't believe it." His voice dropped to a whisper.

Sally took a step closer and squared her shoulders, almost like she was daring him. "Well then, start lobbying the council, the government. Don't give it away."

"There's never any money for towns like ours."

"Bullshit. He who screams the loudest gets it. I know. I screamed, I raved, I shouted at the top of my lungs. How else do you think I got this program up and running?"

Ben took a moment to imagine the impossible. A modern air-conditioned museum right here in Richmond. Those bones laid out in a temperature-controlled environment, and hundreds—no, thousands of visitors every year to view the bones he was about to dig up.

Euphoria ripped and shuddered all over his body. Sally resembled a guiding angel, all blonde and beautiful—almost ethereal. He swooped her up in his arms, held her tight against his chest and spun her around, letting out a whoopie of laughter as he did.

"Ben, are you crazy? Put me down!" She laughed too, its sound reaching into his soul, which had been empty of late. Very empty.

He stopped spinning, placed her back on the dirt and gave himself
a minute to adjust from the dizzying motions swaying his head. Then,
without thinking, he kissed her. Hard, impulsive, her eyes growing bigger
until he closed his and eased up. Heard her whimper, knew this was
affecting her as much as it was him. Liked how her mouth tasted, realising
one kiss would never be enough with this woman.

When the biting sun got too much, even with a hat on, he eased back,
gradually pulling away. "How's your knee? Can you run?" The words
tumbled out gravelly, like he'd lost his marbles.

It took her a moment to return to earth. Her dreamy expression edged
towards another frown. It came out all wrong. *Could she run?* What an
idiot!

"I don't want to run away, Ben. I liked that."

He shook his head. Of course, she'd be confused. "No, I mean, can you
run with me now?" He grabbed her hand and took off at a slow trot. "I
want to show you what I've done since you were last here. Can you run?"

She nodded as a smile lit up her face. They sped up their trot until they
were running, which was crazy in the middle of the day in the outback.
Rivulets of sweat coated his skin, his shirt sticking to his back. Sally was
holding her Akubra with her free hand, running with him as if it were the
most natural thing in the world to do. They were nearly there. Not much
further to go. Ben was keeping a keen eye on where they were going, hoping
to avoid rocks and other obstructions along the path. He didn't need her
tripping again.

They arrived at the timber viewing platform he'd roughly constructed.
A zigzag of framing timber. Something to stand upon and look down onto
the marked-off area of dirt.

Sally's cheeks had turned a mottled rosy pink under the brim of her
Akubra. "You're crazy, Benjamin Reginald Angwin," she spluttered, bent
forward, both hands on her thighs as she gulped in air. "You should at least
warn me when I need my joggers on instead of work boots." She finished
this tirade with wheezing laughter as she lifted her shirt to wipe her face.
"God, it's hot."

Ben caught a glimpse of pale, smooth skin along her belly and swallowed. All the while taking a moment to catch his breath. Running one hundred metres in the hottest part of the day, with no water for a drink, had been a stupid thing to do, but they were here now, and he couldn't wait to show Sally the find.

He beckoned for her to follow him to the shaky structure. It was safe for two people to stand on. Positioned about two metres off the ground, any more than two people and it would never satisfy any safety regulations. But it wasn't about the safety. It was about viewing what he had painstakingly revealed with some removal of dirt from around the one bone Sally had tripped over. There was plenty more to remove before the full picture presented itself, but it was a start.

"Is this thing safe?" Doubt crossed Sally's face, and she hung back from the structure.

Ben grimaced and hesitated for a second, reminded of how he hadn't been able to keep Rhylee safe. Again, that old friend, regret, surfaced. He swallowed it back.

When he looked across at Sally, she was watching him intently, probably sensing his indecision. Snapping out of the past, he grabbed hold of a timber brace and hoisted himself up. He spun around and, still on his haunches, offered to pull her up too. "It's safe. Here, let me help you."

Her warm hand fused with his as she used a lower horizontal timber strut to secure her footing. He tugged a little too hard on her final step up, and she stumbled, falling onto the small ledge. She gasped, grabbing his shoulder to help steady herself. Huffing out a chuckle, she fell onto her bottom, her legs a tangled mess with his on the square metre ledge.

"Well, that went how it should," she remarked sarcastically before giggling. "This thing needs some sort of ladder if you're going to allow others to climb it."

"You're right. I just haven't got to that task yet, but I will." Her smile and laughter tugged at his chest. This was where their adventure started. At this very spot, and boy, was it going to be some venture. Her idea to lobby the government to keep this dinosaur in Richmond resonated with him, and he inched his backside closer to Sally. He wanted another taste of the mouth he'd sampled earlier. God help him; he was drowning as Sally swung her gaze in his direction and connected with his. Could they pull it off? The museum? Seemed hard to believe such an achievement was possible in a small outback town.

Then he remembered her words before they ran. "I liked that, Ben."

His mind was everywhere all at once. Gone was the idea of the museum for now. Other important things were taking up space in his head, like how he was going to kiss her again. Giddy as a teenager with a host of mixed-up hormones, he didn't doubt his intentions. More than prepared to experiment. Happy to learn all over again—after Rhylee.

He reached out, cupping her cheek. Hidden in the shadows of her Akubra, her blue eyes remained steady on his. He took off his hat and sat it down beside him on the crudely made platform. It was too hard to move his legs. Too difficult to move at all, except for his upper torso, which he brought in closer, the heat of their two bodies overpowering and clouding his mind. They were no longer puffing. It hadn't taken long to calm their breathing after their run, and he began stroking her skin with the rough edge of his thumb.

She inched closer, drawn to the magnetic power impossible to ignore. He got that now. Sometimes there were forces outside of his control. This was one of those moments. When his heated mouth touched hers, a bonfire erupted between them, and he lost himself with how good it felt. After so many years without.

When they eventually pulled apart, his nostrils filled with her honey scent. Mixed and fuelled by the smell of dust, dirt, and the treated framing timber used to build the structure. This moment would forever remain etched in his memory.

An inkling of a breeze eddied around them, touching and cooling his sweaty skin. A quick dip in the river sounded like a great idea about now. Anything to distract his body's reaction to being this close to Sally.

For now, he couldn't drag his gaze away from hers. He wanted to sit like this forever. It felt like a safe place, and he didn't foresee any dangers in doing just this. But he had to come clean on one thing. "I should apologise, Sally. I've told you a few times I'm not looking for a wife."

She looked across at him boldly. Assessing, soaking him in, wringing him out. "I haven't forgotten, but that's okay"—her lips curved up, her face relaxing as a smile spread across it—"for neither am I looking for a wife."

Ben smiled too, surprised he was capable of doing so, considering he was a tangled-up mess. "What about a husband?" he whispered past twisted vocal cords that refused to play the game. He cleared his throat, reminded of how parched he was. How totally unprepared they were without any water. Rule number one in the outback? Like he needed reminding.

She dropped her gaze to her lap, fingering the denim covering her knees. "I don't *need* a husband. I'm doing okay without one, but that doesn't mean we can't enjoy each other's company, does it?"

The air rushed out of his dry throat. He could die out here. Happily.

"We're two consenting adults," she added, looking back up.

Never once in the past three years had he ever gotten this close to another woman. He'd closed that door and locked it tight. With a compulsion he couldn't control, he captured her face, tilting it up so she looked at him again. "It's been a long time since I've been sure of anything."

"That's okay." She chuckled like she might be nervous or regretting her suggestion. "I've never been sure of anything either."

Relief was swift as he brought her closer and reached in for a feather-light kiss. He accidentally knocked her hat off, and it fell behind her. "So, we're in the same boat?"

"I can't see a river," she joked.

"There's one close by, or have you forgotten?" he whispered against her lips.

"I haven't forgotten a thing." She pulled away, eyeing him, assessing.

He grabbed her hat, placing it back on her head. He did the same with his own. The sun was getting ridiculously hot, and he never wanted her perfectly clear skin sun damaged like his.

It was time to wrap this conversation up for now. Wasn't sure if he could make her any promises, but he'd have a good, long think about it. No doubt it would keep him awake at night. Something else to add to the worries about his grandfather, who did a good job of keeping him awake some nights.

First, though, he wanted to show her his masterpiece in the outback. She hadn't looked in its direction yet, and he wanted to do the full unveiling. He rose on shaky legs, stretching them and rotating his stiff ankles. She did the same, standing beside him on the small platform.

"Close your eyes."

"Really?"

"Yep, come on, this is special."

She chuckled, closed her eyes, swaying closer towards him. "Turn around like this." He manoeuvred them so they were both looking towards the fossils with her back against his chest on the cramped platform. "Are your eyes still closed?"

"Yes," she groaned, "but hurry up. The suspense is killing me."

Ben laughed, inspecting the work site, hoping the infectious adrenaline resurfacing—like it did every time he looked down from this height—was catching and that Sally would be caught by the bug too. Imagine if this sort of thing excited her too.

"Ben, what's happening?"

He snapped out of his musings and smiled. This was it! Rhylee never fully invested herself in his urge to search for *the one*. Had never been interested in his smaller discoveries, either. Could never make sense of why it was important.

In a split second, the entire earth's vista opened wide. Everything was clear-cut and made sense. He finally got it. For anything to happen with Sally, they had to share this interest. It was what made up his DNA. He lived and breathed digging up fossils and searching for answers. Why had she chosen Richmond, of all places, to set up a teen program? Was the universe talking to him? Is this what they called fate?

He shut down the niggling nerves, ignoring the churning in his stomach. Like the unveiling of a masterpiece in an art museum, he whispered near her ear, "You can open them now."

It took her a few seconds, but with his arms hanging beside her hips, he felt the jolt she experienced. It zapped him, shimmying over his skin.

"Oh, my God, Ben, I can see it clearly."

"I know, right." Euphoria bubbled quietly inside his chest. This was his baby. It was his time.

"Look at those fins."

"Yep, I see them."

"I tripped over *that*?"

"Thank God you did."

"And we have to dig out every single one of those bones?"

"Every single one," he confirmed, wrapping his arms around her waist in a warm embrace. "And look, Sally, the outline shows there are a lot of bones to dig out. This is epic. This dinosaur won't be complete, but what if it's close?"

"It's definitely not leaving Richmond."

"You can't be sure of that."

"I've never been so sure of anything, Ben. We're going to do this. Will you let me help?"

She half twisted in his hold and pushed her Akubra up to see him better. The set of her jaw and the intensity in her eyes spoke volumes about her determination and the seriousness of her proposal.

"Yes, please." It was almost a beg. A plea to get him out of the rut he'd been in for so long. Referring to more than just the find. Was this when his life kick-started again?

Sally turned forward again, pointing out the features so clearly visible from two metres up. Curiosity sparked, she began peppering him with questions, her voice a flurry of words. More than his brain could comprehend. Not sure if, in all the excitement, she noticed that his mouth touched her neck as he inhaled her honey and sweet-scented sweat.

To have a woman interested in the half-buried bones and invested in their eventual outcome was too much to take in all at once. So, he didn't try.

He let her talk. Let her absorb. Let her ask away. Took a moment to enjoy how his heart burst, filling it with her excited chatter and the possibilities of how these newly discovered bones could change his life.

# Chapter 13

Sleepy boys rubbed tired eyes as Sally coaxed them awake one by one, sending them to the kitchen for breakfast. Flora greeted them with a cheery 'good morning', followed by some groans and protests at being dragged out of bed at the first hint of sunrise. Each day's activities began at the fossicking site, and they needed to get started before the heat of the day set in.

"Good morning, Aidan." She gave the last boy who needed waking a gentle nudge on the shoulder.

Aidan groaned, roused and sat in his swag, stretching his arms above his head.

"Flora has breakfast prepared. It's time to get up?"

Aidan gave her a sheepish smile. "We stayed up a bit later than we should have, Miss Barkworth. The jokes were funny, though."

Sally smiled, giving Aidan a few more moments. He was one of the less troubled boys. Without their parents around, some of the others were pushing the behaviour limits to the max. Sneaking out at night, acting up, talking back and being rude. Swearing was not tolerated, but the balance between punishment and reward was a hazy line because these boys had already suffered so much.

There was no easy road for them, but Sally's motto was to keep them busy.

"You must have all whispered them quietly. I didn't hear a thing. But then again, when my head hit the pillow, I was a goner."

Aidan giggled, and it broke Sally's heart. These boys were still so young in many ways. "Same here. The digging, swimming, gardening, and because it's so hot, it makes you very sleepy by the end of the day."

"It knocks us out, that's what it does. Not a bad thing, if you ask me."

Aidan shuffled out of his sleeping bag, his short, spiked hair, messy. The time spent at the old homestead was initially proposed to be more life-experience based, but there were a couple of hours every afternoon spent on traditional learning of the basics, such as maths, English and science. The days were full and challenging—physically and mentally. Full of new experiences and continued learning. A lot for these young boys who had, for some time, been prone to boredom, loneliness, sadness, uncertainty, abuse, and with no incentive for motivation. Without the distraction of technology, Sally strived to teach the boys the importance of keeping busy by other means.

Hearing Aidan's confession about staying up late and joking around was a good thing. This was harmless and would foster good relationships. For those boys who weren't morose and wanted to join in, they played cards, with Uno being a favourite, or a hotly contested game of Monopoly. Some of them read books or comics they'd found in an old wooden box in one of the outhouses. If they left with lifetime friendships, that would be a bonus.

When Aidan scootered off to the toilet, she made her way to her room at the very end of the hallway. One week was all it took for the homestead to change from a hustle to a bustle. The boys had erected tents for the three scientists who'd arrived within days. With six boisterous boys, Flora, Lucy, Ben and herself, the old homestead was well and truly alive.

As for her and Ben, they were too busy to explore what they'd started on that unsteady platform. Instead, there was a touch of a hand here and there, the occasional look from Ben, leaving her insides melting. Added to that was the hum building up inside her just being at this momentous digging site. History was in the making.

With satellite access to the internet, she could progress her campaign to keep the bones in Richmond. She had months up her sleeve, but she needed to get the ball rolling now!

Sally was fast learning what a painstaking process digging up the bones was. The initial excavating involved the removal of the soil around and underneath the fossil, mostly with a hand trowel and a soft-bristled brush. Gently exposing the entire fossil. Only then would the tedious task of removing each bone begin. This kept Ben and Lucy, and their team, very busy, which Sally understood. She was busy too and couldn't believe how full her life had become in a matter of weeks. Being a teacher and house mum to six boys was no easy feat.

Thoughts raced through her mind all day, a relentless whirring that left her head buzzing. Only after dinner, when she left the boys to enjoy their own time, did she find some quiet space to catch up. Never-ending paperwork, writing up notes, reports, and the letters needed for keeping the bones in Richmond. Had she taken on too much?

Frustration mounting, she groaned as she scrummaged around in her small room for her day pack and empty water bottle. She'd devised a list for the boys so they could check everything off before they left the homestead. She quickly scanned her copy. This was crucial for saving time and lives.

The day she and Ben had crazily run to the dig site without water, she should've been parched, almost on her deathbed, so unused to being in those outback conditions. It might have happened, but Ben's kiss obliterated any common sense.

Relief washed over her, and she smiled when she found her water bottle which had rolled under the bed. They'd cautiously returned to the homestead, trying to keep their new development under wraps. She'd heartily eaten Flora's lunch and drank enough water to satisfy her intense thirst, but nothing could remove her goofy smile, which probably gave away too much.

With so many adults around, not forgetting inquisitive boys on the cusp of developing into fully fledged hormonal young men, Ben and Sally had no option but to put a hold on trying anything.

She ran a comb through her hair, grimacing at the knots she was having trouble freeing. Hopefully, she could give her hair a good wash before the drive back to Malanda for Roberta and Nate's wedding where she was a bridesmaid. *Oh, boy.* Hadn't her grooming regime vastly declined in the outback?

"Psst!"

Sally spun around to find Ben filling her doorway. In an instant, her heart started pumping more beats from being so close to him. Despite her sleep deprivation, it was hard not to smile.

"It's my turn to check up on Grandad in Malanda. Would you like to come with me and I'll get you to your friend's wedding? We could leave early Thursday morning and be back at the main homestead by Sunday night for dinner with Mum and Dad. We'll sleep the night there, then get back here early Monday morning. Could that work?"

She'd mentioned the wedding a week ago, furiously organising her leave, how to get there and who would look after the boys in her absence. "Yes!" she exclaimed, relief washing over her.

It was hard leaving in the middle of the program, but it was a matter of ensuring the boys had a schedule to follow while she was away. Flora and her versatile skills would fill the gap and take on the extra duties. Getting a lift with Ben solved all her logistical problems. Not to mention the added buzz of having time alone with him for some of those four days.

Ben took a step inside her room, grabbing both her hands. "It's been hell trying to find a moment alone with you. Even now I'm scared I'm being watched."

Sally laughed as their foreheads touched and their gazes caught. "Can you rustle up a decent outfit?"

"Huh?" Ben touched his mouth to her lips for a brief kiss.

"Roberta has been nagging me to bring a plus one to this wedding."

His kiss deepened, and she sighed into it, forgetting her train of thought.

"Ah ... could you run that by me again?" Ben asked when he pulled back a fraction, a worrying frown marring his forehead as the warmth of his breath fanned her face.

She clutched his fingers. "Would you like to come to the wedding with me? I'll be free once the formalities are over. I realise you only see your grandfather occasionally, and I—"

"Shh," he pleaded, keeping his voice low.

Her eyes widened. Had she said something wrong?

"Would you really like me there?"

She swallowed and nodded, realising what this meant. To Ben, to her. She still knew nothing of his previous life with his late wife. There was so much to sift through. Without five minutes to spend privately in the past week, any conversations were impossible.

"Our lives are crazy right now, but yes, I'd love to come. Will you—"

Words caught in his throat, and he cleared it. "Will you give me time to get my shit together?"

"Of course," she whispered in the quiet bedroom, while only metres away, the noisy bunch of teens and adults eating breakfast filtered around the old homestead.

He brushed his mouth against hers once more. "Thank you," he said before taking her hand. "I can't promise I'll be good with crowds, but I'd like to meet your friends."

"Oh, Ben, I can't wait for you to meet them. I'll tell you all about them on the drive. And don't stress too much. It's going to be an informal wedding where the guests will mingle and eat finger food. The teahouse on the shores of Lake Barrine is a beautiful venue."

"Okay, let's do this. But now, it's bones, bones, bones."

"I started drafting letters to everyone important. The quicker you dig up those bones, the sooner we can demand they stay in Richmond."

They grasped hands once more before letting go and heading for the kitchen. "I hope so. I'm holding onto that dream."

Sally's heart sang. She'd made a promise, and she would see it through. Her, the boys, and everyone involved would look back on this time with pride. If Ben's intuition proved correct, and this discovery was as huge as he suspected, what a moment it would be when the bones were on full display for all the world to see in this small outback town.

She made a mental note to drop by the council chambers on the way through to Richmond and make an appointment with the mayor.

The mayor had no idea how his small outback town was about to change.

# Chapter 14

Sally took another sip of the champagne and giggled. "Oh man, I need to stop sipping this stuff; it's going to my head." It wasn't like she'd never drunk beers or spirits before, but her hormones were zapping around her body so fast, and a few sips of champagne had turned her into a giddy teenager.

"Tell us more, Sal; you're holding out on us," Liz demanded.

It was the three of them, all ensconced in the small cottage beside the Lake Barrine Teahouse, as the hairdresser and make-up artist went about their thing. The beautiful bride-to-be, Roberta, and Sally's first cousin, Liz. Thick as thieves they'd become ever since Liz stumbled onto a train a few years ago on the way to search for hidden jewels in a small southern Italian village, changing all their lives forever and sealing their friendship.

"Nothing is happening," Sally insisted, flopping down onto the only couch in the cottage, making sure not to crush her hair, which was pinned up in a stylish updo.

"Doesn't look like it from here. Here, give me that. There will be no more drinks for you, girly." With Roberta all done, glowing and smiling brightly, she came over to take the half-empty flute from Sally. Which was a good thing because, with the way her hand shook every time she thought of Ben, she'd likely spill it.

They waited until Liz finished her make-up before they put on their dresses. In less than an hour, Roberta would walk down the aisle. Well, the beautifully prepared path leading from the cottage to the shores of the lake, where her man, Nate, waited for her.

Sally wistfully closed her eyes and leaned back. If only.

"What does he look like?" Liz asked, toying with her pendant necklace.

"Hot!" Sally's eyes shot open at her admission, and they all laughed again.

"Yep, she's holding out on us, Liz," Roberta said. "Now I'm going to be too distracted to get married because I'll be busy checking out this plus one you brought."

Sally sat up straight, trying to hold a straight face. "You will do no such thing. It's early days to check out anything. Anyway, bones are more important to him."

This set Liz and Roberta off again in a fit of giggles, and Sally groaned at her choice of words. In the context of the discovery, they wouldn't understand what she meant. She was keeping the exciting news quiet for now. The time would come when she could explain.

The door opened and Roberta's mother, Lily, came in. "Are you girls almost done? Ready for the dresses?"

They all greeted Lily with a resounding yes. Sally rose. It was time to get the show on the road. In all the excitement, Sally remembered that Roberta's newfound biological father, Bob, would walk Roberta down the aisle. What a discovery that was for Roberta. Sally couldn't be happier for her friend. Bob proposed to Lily recently, bringing everything full circle after a one-night steamy encounter almost thirty years ago, resulting in Roberta being conceived.

Life had a funny way of turning everything on its head for some people. Her life was certainly being turned on its head. Look at how she'd tripped over a rock, and it'd turned out to be so much more. A shiver of apprehension shot up her arm. Suddenly, she wanted to be out in the sunshine where she could feel its warmth and ogle Ben from where the bridal party would stand.

Liz's husband, Connor, would be there to greet Ben when he arrived. Connor was also in charge of their adorable daughter, Harper. This was a full-time job now that Harper had found her legs and didn't want to stand still. Gosh, life was moving full steam ahead, and she wanted to be on a similar path.

"Arms up." Lily took the magenta filmy dress from the hanger and helped Sally into it. The bottom half was designed with soft layers, giving a gentle, cascading effect. She lifted them waist high and watched them fall gently around her legs as each layer fell from her fingers. Today, she would look and feel beautiful. Would Ben see something special in her? She mentally crossed her fingers, hoping it would be enough to engulf the painful memories of his late wife.

An overflow of joy filled Sally's heart as Roberta and Nate exchanged their vows. She snuck out a tissue from a hidden pocket in her bridesmaid's dress, using it to dab her eyes. It was a perfect day on the shores of the lake, with the midafternoon sun striking its gentle autumn rays across the shimmering water, its warm edges feathering them as they faced the guests seated beneath the ample teahouse awning.

The instant Sally and the bridesmaids left the cottage, she'd sensed Ben's eyes on her. She hadn't seen him since late Thursday, after briefly introducing him to her parents, amid raised eyebrows, and before he left to spend time with his grandfather.

Standing beside Connor, the two men chatted and took care of Harper. Just when the rings were being exchanged, Sally almost burst out laughing when Harper squirmed her way out of Connor's arms, landed on the ground and took off. It was Ben who swiftly picked her up and handed her back to Connor, both men wearing a sheepish grin.

Once Harper was back in Connor's arms, Sally found it hard to concentrate on the bridal couple. Every time she looked in Ben's direction, her cheeks tingled, and heat rose behind her neck. She tried to pretend her heart wasn't beating like crazy.

At this very moment, she needed to fan herself, and it had nothing to do with standing in the warm afternoon sun. Did he have to wear the stylish moleskin-coloured chino pants? She didn't doubt they came with an R.M. Williams label. All she had to do was look down to see how they perfectly matched the leather boots he wore, where the sun glinted off their polished shine and struck her in the eye. She blinked, moving her gaze towards his top half. The off-white long-sleeved button-up shirt, which completed the outfit, was leaving her hot under the collar, if she were wearing one. It moulded his torso, leaving little to the imagination of what was underneath. She was a desperate woman. Yep, she wanted to lick at all the deliciousness that was a dressed-up Ben, like he was a scoop of ice cream ... then go back for seconds.

"Congratulations. You may now kiss the bride."

Sally jolted at the realisation she was missing an important moment in her friend's life. The wedding ceremony was over, and now there would be blanks in the day. She inwardly groaned, pointedly turning away from Ben to watch Roberta and Nate share a romantic kiss, much to the delight of all the guests cheering them on.

The guests threw rose petals over the bridal party as they hovered around the happy couple, hugging and cheering. Sally chuckled alongside Liz as more than rose petals landed on their hair and bare shoulders. It was Bob's mother, Roberta's newly found grandmother, busy scattering rice and sugar-coated almonds, much to the delight of the young children who scrambled for a lolly.

Sally, Liz and the two groomsmen stood aside while Roberta and Nate signed the official paperwork. The general noise and hubbub of the good-sized crowd of about seventy guests rose a notch now that the formalities were nearly over, and the guests could stretch their legs and mingle.

She gasped when a hand fitted snuggly over her shoulder and a warm breath tickled the side of her face.

"I just want to say you look beautiful today."

Whispered near her ear, no one else heard Ben. Liz was too busy keeping an eye on Harper, who, to the delight of everyone, was determined to set foot in the lake.

Sally turned on her heeled shoes and blinked rapidly. They were the exact words she wanted to hear. "Thank you." She swallowed, the unexpected joy of hearing them making her emotions flit in every direction.

A slight afternoon breeze whispered around her bare skin, and goosebumps rose when Ben clasped her arm. He'd tried to tame his unruly brown curls, but they sprang out in all directions with the assistance of the breeze. She couldn't help herself. Her fingers, with a mind of their own, twirled through his curls, freeing them further.

His mouth briefly touched hers. "I'm guessing you have bridal photos to get through?"

She nodded, pressing back for another brief kiss.

"I'm helping Connor take care of his cute little monster," Ben added, the creases around his eyes deepening with laughter and bringing out a twinkle.

"Which one of you will end up in the water? She's not going to stop until she's soaking wet." Sally fingered his well-fitted shirt and licked her suddenly dry lips. "Would be a shame to mess this all up."

Ben released a little snort of laughter. "Harper messing it up, or the water doing so, or someone else ..."

Oh, she would so love to mess everything up about this man. She gulped. There was no battle to fight if Ben made the first move. Zero chance of warfare happening inside her head if he gave the nod of approval. She was ready for this. The conditions were perfect for what she wanted, but was she brave enough to make the first move if Ben showed any hesitation?

How did you bring up such a subject? She didn't want to risk pushing him too quickly. Was he emotionally stable after losing his wife, or was he still grappling with the grief?

Harper tugged on the legs of Ben's pants. They both looked down at the serene face of the tiny rascal as she gurgled unintelligible words.

"This kid's killing me." Ben ruffled Harper's hair.

"You love it."

A brief spasm of pain crossed his face, and Sally sensed he made a herculean effort to mask it.

"She's growing on me. Might have to make one myself one day." Ben scooped up Harper into his arms before reaching across for another quick kiss. "I'll leave you to it."

Sally's jaw dropped as Ben walked away towards Connor. The brief look of pain confused her, but she let it go. Maybe she'd drunk too much champagne and was seeing things or not seeing things as they were. Was this an admission of sorts? That one day he wanted children?

Harper's little arms wrapped around Ben's neck caused a sharp tug inside her chest. She clearly had no problems seeing this. Sally's fingers curled, nails digging into her palms as she concentrated on regulating her breathing.

*Might have to make one myself one day.*

Oh, she could so help him with that. Was it an invitation?

She was taking it as one.

# Chapter 15

Ben took another mouthful of his beer, leaning against the shadowed wall of the teahouse, away from the crowd. He stretched his right leg before butting the sole of his boot against the cladding. Multicoloured bright lights flashed from the DJ setup, the music weaving its sound on the breeze, dancing alongside the more tipsy or brave guests jiving to the upbeat music. Couples, singles, it didn't seem to matter. Everyone knew someone here and dancing was free for all, a way for everyone to let their hair down.

He was the designated driver, so this would be his last drink if he were to get Sally back to her parents' farm, as promised. Breaking that promise and taking her somewhere else had some appeal, though. Only if he took a few moments to sort out his head and all the mixed messages flitting around.

He took a moment to enjoy a breather and take in the jovial atmosphere, the new people he'd met. Harper was asleep, finally, in one of those portable cots set up in the cottage, complete with a baby monitor. Dead to the world, where all small toddlers should be this late in the night.

A small smile, slow and subtle, lifted the corners of his mouth. She'd been a handful, and he'd been more than willing to give Connor a break while Liz and Sally were busy with bridesmaid duties. Somehow, the two of them managed to keep her from flinging herself into the lake on those unsteady toddling legs.

Ben scraped a hand over his face, the needle pricks of late-night stubble biting into his palm. Had he really made that bold statement to Sally?

About making a baby of his own one day? The muscles inside his chest contracted, reminded again of the tiny life he never got to hold—and the same question circled his head over and over.

Why did Rhylee keep the pregnancy from him? He'd known nothing of her visit to the doctor. It was the last thing he expected to learn after her death. They weren't planning for parenthood at that stage and were following precautionary measures. *Fuck!* If he'd known about the pregnancy, he could've helped her overcome the uncertainties. Supported her, been her rock. The discovery that she hadn't turned to him for support was probably more crushing than her death itself.

His fingers tightened around his beer, its coolness dampening the surge of anger that accompanied these thoughts. Their final argument had been fierce, especially when she flung the accusation across the room that night: she hated his family property and regretted ever thinking she could live her life in the outback. Had she contemplated abortion? The doctor neither confirmed nor denied the question when asked. If she'd gone down that path, it would've been a betrayal of the worst kind. One day, the secret would've unravelled. They always did.

On better days, when he was feeling stronger and could view her death as an outsider, he accepted that karma stalked his home that night and took matters into its own hands. But whose karma was being dealt with? He was left behind to find the answers to questions that were never asked. No one knew of their struggles. Or their last argument. *He* hadn't been aware of her internal struggles. All the while, her resentment must have been brewing. Too busy building up their share of the property, the cattle, digging up bones, he hadn't seen it coming either. Life was hectic, but he was left with no closure because she was no longer there—nor was their unborn baby.

The authorities recorded her death as an accident, but he would always question Rhylee's actions. Her delirious talk that night had sent him after her only minutes later. Enough time for her to make an instinctive decision to jerk the steering wheel a little to the left on the causeway, sweeping the car away on the rushing flow of flooding water.

Sally wasn't to blame for any of this; Harper's presence brought this all to the forefront of his mind, making him confront these issues. His shoulders slouched against the cladded wall, and he wriggled them, looking for a more comfortable position. A cheer went up from the makeshift dancefloor. It looked like Roberta and Nate weren't far from leaving their wedding party.

Spotting Sally winding her way around chairs in his direction, he straightened. There weren't too many moments during the night when he wasn't aware of exactly where she was. For a split second, a slice of uncertainty knotted his stomach. He knew he wanted to cross that line with her. Had sensed it happening against his will. What if he got it wrong again? Missed something important along the way?

He could do this. He was a much stronger person because of what happened with Rhylee. But God help him, he wouldn't make it through a second time if he got it wrong again. Of that, he was certain.

Placing his half-finished beer on a nearby table, he welcomed Sally into his arms with a fierce hug, filling his lungs with the rich smell of tropical rainforest, which hung in the cool, crisp night air. He would work hard not to make the same mistake twice, but how much should he share? He didn't want to open that black box. After Rylee's death, he'd spiralled so much that even the counsellor had struggled to help him out of the vortex of self-hate and the consequences that spun inside his head. No one needed to know the contents of the box. Now reconciled with it, he didn't blame himself anymore. Yes, he would talk until his voice was hoarse with his next relationship, but there was still that ugly space he never wanted to visit again.

"Hmm, that's nice," Sally whispered near his ear, snuggling up and setting things off below when she rubbed against him. He breathed deeply, soaking in the scent of a fruity hair product, when he tucked her face beneath his chin. He filled his chest with its potent smell, reminding him of strawberry fields and the few times he'd taken his grandad for a pick-your-own strawberries afternoon. That was another matter deeply troubling him. For now, he pushed those concerns away.

"The happy couple are about to leave. They're going to play a couple of last songs. Slow numbers." Sally looked up with a mischievous smile. Inviting as all heck.

He chuckled, dropping his mouth to touch hers lightly. "I normally step on toes, but if you're okay with sore feet, would you still like a dance?"

"I thought you'd never ask." She kissed him back while he tightened his hold.

Already, Sally was different on so many levels, and they could take it slow. Hadn't she told him she was doing fine without a husband?

She pulled back, her warm breath washing over his cheek. "Come on, it'll be over if we don't hurry up." She grabbed his hand, leading him to the group of guests already dancing only metres from the water's edge. Ben tugged on her arm, halting her. His heart thumped, and her eyes opened in question. "What's wrong?"

He tried his hardest to lift his mouth into some semblance of a smile but failed miserably. Grim was what she'd be staring at. "Sally ..." He wavered, dropping his gaze.

"Ben?" Sally reached up and spoke over the softer music. "What's up?"

"Will you tell me if I get it wrong?"

"Where is this coming from?"

He shrugged. He thought he had this, but his vulnerability wasn't going anywhere yet. "What if I get it wrong?"

"You will, Ben, and so will I."

"But will you tell me along the way? Not keep it locked inside until it blows up?"

Sally trailed her fingers down his arms, taking both his hands in hers. She squeezed, and he applied the same pressure back. "One day, will you tell me what happened?"

He nodded, overcome with relief that she wanted to hear it.

"I promise, Ben. I promise I'll always be open."

He delved into her dark blue pools and lost himself a little more, liking her answer. "Would you still like to dance?"

"Yes, please," she whispered, Ben relying on reading her lips as her words got lost in the music floating around them.

So engrossed with their conversation, the rest of the world faded into the background. But now he wanted to smile again. With that off his chest, he could breathe too.

They joined the other couples, including Roberta and Nate, who were lost in their own world. He wound one arm around Sally's waist and clasped her hand with the other. She placed her face against his chest, moving small steps in time with his. The words to John Legend's 'All of Me' seeped into his skin with a new level of meaning.

The lyrics resonated with how his head was spinning. He would climb mountains to know what was going on in her beautiful mind. Being this close to her was making him dizzy, like his head was under water, but otherwise, with Sally by his side, he was breathing fine.

Already, he loved her curves and her edges and all her perfect imperfections. With this thought, his hand left the safety of her waist and slid down until it touched her hip. She gave a small whimper when he pressed against it.

As the lyrics wound their way around his core, he wanted her to be the beginning and the end of his every day, whether he was losing or winning. If she would give her all to him, he'd give her his all. That was the promise he would make to her that night.

He disentangled his fingers and cupped her cheek, tilting her face up. Her eyes fluttered closed, and she leant into his touch. Her warm, soft lips tasted of champagne and fire, but he plundered further, deeper, harder, wanting more, needing everything to bolster his crushed spirit.

It'd been a long time.

As the last note faded, Ben reluctantly pulled away from her, a lingering warmth on his lips. The dancing crowd yelled for another song. This brought a lopsided smile to his face.

Sally gave a wistful sigh. "Why did we wait for the last song before we danced?"

A little breathless, he tugged her closer. "Would you like to come over to my grandad's when we're finished here? I'll put my playlist on so we can dance some more."

Her pupils dilated, and a small pulse ticked on the side of her neck. He put his mouth against it, its flicker heating his lips.

Sally tangled her hands in his curls. "Yes, please," she whispered in his ear, "and I'll choose the music."

He buried emotions as thick as the muscles in his arms as the DJ relented and played another song. Robbie Williams' 'Angel' came through the speakers. Ben didn't doubt Sally was an angel in his eyes, come to save the shell of a man he'd become. He'd been weak for three years now. The constant pain, doubts and uncertainties had walked by his side all this time. A one-way street with no place to turn and find his way back. Until now.

Was Sally a woman who might bless him with love? Taking her in his arms again, they swayed with the music, losing themselves amongst a dozen other couples. Before the song raced to its last verse, thereby signalling the end of the party, he found her mouth again and ravaged her in the soft darkness. The DJ lights no longer flashed, and the only light came from the occasional sliver of moon that broke through the moving clouds, illuminating the secluded dancers. Glad of the shadows, he kissed her hard, his tongue darting inside, causing tremors to rip along his arms. The chilled air couldn't douse the heat flaring between them, and he hardened against her, groaning his impatience that he wasn't alone with Sally.

When the song ended, Ben reluctantly stepped back, still holding one of her hands. They locked gazes while his thumb made small rotations on her palm. Chatter and conversation picked up around them. A slight breeze coming off the water tangled around the satiny length of her bridesmaid dress, getting caught up around his legs.

There were shouts of something being organised which he didn't understand. In his periphery, the couples lined up in two rows.

Sally tried to ease the frown on his forehead with her finger. She chuckled before kissing him on the mouth. "They're creating an arch so

Roberta and Nate can walk beneath it and say goodbye to everyone. Want to join in?"

Ben nodded. "I'm all yours. Show me what to do."

She led him towards the steps leading up to the top car park. The archway was in full swing, with the married couple hugging and kissing friends and relatives as they said their goodbyes.

"We'll go to the top of the steps where their car is waiting."

A surge of excitement spiked his adrenaline. He easily supported Sally up the uneven steps, gripping her hand tight because she wore heels. Now he couldn't wait to leave. He'd take her back to his grandad's home for some dancing, then ask if she wanted to stay the night or at least part of it. He hadn't felt this stirred up in a long time, and he released a gust of pent-up air, intrigued by this wedding tradition which he assumed came from Roberta's Italian heritage.

When the bridal couple finally arrived at the end of the human archway, where he and Sally waited with Liz, Connor and the parents, Ben gave Nate a solid handshake and received a tight hug from Roberta.

"Take care of Sally, she's our everything," Roberta said, her gaze looking deep into his. He dipped his face, overwhelmed by the lump of responsibility Roberta hoisted onto his unsure shoulders. That was all Roberta had time to say before her parents swept her up into their arms. More hugs, kisses and happy tears.

In a matter of minutes, Nate was driving away with the rattle of empty beer cans strung together, dragging along the road behind them, noisily announcing their departure.

Guests chatted, smiled, joked and laughed, slowly making their way back down the uneven steps to the teahouse. As the reception wound down, Ben assumed guests would begin to leave.

With the wedding couple gone and the human archway collapsed, Sally wound her arm around Liz. Ben felt the weight of their goodbye. Liz, Connor and cheeky Harper were returning to Canada in a matter of days, but Sally was coming back to Richmond with him the next day, so tonight was their goodbye.

Connor came up beside him and said with a wry chuckle, "This could get a bit messy with these two."

Ben smiled back, already warmed to the Canadian man and his humour. His state-of-the-art prosthetic arm was the butt of many jokes as they'd bonded over Harper and the million-and-one dad jokes Connor came up with. It also hadn't taken Ben five minutes to realise how much Connor loved Liz.

Sally had filled him in on the long drive from Richmond about all the people he would meet that night. Ben had shaken his head when Sally talked of a tiny Italian village, buried jewels and the anguish Connor suffered before finally claiming Liz as his own.

There was more head shaking when Sally told him of Roberta and how she'd come to the north to unearth a hidden box at Lake Barrine. Meeting Nate and discovering her biological father and the entourage of his large family.

The soft moonlight illuminated Sally's tear-streaked face, confirming Connor's assessment of the situation as 'messy'. For a moment, his desire to take her in his arms and comfort her was overwhelming. Instead, he shoved his hands into his pant pockets, giving Sally and Liz the space they needed to say their goodbyes.

"I've never been to the outback before. My sister is coming over from London to complete a private project for her boss. I think we should all make a special trip when she arrives and come visit you both."

Ben swallowed hard, surprised by this couple's inclusion. "You're welcome any time. We're doing some exciting stuff out there."

"Deal!" Connor clapped him on the shoulder. "But I really need to get to sleep tonight. I wish we had another day to catch up properly, but right now, that rascal has burnt me out."

Ben laughed just as Liz and Sally disentangled themselves and came over. Liz automatically went to Connor's waiting embrace, and God help him, it felt natural to take Sally in his where she fit perfectly.

Where he wanted her to stay forever.

# Chapter 16

"Are you ready to leave?" Sally snuggled against Ben's neck, exhausted. It'd been a long day.

"Only if you are?"

"I'll go grab my overnight bag, which I left in the cottage. I'm pretty sure Liz and Connor are past tired, too. They're staying in there tonight."

"How about I get it?" Ben glanced down at her heeled shoes. "You wait here and save your feet. Which one am I looking for?"

Sally pulled back and grinned. "It's the purple one you told me looked 'typically girly' when you put it in the back of your ute."

"Oh, that one." Ben matched her smile with a sheepish one. "I should recognise it."

"It's inside the front door on the left. Liz will show you. And thank you, Ben. I honestly can't take another step in these shoes."

Ben shook his head, tutting.

"I know, I know, you'll never understand why women wear heels. By this time of the night, I'm wondering the same thing too."

"Goodbye, you pair." Liz wound her arms around Sally for one last hug while Ben and Connor shared a final handshake. "Until we meet again, hey?"

"Ooh, I hate goodbyes. Why did you have to live on the other side of the world? Keep your phone charged, always."

"I promise," a tired Liz assured her as they gave each other one final goodbye hug.

"Ben will follow you down and grab my bag. Then we can leave you in peace to get some sleep."

"Here, Sal." Ben handed her the ute keys. "You can wait in the ute where it's warmer. I won't be too long."

Sally took the keys from Ben and then hugged her arms around her chest to ward off the night chill as the trio walked off. As exhausted as she was, heightened anticipation was hard to ignore as her grip tightened around the keys. What would tonight bring? She'd stay awake for eternity if it meant she could take her fill of Ben forever. Everything about him sat right with her. She was so ready for what lay ahead.

She looked across the wide expanse of the lake shimmering under the moonbeams and allowed its soothing effect to wash over her. Nerves and anticipation had her heart rate picking up, and a thrum of excitement settled in nicely.

She waved to some of the guests leaving and received a hug from Roberta's grandmother, inviting her to visit one day. The love Roberta received from her newly discovered grandparents and the entire family always blew Sally away. So much love, so much joy in life. Roberta fit in easily after discovering her biological dad.

"Are you still standing here? You crazy woman."

Ben's sudden appearance behind her, his arm wrapping around her, caused her to gasp in surprise. "How did you get back so fast?" She giggled, the headiness of the coming night already affecting her.

"I don't know. I walked down, then came right back up. Now come on, can you walk?"

"Only just."

Ben continued to shake his head. "I'll never understand."

"You're right, you never will." Her smile was hard to dislodge as he increased his stronghold around her waist, leaving her almost floating as they walked to the other side of the car park.

Ben released her at the passenger side of the ute and went to stow her case on the tray. As he wound a secure strap around it, he said, "I guess it'll have to be little old me who has to rub your feet."

*Rub my feet? Hmm.* This was something she would encourage. Sally leant against the ute watching Ben fasten the ratchet. Openly staring. Enjoying every single second. Tie loosened and slightly askew. Sleeves still buttoned up and not rolled up to his elbows. His go-to every other day. This formal version of Ben was stirring up a lot of heat inside her. Enough that the late-night chill couldn't tamper it. All the fluttery bits were a real thing in her stomach every time his shirt stretched across his shoulders as he tightened the ratchet around her suitcase.

She fingered the delicate halter fabric resting against the skin of her neck. Like moving the soft fabric would bring any reprieve from the hot flush coursing across her neck. How had another woman not snapped him up sooner?

With the case secured, Ben sauntered to where she stood and planted his feet on either side of her aching ones. "Did you want to get inside the ute, or did you want to stand out here all night ogling me?" He placed his hands flat on the glass window, either side of her face, pressed up against her, holding her captive between him and the ute.

"All night, ogling," were the only words she uttered before Ben captured the sides of her face and lowered his. Turbulent heat rippled through her, leaving her charged ... electric ... begging for more. His lips teased. She feasted. Their tongues tangled. This late at night, her mind was a jumbled mess.

Only the sound of a wolf whistle close by prised them apart. His gaze raked over her. Searing every inch of her face. Her neck. Her breathing was unsteady. If her heart thumped any faster, she would pass out. Heavy limbed, she wasn't sure if she could move.

To think this all began with the offer of a foot rub. The thought of Ben's supple, tanned fingers doing anything to her feet sent a shiver along her skin. "I'd really love a shower first to remove all this gunk out of my hair and off my face. Will that be possible without waking anyone up?"

Ben groaned, dropping his forehead against hers. "Oh, please, I was only going as far as a foot rub."

Sally winced as she tottered the two steps, entwining her arms around his neck. "Thank you for taking care of me tonight."

He tightened his grip, growling into her ear, "Hop in, please," when she pressed up against him, knowing full well it would set him off.

"I would, if you'd let me."

"You had one job when I went to get your case."

"Yeah, I know: get inside the ute and wait. I couldn't even get that right." She smiled against his cheek, reluctant for the moment to end.

Ben's continued growl made her heart sing. She'd do anything to help him hide the sad streak that constantly coloured his aura. She'd witnessed it firsthand the day they met when he collected Moby. While she didn't know all the nitty-gritty of how and why his wife died, whatever happened still haunted him.

Ben gradually dropped his arms, but not before running his hands over her hips and opening the passenger door. Turning back, he lifted her, cradling her against his chest. Ridiculous, really, as she was quite capable of walking the few steps to the open ute door, but Sally tangled her arms around his neck again and snuggled against him, happy to stay this way for the night.

"Um ... did you want to get in?" Ben asked with a jovial huff.

"If I have to," she teased, slackening her arms so she could stand. Once inside the ute, she strapped herself in while Ben remained perched against the doorframe, leaning against it.

"All good to go?"

"Yes, please, take me anywhere I can take these shoes off. I'm never usually this helpless."

"That'll be *my* one job tonight."

Sally caught his gaze and snagged on it. As little as the lighting was at the top car park, she could see enough depth. Enough for her breath to catch in her throat. "Is that all you want to take off?" She bit her bottom lip, heat coursing up her neck. Not sure she should've said that, despite wanting it so badly.

Ben traced a finger down her cheek, tucking a loose strand of hair behind her ear. No smile. All serious. "I was hoping not."

He broke the connection and went around to the driver's side, leaving Sally struggling to breathe. God help her, he was one hundred percent all male, and she sucked on her lip, hoping to settle her nerves. After being so ready for this, now she wasn't so sure. She'd harped on before how she didn't need a husband, and they were two consenting adults, so what was the problem? He wasn't the first man she'd been with, but this felt so different from every other time.

Maybe it was all the baggage she was taking on with Ben. She knew so little. Should she learn more before committing?

"Hey, are you okay?" Ben asked as he clicked in his seatbelt.

To hell with needing to learn more. Just do it! She put her hand on his thigh and swallowed. "Yep, sure am. Let's go, please."

There! She committed! Any fallout after she'd deal with. She wasn't missing the opportunity to sample this hot man. The way his shirt hugged his muscled torso. How his pants stretched tight over his thighs. Oh, and those well-polished formal boots. She'd drooled over them all night, elated when she finally found the courage to ask him to dance.

Some men never made the first move when it came to impromptu dancing, so she was glad she made the first move. It would be hard to forget how the breeze whispered in her hair, danced along her arms, and how Ben's touch scorched her skin. Dancing in the outdoors lent a magic of its own. She may not be as country as Ben was used to, but she could get used to it. She loved everything outdoors, the wide-open spaces and the star-studded skies of the outback. How it hadn't rained a single drop all night was a miracle in itself.

Once Ben drove onto the open road, he took his hand off the gears and covered hers still sitting on his thigh. A comfortable silence settled in the ute cab, giving Sally the space to contemplate how fast her life was changing after deciding to take her project out to Richmond.

A year ago, when a fellow teacher took his family out to Winton to experience the dinosaur tourism explosion with his preteen boys, his story stuck. Further investigations revealed Richmond was another hotbed of dinosaur bones. Then, someone put her in touch with Ben's dad, and things snowballed from there. Like it was all meant to be.

That morning, when she spoke to Flora on the sat phone, she'd assured her all was going to plan out there. Tomorrow would come soon enough, and she'd be out there in the excited fray of boys and geologists. As exciting as the wedding was, she missed the exhilaration of the dig and the dry heat.

Rain speckled the front window as she gazed out into the night. "I knew the good weather couldn't last forever. Thank goodness it held out for the wedding."

Ben squeezed her hand before changing gears at an intersection. "Sometimes you strike it lucky. Like I have ..."

She glanced his way, and the quick look she received in return set off a flutter around her heart. She gulped. *Good Lord, this man is saying all the right things.*

"Do you miss it here?" Ben asked.

"Yes and no. There's something special about those star-studded skies, though. I might be a little hooked."

Ben turned to glance at her again before turning back to the front. That look? Like he didn't mind her answer. "We're nearly there."

"It's quite a drive and isolated. Should your grandad be this far away from services as he gets on in age?"

"Those exact concerns worry us all. So far, he's holding up, and his new wife is an ex-nurse. He's not keeping too well at the moment, though."

"I'm sorry to hear that."

Ben navigated a narrow driveway where heavily forested trees arched above. He dimmed the lights and turned off the ignition, parking the car under a temporary cover near the main house.

They hadn't driven with any music or radio on, but the quiet in the ute blanketed them as tiredness crushed down on her shoulders. "Will he mind me turning up for breakfast unannounced?"

Ben turned in his seat, but darkness prevented her from reading too much. He took her hand and brought it up to rest it against his warm cheek. "Grandad will be ecstatic. I can't be too sure about Gwen. Please don't ask me to explain why because, in my mind, it feels too complicated. It doesn't stop me worrying about Grandad all the time. Some days, I just want to take him back with me and take care of him, but he won't budge, and I can't make him. But I'll be forever grateful for how he took care of me when I needed him most."

Sally nodded slowly because each time Ben brought up the past, a little more was revealed.

"Is it okay if we talk about Grandad tomorrow? Tonight, I'd like to concentrate on you because I'm as nervous as all crap."

Sally smiled in the darkness and knew by the whites of his teeth that he smiled back. "That makes two of us."

"I'm so out of touch; I don't even know how to start this conversation."

"I'm sure we won't need to," she whispered in the quiet of the cab, her smile slipping. "How about I start with a shower? I really need it."

"How about I cover my eyes and block my ears and *not* picture you in the shower?"

"How about you show me to the room? I'm actually dreaming of life without these shoes on—and what are you're going on about?"

"I can guarantee you it has nothing to do with shoes but everything about taking everything else off."

Sally laughed quietly, keeping her voice low as she opened the door and stepped onto her hurting feet. Never again, she wanted to claim. She longed for flat, sturdy outback boots where her feet never hurt and she could clock up enough steps to break any step tracker.

"This way." Ben took her arm in one hand and her suitcase in the other, leading her to a set of steps away from the front of the unique-looking property. In the dappled moonlight peering out from behind the thick clouds, it appeared to be an attached add-on quite separate from the rest of the house.

Already Sally imagined making lots of noise, grateful the room wasn't in the heart of the house. Ben walked behind her, securing her every step, building up the anticipation of the night ahead as they climbed the steps.

Whose idea was it to shower first?

# Chapter 17

The chirping birds outside the window slowly brought Ben awake. Disorientated for a moment, the solid length of warmth along his entire side jolted his memory as to where he was. Who he was with.

His eyes fluttered open. Through the crack in the curtains, the new dawn seeped through the tops of the trees. He smiled in the semidarkened room, snuggling closer to Sally's side.

It had been close to midnight when they arrived last night. Sally showered first. When Ben finished his, he'd come back into the room to find her sound asleep. The muted light of the bedside lamp gently highlighted her relaxed sleeping face, mostly hidden underneath the towel wrapped around her wet hair. He didn't have the heart to wake her.

With nerves a real thing, he hadn't lied to her. He'd carefully climbed into bed without disturbing her, inching closer, doing everything possible not to rouse her. These were the last coherent thoughts he remembered before sleep claimed him too.

Sally murmured in her sleep and gravitated towards his warmth, allowing Ben to spoon her. The towel had long since been relegated to another place. Probably on the floor. He wrapped an arm around her waist, wedging his body along her back until they fit perfectly.

He inhaled the scent of her warmth. Reminded of sweet honey, it filled his senses and went to his head. Closing his eyes, he enjoyed the headiness that came with it. Accepted the faint dizziness. Disbelief that Sally was in his arms. The urge to touch her was out of his control. He began leaving soft kisses along her hairline; at the same time, he flared down below, firming up and jutting into Sally's back like a steel rod.

He wasn't even frustrated because he'd slept soundly, unheard of in a long time, but he had every intention of enjoying some morning time if Sally agreed. Totally prepared from the previous night, he called for all the confidence he could muster and began touching her under the warmth of the covers. He had every intention of waking her up now.

"Ben?"

All his cylinders were running. "Good morning," he whispered.

Sally shuffled around and turned to face him. "Oh, Ben, I'm so sorry. Tell me I did not fall asleep before you finished your shower last night?"

Ben gathered her in his arms, tightening his hold. "I had the best night's sleep ever. But I'm awake now," he added, leaving more kisses along her forehead.

"What time is it?" She spoke softly, her voice gentle in the quiet room. "Do we have to leave soon?"

Ben snuck another glance towards the window and hazarded a guess it was close to six am. So deep and untroubled was his sleep he was confident he wouldn't tire on the drive back to Richmond. "We've got all day to reach the station, and Mum will have dinner ready for us. So, I think we can relax."

"What about your grandfather?"

"He's not going to barge in if that's what you're worried about."

Sally chuckled, winding her arms around his neck. "Okay, I'm relaxed if you are."

Ben smiled against her hair, his chest puffing out to bursting point. How had he gotten here? This beautiful, caring and intelligent woman was in his arms. Like a beacon of light leading him forward. They were both already naked, and with his heart in his hand, he pulled back, searching her face in the dim light.

"What's up?" she asked, her hands tantalising his hips, her tongue wetting her lips enough to raise goosebumps along his arms.

"I want you to be absolutely certain you're okay with this. That I haven't put you in a position where you don't feel you can back out from."

"Oh, Ben." Her whispered plea ended when she touched her lips to his. She began a sensuous kiss that sent rocket fuel screaming through his already charged body. The kiss went on and on. Hard and open mouthed. He'd long forgotten how kissing made him feel so damn good and built up a tremble deep inside.

The longer they kissed, the more intense it became until they burst apart for much-needed air.

"So, that's a yes?" he asked one last time on a puff of air.

Sally's groan touched a nerve, her words spearing him in the heart. "Don't you dare stop now."

Her plea was his undoing. He was all in. There was no backing out as he fumbled for the condom on the bedside dresser and hastened to get it on. A sense of rightness settled over him. This didn't feel like a mistake, and God help him, he didn't want it to be.

Sheathed and ready, they came together again in another long, deep kiss. Brutal. Raking her arms, back, backside. Clutching her tight against his rock-hard erection, holding off, until he couldn't anymore. His hand travelled to her front and found her warmth. So wet, so ready. Now it was his turn to groan, his lips leaving hers, his hands greedy for all she offered.

He took it all. Giving back too. Took her plump nipple in his mouth and savoured its softness. Going out of his head while his fingers pulsed inside her warmth, pushing in and out, revelling in the delicious wetness continuing to sustain his hardness.

A twitch from Sally. She grabbed his face and forced him away from her breasts, taking command of his mouth and kissing him with an energy he didn't think possible.

He settled on top of her and gently nudged her legs apart. She opened willingly, raised her knees on either side, lifting herself to make his entry easier. He moaned with the intimate pleasure of what they were doing. It'd been a very long time. Couldn't remember the last time, to be honest. With the warmth of Sally's hands pressing into his backside, they rocked, pushed and kissed until she shattered beneath him. He followed without delay, seeing stars, and feeling a headiness that left him panting like he'd run after stray cattle on foot.

Behind his closed eyelids, pinpricks of light flittered, giving the sensation of sitting at the stargazer's lounge and gazing upwards. He gently eased himself down over Sally, hoping he wasn't too heavy. But it felt like the right thing to do as he squashed her into the comfortable mattress.

"Hey," he whispered, his breathing evening out as their chests rose and fell in sync. "Do I need to move off?"

Sally wrapped her arms around his neck and hugged hard. "Not yet."

They lay this way, Ben soaking it all in. Unbelievable really. He closed his eyes and settled his face in the crook of her neck, the rhythm of her heartbeat almost lulling him back to sleep. She tangled her fingers in his hair, her gentle massage another action to help shut his body down.

⁂

He jerked awake. It might have only been a few minutes or longer, he couldn't tell. He was still partially inside Sally. Just thinking about where he was caused his crotch to twitch, and he began to harden again.

"Did we sleep long?" Sally whispered.

"Not sure."

She smiled seductively, loosening her hold and running her fingers down his arm before testing his firmness for herself. "Do we have time for this again?"

"Not sure we do."

"Pity," she said as she found a spot below his ear and kissed it.

"I have an idea for later, though. Will that help if we get up now and have breakfast?"

"Will you share the idea?"

"We can treat it as a surprise. Do you like surprises?"

"Not really." She reached for his mouth. A firm yet gentle reminder he was on notice, and the surprise better be a good one.

She pulled back, looking at him. All his morning messiness was on full display and not an ounce of nerves left. "Any regrets?" he asked, heart in mouth.

She fingered his eyebrows, neatening them towards his temple. She shook her head, her smile warming him up. "None at all."

*Phew*! Ben smiled back before rolling off her and nestling beside her. "Not sure how we're going to get up, but we should get moving, or we'll never get back to Richmond by tonight."

"Okay." Sally kicked the blankets off, squealing when the cool morning air licked over them both. "I'll have a quick shower."

"I'll have one too."

"With me?" Sally threw back as she sat up and swung her legs over the side of the bed.

Ben growled as he took the blankets back. "No, definitely not. Hurry up, Sal."

"Two minutes, I promise." She grinned.

"I'll hold you to it." But not before he hurled himself out of the warm bed and halted her progress to the bathroom, ravishing her all over again. Rubbing against her, inhaling her womanly scents after their morning capers, and expanding his chest with everything Sally.

Totally his fault if they never made it back to Richmond in time for dinner that night.

# Chapter 18

Sally continually added music to his playlist on the long drive home, and Ben didn't mind. He was fully prepared to find a mix of everything added to his staple of country music the next time he plugged it in. For now, he listened intently to Pink's lyrics for 'Just Give Me A Reason' as it blared around the enclosed ute cab. He kept running some of the words around his head as Sally sang along. The line about not being broken, just bent, and learning to love again resonated perfectly with how he was feeling.

They'd shared a hurried breakfast with his grandfather and Gwen, including some cuddle time for Sally and Moby. Followed by the usual throw the sheets in the washing machine and remake the bed for the next guest before an even quicker stop at the hardware store for Sally to purchase some gardening things to make a start on the lawn at the old homestead. Only then did they hit the road.

All was perfect, if it wasn't for the small niggle that wouldn't go away. His feel-good thermometer, after their amazing start to the day, nosedived. His grandfather—gardening that morning before Ben and Sally rose from bed—scraped his leg along a piece of steel protruding from the small garden shed. Not a big deal any other time, except the bleeding didn't want to stop. Not bucket loads coming out, but a thin steady stream not clotting.

Gwen assured them she would take care of it. She was an experienced nurse, she reminded them, and if it didn't slow soon, she'd drive him to the emergency department. She was an ex-nurse, right? He should be able to let it go, right?

He couldn't.

Sally silenced the music. Ben glanced her way before looking back at the road.

"Is the music too loud?" She gave his thigh a tender rub. "You're a bit quiet."

Ben wriggled his back against the seat and adjusted his position. With the progression of their relationship, he could confide in her. "I'm worried about Grandad."

"Gwen's assurances that she would take care of his bleeding aren't enough?" She looked over at him with a frown.

Ben grimaced. How did he explain what he couldn't work out himself? "He's going downhill so fast. Way too fast considering how he was only six months ago. I just don't know anymore." He shrugged and tried for a reassuring smile in her direction but barely held it. "Anyway, it's nearly time for a break."

The drive always took it out of him, but the last few hours had disappeared quickly with Sally beside him. They were over halfway, and it was time for a stop and a driver change. Sally insisted and he wouldn't argue. The road was a straight line and very manageable if she wanted to drive.

"I know of a spot where there's a creek and some shade." He pointed through the front window to a patch of trees in the distance. "Not much, and there should be some water this time of year. It's about a kilometre off the main road, but it's always peaceful and a good place to refresh and recharge. We can eat the lunch we packed."

Sally gave him a gentle squeeze on the shoulder. Another reassurance of sorts. It was hard to ignore her kind and caring nature. Ben embraced the lump of gratitude that being around Sally brought to the forefront of his mind. How had he gotten so lucky?

The promised surprise was in this spot, if Sally was up for some adventure. The thought of what he planned was enough to divert his worries for the moment. He'd only discovered this secluded place in the past six months, and the idea crept into his mind.

He turned off the main highway and hit the dirt road. Rough, corrugated road always had him rethinking if this diversion was a good one. Each time he stopped there for a break, he always left refreshed and ready to tackle the road again. Isolated as it was, there was a good chance no one else would be there, and they'd have the spot to themselves. Today, he planned on leaving this spot more than just refreshed.

"Gotta love these outback roads," Sally said, breaking his thoughts. "Lucky your ute is built tough to handle it."

Ben grimaced, glancing in Sally's direction for a split second before turning back to the dirt track. "It's not in too bad a condition. I've driven on worse."

"Do we need to watch out for crocs where we're going?"

"Yep, always. But in this section of the creek, at the moment, you won't find any. That happens much further down the tributary where it gets deeper and there's always water. This section dries up in between wet seasons."

"Okay, so we should be good for today." It was hard to tell if this was a statement or a question, but her voice was slightly hesitant.

"Yep."

The rough track led to a small clump of trees. Mostly gums, with their arched trunks leaning heavily towards the small creek barely three metres wide. A variety of browns, off-whites and every shade in between dominated the small clump as flaking bark peeled off in strips along their sturdy trunks. Even the shallow water was more murky-brown than clear, but this was the normal way of things the further west from the coast you drove, as the small tributary slowly disappeared, reverting to a dry sandy riverbed in anticipation of the next wet season.

Ben braked and turned off the ignition. Unbuckling his seatbelt, he turned to Sally. "Are you ready for the surprise I promised?" Suddenly assailed with nerves again, which was ridiculous after what they shared that morning, he buried them. Always at the forefront of his mind was the concern he didn't deserve this.

Sally opened her door, and he did the same, the enclosed cab already stifling with heat. "What did you have in mind?"

He cupped her face, leaning in to kiss her sweetly. No rough play yet. Despite the turbulent thoughts of how he really wanted to kiss her, he ventured to suggest, "I have an old rug, and I plan to lie down for a rest."

Sally jerked away from the heat between them, crossing her arms. "Out here? In the open? Benjamin Reginald Angwin, have you gone mad?"

He shook his head, a wry grin beginning to grow. "It would be something to write home about."

Sally laughed, playfully punching his shoulder. "Like I'd add that in."

Ben fully grinned now, rubbing the spot she'd tapped. "So, maybe a yes?"

Sally groaned and got out of the ute. "I thought I was getting mixed up with a nice guy."

Ben got out too, going to the locked box on the back of the ute. "I am a nice guy. But after this morning, I'm not sure I want to stay one." He unlocked the box, pulling out the outdoor rug with canvas on the bottom and fabric on top. His body pulsed in preparation. She'd come around. It was just the thought of being out in the open that had her baulking.

"How much time do we have?"

With the rug tucked under his arm, Ben came around to the other side of the ute where Sally was dipping her toes in the creek. "We can always eat lunch on the run to make up for time." He found a decently shaded spot and spread the rug over a small patch of sand. It wasn't ideal, but his body was already prepping, and he couldn't hide the rush along his skin when Sally came up behind him and wrapped her arms around his waist.

The sun beat down on their heads, the limited shade barely enough to provide them with a complete canopy. This was the least of his worries as he turned her in his arms and tightened them around her waist, bringing her in contact with his growing erection, making no bones about how she was affecting him.

She snorted, a gurgle of laughter escaping. "Ben, this is crazy."

They wore negligible clothing, just shorts and tops. Nothing like how they were dressed last night for the wedding. Even that felt like a lifetime ago. He pulled her cheeky yellow shirt up, hiding the funny meme on its front—*I enjoy women's rights ... and wrongs*—that made him laugh when he'd seen it that morning. There was no laughing now. Relaxing and taking his time were proving difficult. He wanted to rip everything off her and attack her like a crazed animal. When he looked deep into her eyes, he could've sworn she carried that crazy look, too.

"Ben, you look like you want to eat me whole."

"I do."

She helped him and pulled her shirt off, dropping it to the rug near their feet while Ben took a step back, giving her the space.

He took a deep breath, doing his best to slow it all down. *Make it last the distance, make it memorable* he reminded himself before his brain switched off and his body took over.

He wanted to create the forever kind of thing where they didn't hesitate to take this road every single time they drove between Richmond and Malanda.

Slowly expelling the trapped air, he stepped closer, running a hand along her bare neck, taking her bra strap with it and sliding it off her shoulder on one side and then the other. Finding the spot irresistible, he latched onto it. Soft skin, gentle nips as Sally sucked in a breath. Her fingers tangled in his hair, doing a good job of keeping him close. She wasn't objecting to what he did until she lifted his face away from her bare shoulders and took a step back. Twisting her bra around to the front, she undid the clasp, letting it fall. He made a beeline for her plump nipples, but she stopped him.

"Uh-uh, let me."

She began the arduous task of undoing his buttons, one by maddeningly slow one. A groan tore from his lips, and she tutted at his impatience. When his shirt fell open with the last button, she teased him with her fingertips. Touching, kneading, tweaking his tiny nipples, springing them to full size. He had a few spare brain cells still working, enough to remember the condom he'd secured in the top lefthand pocket. He fumbled with the button, elated when he had it undone, and pulled the foil package out to show her, like revealing the holy grail to a religious fanatic.

Sally chuckled as she latched onto his nipple and took a firm hold. He dropped his face, all his strength gone, except for the bit needed to hold onto the silver packet he gripped tightly in one hand.

With her mouth firmly attached to him, he moaned when she trailed her hands down and attempted to pull off his loose board shorts and jocks. He offered to do the same with her cute cutoff denim shorts and knickers. He undid the button and zip and slowly slid them both down her thighs.

Once they'd both kicked them off their ankles, all that was left was his unbuttoned shirt. Taking it off and dropping it to the rug, they stood staring at each other. Naked. Wide-eyed. Disbelief for Ben that they were at this juncture so soon again. Terrified of doing something wrong and losing her.

"Ben, I have never done anything so daring. What if someone happens to come this way?"

He swallowed, needing to brave it out and trust himself. "We'd hear them coming."

"Would we? I'm not sure I'd hear anything."

Ben managed a chuckle, reprimanding himself for his self-doubt. He was so primed for this and was confident Sally was, too. He took hold of her hand and tugged it.

She didn't budge. "You get that thing on first. I'm not sure I'll have any control left once I take a step closer."

"Here." Ben handed her the foil package, prepared to suffer the torment. "I can't be trusted to move that fast."

She tore it open and fiddled with the condom to check it was the right way up, while Ben kept an eye on her actions. His heart thudded harder when she finally took a step closer and reached for him, a grin wide enough on her face to make him groan in frustration. He never considered how tortuous this was going to be, while she enjoyed every single moment of it. He should've been smart enough to do the job himself. It was going to nearly kill him to remain still while she rolled it over his erection.

She released a satisfied gasp when she touched him firmly. True to his word, she was excruciatingly slow as she rolled it over him. Humming quietly to herself, wetting her dry lips, a sheen of sweat forming along her forehead.

His face fell onto the top of her head, struggling to breathe out and back in. "Hurry up, Sal," he hissed, the gentle touch of her warm fingers along his hot, throbbing skin sending his mind into a spin as he grabbed her by the thighs, hoping he could hold them both up if needed.

When she was done, she clasped her hand around his testicles, giving them a gentle squeeze. He emitted a long, pain-filled moan and stumbled back, his legs buckling as he fell back on his bottom, taking her with him. That was where all the niceties ended when he rolled her over, using his weight to sink them into the sand.

He took her mouth in a hot, demanding way, matching the tropical sun, causing a ripple of sweat to break out on his back. When he pulled back a fraction and stole a look at Sally, scant shades of dappled shadows fell over their bodies. She opened her eyes too, observing, all smiles gone as the serious task of completing this surprise took over.

"You ready for this, Sal?" he choked, emotion blocking his airways. It'd been forever since he believed he was worthy of this again. Had denied himself for so long. Missed it like crazy.

She combed her finger across his eyebrow, something that was uniquely her, brushing the tiny, short hairs neatly towards his temple. "Whoa, Ben, I never thought doing this out in the open, under a hot, burning sun, would turn me on so much. I am so ready for this."

He smiled at her tenderly, sweat pouring from their bodies, coating, pooling, slicking between them, and began kissing her slowly. Everywhere. He moved from her temple down to her cheek. Light butterfly kisses, dragging it out, wanting it to last into eternity. Slipped his face in the crook of her shoulder and kissed her there. She groaned impatiently, writhing beneath him. He persisted. Slid easily down her body until he hit the jackpot and closed his mouth over his nipple.

Her fingers tightened in his hair. Tugged on it. He felt no pain.

He sucked until his teeth gently scraped over her nipple, and she moaned some more. Releasing the swollen bud, he slipped a little further down. Tasting the heat and burn firing off her skin as he moved lower, his tongue licking its way down until it caught on her belly button.

"Ben!" she gasped. "I'm not going to make it, and I need you inside me. Please!" she begged in a raspy voice as she cradled him between her raised knees and rubbed against him.

With the fantasy of where he was headed clouding his mind, the tugging on his hair finally penetrated the thick fortress of fog, and he pulled back. Looking up, he got tangled in her fierce gaze burning with desire. He slid up her length again, slowly, easily, his erection throbbing impatiently at her dripping wet entry. He took a moment to take in some much-needed air, trapped in the liquid of her eyes before she pulled his head down to claim his mouth.

Desire heated his blood to boiling point, and he sank into her kiss as raw need slammed into him. He slipped inside her with a rush, clenching both her hips, fusing her body with his. A slight breeze wavered over from the fresh water in the creek and whispered around the sweat dripping off his back, giving him a hint of relief. He took it while hating it. He didn't want to cool down as he thrust further in, still kissing deeply.

A kiss that wouldn't end, leaving him dizzy from lack of air. He continued to press against her, sinking them further into the sand. Moulding their bodies as one. A moan tore from her. Enough to shut down his thoughts and concentrate on one thing and only one thing. The tidal wave was coming back into shore. He would happily drown under its weight when the relief came. The tsunami of his pulses had reached breaking point, and it was time to end the climb of that gigantic wave. But not before one last shot for that one shooting star as it sped across the sky. It would only take one more thrust. They were nearly there—and then they were.

Sally came first. Her guttural cries broke across his face, her hotter-than-hot breath streaking across his skin when she shattered and pulsed around him. He was there with her in seconds, his voice sounding like the roar of a proud lion as he pounded into her soft flesh.

A rattling tremor passed over his back as he registered the coolness of the breeze gusting over their sweat-covered bodies, bringing on a flicker of goosebumps along his arms and neck.

Then he was done. Crushing down upon her. Protecting her from the sun. A fierce surge passed through him of needing to take care of her forever. It took over his senses as he cradled his arms around her, squeezing her tight.

Her cry of alarm broke him, and he pulled away.

She smiled immediately, wriggling against him like a Cheshire cat. "Sorry, just couldn't breathe there for a second."

A grin spread across his face as he rolled off her, settling into her side, allowing the breeze to cool them.

"Good gosh." Sally giggled, turning towards him, leaving kisses along his temple. "Do you think it'll be this good all the time?"

Ben snorted with laughter. Maybe it was more from relief; he couldn't be sure. But a weight lifted off his chest and rose, disappearing into the canopy of the overhanging gum trees. He was glad to have it gone. For good, he hoped. Three cheers to new beginnings, he wanted to chant.

He rolled inwards, taking her face in his hands. "Thank you, Sal. That was out of this world, and—"

"And now we need to get going?" she cut in before smacking his lips with another fierce kiss.

"I guess we do."

"We have six boisterous boys waiting, dinosaur bones to keep digging for, and—"

"A lot more of this, I hope?" Ben quirked an eyebrow, his gaze never leaving her.

"You bet, cowboy, but now I'm starving, and I might venture into the creek for a little rinse off."

Ben moaned, worried they'd never leave this haven. The thought of her rinsing off in the creek would be enough to set him off again, and he didn't trust his libido to slow down one iota.

"You don't want a quick rinse, too?"

"No! I do not. What don't you understand?"

Sally chuckled, rising from the deep rut they'd created in the sand in all her naked glory. He found it difficult to stray from her swaying backside as she sauntered towards the water's edge. His awakening mind was already devising ways to do it all over again on the edge of the creek bed.

*Christ!* How was he supposed to sit quietly for the rest of the drive home with a hard-on?

# Chapter 19

Painstakingly slow. This was the best way to describe their task. Crouched, Sally used the sleeve of her shirt to wipe sweat from her brow. She eyed the grid system set up on the ground. Over the past week, they'd set up the grid, dug around the circumference and down about half a metre around the fossil. Now came the critical stage of digging out every individual bone. There were plenty. Nothing could contain Ben's excitement when it was discovered how almost complete this find was *and* fossilised in life position.

The digging site was a bevy of activity from early in the morning until about lunchtime. Lucy and her team of three scientists worked side by side with Sally and her boys, and Ben oversaw the entire project. When the heat got too much, they all plodded back to the homestead where Flora would have lunch ready.

"Like this, mate."

Sally glanced over at Ben who was showing one of the boys how it was done. With a hand trowel and dustpan brush at first, then a smaller paint brush to remove more soil, Ben showed Cole, the quieter of the six boys, how to carefully remove the dirt away from each bone.

"Then we hand it over to one of the team. They will plaster cast it to protect it in transit to the lab."

Cole nodded, moving on to the meticulous task of removing the next bone in the dinosaur's fin. Sally's heart cheered. All six of the boys were grossly engaged. Not once did they whinge about how hot it was or that it was boring. There was an undercurrent of excitement they'd never experienced before. A close family connection to the team working around them and the dinosaur fossil Ben had dubbed *Penny*.

Which kid didn't want to find their own dinosaur? Sally blinked, overwhelmed with how life-changing this experience was for herself and her team of boys. This would stay with them forever.

Down on his haunches, Ben glanced up, a warm smile crinkling the corners of his eyes. Impossible not to smile back. She buried the feelings of gratitude stirring inside her for now.

It had been one entire week since that glorious day at the creek.

Sex. Every. Single. Night. Since.

A ripple of goosebumps rose along her arms and neck thinking about how they spent their nights.

She chuckled, falling onto her backside. Crouching was a difficult position to maintain for too long, and she found herself alternating from crouching to sitting on the ground to standing up to stretch her legs. Her task was to collect the soil from around each bone. They collected it in bags, taking it back to the lab for possible teeth, marine life, other life forms, and evidence of the environment that existed around that time. By the time this dinosaur fossil was put back together, the team of palaeontologists will have reconstructed how it lived and died by using all their findings. Quite remarkable, really.

While removing the bones was monotonous and slow, you couldn't hide the palpable hum of excitement. The tangible evidence that life existed thousands of years earlier. So hard to dismiss when it was staring you in the face.

Ben rose, coming over to where she was sitting a little away from the others, and sat next to her. She swore black and blue that it was Ben's constant buzzing transferred to her every night when they lay together. This find was major news, so for now, they were keeping it from mainstream media and within the scientific community.

Sally strategised how to keep the bones in Richmond while she and the team gently removed them. Writing letters, making appointments, planning and more planning. There had to be a way to keep this fossil in Richmond.

Ben squeezed her hand. She tilted her hat back to better look at him. They didn't have to say a word. It was enough for her skin to tingle, her heart rate to pick up and her mind to dwell on what was happening between them.

They were two consenting adults, she reminded herself often.

In a few days, the boys would return to Richmond, and Sally wasn't so sure how she felt about it. Their return to town would see them continuing their schooling with more depth, further intense counselling and enjoying different activities—water sports on the lake a top priority—and a chance to train alongside the local boys with the footy club.

"Are you okay?" Ben asked, bumping shoulders. "That looks a little like a frown right about here." He touched her forehead, smoothing out the crease lines.

"I'm going to miss the boys." She spoke quietly so only Ben could hear. "I'm not sure how I'm going to cope when I have to say goodbye to them for a month. Without the distractions and their horrible family lives, they really are great kids."

Ben cupped her face, gently massaging her cheek with his thumb. "You're a good person, Sally. I see how you interact with the kids. You're saving them. Just like you're saving me," he whispered for her ears only.

Sally covered his warm hand with her own. Entwined her fingers with his and held on tight. Held onto her emotions that were fluttery as all heck and wanting release. She blinked some more, swallowing back a thick wad of them. They weren't showing huge amounts of affection publicly, but everyone was aware they were an item, so Sally wasn't surprised when Ben leant closer to leave a chaste kiss on her mouth before disentangling his hand.

"This is nuts, Ben."

"I know, right," he admitted with a grin. "I have bones to unearth and a digging site to supervise. I need my head in the game, and all it wants to do is stray to other things. Like tonight. After dinner. After our team meeting. When we can finally be alone again."

Sally chuckled. "It'll take my mind off saying goodbye to the boys."

"Is telling you it's only for four weeks going to help?"

Sally shook her head. "Not really, because then I'll be saying goodbye to the next half a dozen boys. I'm going to be a wreck."

"Looks like I'm going to have to work extra hard to keep you distracted."

"I think you're already doing that just fine."

They grinned at each other like the love-struck loonies they were. Even though they never discussed what was happening between them, Sally was more than okay with only sex. This was the new her. Live life to the fullest. Sometimes she dwelled on Ben's past, but no way would she demand anything more from him. This early in their relationship, she didn't feel it was her place to ask too many questions.

"What's the plan for this afternoon?" Ben asked.

"I discovered a pile of used ironbark fence posts behind the homestead. I thought the boys could construct some garden beds to separate the lawn. Some native shrubs will arrive in my next delivery. I hope you don't mind," Sally added with an extra wide cheesy smile.

Ben chuckled. "Not at all."

"I didn't think you would. They've increased my budget to allow for more gardening expenditure, so along with the native shrubs and organic fertilisers, I also have a stack of sugarcane mulch coming at the same time. I hope to have enough to put around each of the shrubs. The poor little plants will need all the help they can get out here."

"Flora is hanging out for this same delivery. She was saying food stocks were getting dangerously low, that we might all have to starve for a day or two if it doesn't hurry up."

Sally let out a snort before reaching behind for her water bottle. "I reckon Flora can conjure up a meal from nothing." She unscrewed the cap and took a long swig of water, the deliciously cold liquid flowing down her throat, giving her instant relief from the hot, dusty conditions of the work site.

"Yeah, she's God-like alright—and a mothering, interfering, meddling woman at the moment with my mother in her ear too."

Sally's eyes widened. "You don't mean that. Flora embodies everything good in a woman in the true spirit of the outback."

Ben's grin spread wider. "*If* she stuck to what she's supposed to instead of harping on about me moving on and taking you seriously."

"You're not taking me seriously?" She grinned back. What they had going on between them was too special to screw up by getting needy. She did her best to ignore the way her heart thudded harder inside her ribcage. Forever, she forcibly reminded herself. They could carry on this way forever. She wouldn't push Ben. Promised to give him time to sort his shit, and she was sticking to her guns.

Ben's grin disappeared completely. In its place, he wore a look that told her he was mentally undressing her, right here, right now. Her smile slipped too; her mouth opened slightly, and she lost herself a little more in the watery depths of his green eyes. Forget about the heat bearing down on them. She was more concerned about the heat brewing inside.

Ben quietly groaned, loud enough for her ears only. "Oh, I'm taking you very seriously." He roughly scrubbed a hand over his face. "And I need to get my head back in the job. You really are very bad for me, Sal. I can't concentrate on anything."

Sally rubbed her earlobe, doing anything to distract the headiness attacking her. "You better get back to the other side of the grid. It'll be safer if you're over there," she added with a resigned plead. "I have a job to do here, and I don't need any reminding of what I'd rather be doing."

Ben emitted another soft-sounding moan and scrambled to his feet. She huffed out trapped air, attempting to control her erratic pulse.

"Along with our food order and your gardening stuff, Lucy's girls are on their way out for the two weeks of school holidays."

"Does this mean I'll have to share you even more?" She pouted.

"Unlikely," was his parting word as he finally left her alone, walking over to where Lucy and the group of scientists worked on the other side of the grid.

# Chapter 20

"Miss Barkworth, when will we see you again?"

Sally put an arm around Jack's shoulders, giving him a comforting hug. "Four weeks exactly." Jack was the comedian of the group of boys, always making the others laugh with a joke or a silly antic. This morning, he wore a serious and troubled look, and Sally's heart clenched tighter. She didn't doubt the boys experienced a month of relaxed casualness while their minds and bodies were kept busy.

Fossil digging, gardening, taking turns helping Flora prepare the meals, teaching them how to wash and care for their clothes, swimming and fishing. Ben even started giving them driving lessons out in the open backyard. A lot of stimulating and engaging activities, a stark contrast to their lives before this program. Engulfed by a technologically driven world that had forgotten how to enjoy the basics of life, it seemed there was no space left for anything else. It would hurt even more when she had to finally release them back into the system or their families, if it was safe.

"Have you packed all your gear, boys?" Sally directed to all six as they milled around the front of the homestead.

"Who owns these socks and shorts?" Flora came down the homestead stairs carrying an armful of belongings. One by one, the rightful owner was found for each item, but not before Flora engulfed each boy in a rib-breaking hug as she kissed the tops of their heads, demanding they hurried up and come back soon.

Flora soon had Jack's sad face converted to a bright and happy smile. Sally bit down on her lip, doing her best to hold it all in. Now, to deal with this goodbye in a responsible adult way. But heck! She didn't want to adult today.

"You okay?" Ben sidled up to her as columns of dust in the distance drew closer.

Six new boys would arrive in the next twenty minutes, along with Lucy's two daughters and all the requested supplies.

The drivers would pretty much turn around once everyone and everything was unloaded and drive back to the main homestead, where the second teacher waited due to lack of space in the vehicles. There, Ellen would feed the boys and drivers lunch before they trekked into Richmond.

Sally shook her head, not able to say anything, as every emotion possible bubbled below the surface.

"You've done an amazing job with them these past weeks. They're going to be fine." Ben put his arm around her waist, pressing her closer to his side.

"I know all this. Your mum even promised to visit them in Richmond a couple of times during the next month with heaps of home-baked goodies, but it doesn't change how much I'm going to miss them."

"Donna is an excellent role model too."

Sally didn't dispute this. Their second teacher, known to the boys as Mrs Bartlett, was a mid-forties dynamite with many years of teaching under her belt and a caring passion that never dimmed.

"And you get to sink your teeth into learning all the habits, good and bad, of the next lot. More challenges for Miss Barkworth." Ben grinned, dropping a quick kiss on her temple.

Sally knotted her fingers with Ben's and clasped them tight. When the moment came, it was going to be hard.

Thankful for Ben's support, she disentangled herself from him, taking a moment to admire the great work done in the front yard. This time, when she inhaled a lung full of dry, dusty air, it was tinged with the fresh scent of the beginnings of a green lawn. What would hopefully be a permanent feature of the property provided water was in good supply.

Gardening was a therapeutic approach for a lot of people, and there was plenty of space for her and the boys to work with. With the front of the old homestead now sporting more grass than dust, their successful start was beginning to show. Garden beds, waiting for the arrival of the native shrubs, had also been sectioned off by the boys. Barely a dent was made in the pile of old ironbark fence posts, so Sally had plenty of ideas on how to use them to continue making borders, neatening the entire homestead yard.

She released the dry air, and the tension in her shoulders dissipated. "Thank you," she said, facing Ben again. "Thank you for standing by my side. It's still going to be hard, though."

Ben cupped her cheek, smiling with encouragement. They'd shared some heady nights over the past couple of weeks, and she lost herself a little more in his iridescent eyes. On some nights when they didn't want to tempt fate with the noise they tried so hard to keep low, they stole outside, under the stars, with a rolled-up rug they kept at the ready. One night, they ran as far as the digging site, allowing Penny to keep an eye on their shenanigans.

Ben's thumb continued to stroke her skin in soft rotations. She wasn't sure if this thing between them was long term or short, but she grabbed the notion with both hands, bringing it close to her chest. "I better go check they're ready to leave. I'm sure they have everything because Flora won't have missed a thing, but it won't hurt to double-check."

"Except Flora can't give them a Miss Barkworth hug."

"No, but she gives a damn good Flora hug. I'll need one from her after they leave."

"You'll be too busy with the new boys, and knowing Miss Barkworth like I do, I may have to miss out."

This was enough for Sally to completely loosen up and chuckle. "I doubt it. You're persistent *every* night," she added with a cheeky grin.

Ben grinned back, drawing her in for another kiss. A quick one, probably just to remind her he was going to be insistent again that night. "I'll try to tone it down then, will I?"

"Don't you dare," she whispered for his ears only, almost running into Lucy when she turned to walk away. Lucy had spent time at the digging site this morning and was back in time to meet her daughters.

"Morning, Lucy, the girls are nearly here. I'm looking forward to meeting them."

Lucy ruffled her already sweaty dark hair, kept short and neat, before shoving her hat back on. "They've been talking of nothing else for the past two weeks. It's been a merry dance getting a tag team in place to accompany them all this way. So, beware, here they come."

Sally glanced up at the approaching dust spirals and frowned. "Is it my imagination, or can I see three spirals approaching?"

"That *is* weird," Lucy confirmed. She removed her hat and squinted some more, gently massaging her scalp before shrugging. "I guess we have a visitor. What do you think, Ben? Know anything about it?"

"I just spotted it, too. Might be Mum or Dad coming for a cuppa." Ben joined them as they all stared at the approaching dust plumes.

"It won't be your mum. She'll be busy getting lunch ready for this returning crew," Lucy reminded them.

"Yeah, good point. It's not another one of your pals come to take our glory away, is it, Luce?" Ben joked.

"No one I've invited. If it's someone coming to sniff things out, they can turn around and go straight back to where they came from."

Lucy, with her no-nonsense retort, brought a smile to Sally's face, but she had a good point. The secrecy of this discovery was contained to a small section of the scientific community and a few members of the council. Very few people knew of it, which was a good thing. The homestead was already at bursting point. They couldn't sustain too many more people without bringing in more food and bedding supplies.

"Anyone you invited, Sal?" Ben asked, wrapping his arm around her waist again. Sally inhaled everything that embodied Ben and the outback, helping to boost her flagging spirits at the coming goodbye.

"Nope, nobody I know. I'm making arrangements for Dean to come out for a few weeks, but the plans are still in progress."

There was no mistaking the third trail of dust. Now only minutes away from arriving.

"Is this another mouth to feed?" Flora asked as she joined them. "Feels like a permanent addition if they bothered getting a third vehicle."

"Just tell them to go right back to where they came from, hey, Flora," Lucy said. "I'm not sharing your chocolate cake any further than I need to."

Sally smiled some more. Flora's cake was legendary, and Lucy had a point. But now she, too, was curious. As the first 4WD troop carrier with a trailer parked and turned off the ignition, her attention was distracted by the new boys. She left the security of Ben's hold, walking towards the vehicle where doors popped open and boys tumbled out, a couple even tripping and falling to the lawn in a fit of giggles.

*Well, this is a good sign.*

The other two vehicles arrived one after the other. There was more activity as doors opened and shut. Boys talked over each other, and the drivers began the arduous task of unloading.

Flora was already in amongst the fray of boys and bags when Sally swung around towards the sound of two young girls squealing, "Muuuuuummm!"

Two middle-grade miniature versions of Lucy tore out of the mysterious white vehicle and hurtled towards Lucy. She caught them against her chest, raining kisses over their faces.

Sally didn't recognise the man coming out of the driver's side until Lucy's screech split the air in a delighted squeal. "Rodney, oh my God, you came too?"

"You didn't think I'd let the girls have all the fun, did you?"

Sally watched on, fascinated, as Rodney and Lucy embraced over the top of the two girls and kissed.

"I've missed you like crazy," Rodney added when Lucy took a step back to give her girls some more attention, inconspicuously wiping a tear away.

The family reunion filled Sally with a rush of emotional warmth. Was this what happy ever after looked like?

"Is there room for me?" Rodney turned towards Flora with a hopeful smile.

"Always room for you," Flora assured him, coming up and getting a hug from him, too. "But does this mean I have to cook that damn pumpkin fruit cake you love so much?"

Ben and Lucy laughed at a shared memory while Sally basked in the good feelings surrounding the arrival of Rodney and the two girls, but now it was time to shift her attention to the six new boys.

Before she could approach the chaotic scene of boys, gear and drivers busy unloading, someone tapped on her shoulder and she spun around.

A memory fought its way to the surface as she stared into the boy's face. Dizziness threatened to destabilise her, and she swayed as she struggled to catch up with what she was seeing.

He was taller. His once-clear skin showed signs of acne. His eyes spoke of sadness and suffering. Her heart began to crack and fall to pieces, each shard a painful memory.

"Hello, Miss Barkworth." His voice caught on a slight catch, like it was breaking with approaching puberty.

"Jacob," she whispered. "Oh, my God, Jacob, is it really you?"

He nodded once. A solemn face etched in that expression. Like he hadn't had a reason to smile for a long time, and it tore at her heart.

"Come here," she demanded, her arms open wide. Taking him against her, she did her best to keep it together, fighting back tears. "Where have you been?" she asked, reluctant to release him, just in case he disappeared again.

Jacob shuffled out of her arms and stepped back. He lowered his gaze, and his cheeks reddened slightly. "Everywhere, Miss Barkworth, but ... nowhere."

Nothing could hold back the tears trickling past her eyelids, even though she did her best to contain them. His words carried the anguish of a tormented adult, not a child. How much had he suffered these past years? If he was here and part of this program, what did this mean?

She valiantly sniffled her tears back, dashing a sleeve across her eyes to wipe away the evidence. Now was not the time or the place. "Have you been okay, Jacob? Oh, my God," she whispered so only he could hear her, "it almost destroyed me when you disappeared. Where did you go?"

He shrugged like there was no straightforward answer. As if he could explain in a few words. She berated herself. She knew better. "I'm sorry, Jacob. We'll talk later." She gave him another hug. This time, it was a quick one so as not to draw any more attention from the others.

She stepped away and almost crumbled again when Jacob swallowed enough times that his Adam's apple trembled. God help her; if all this program ever achieved was to right the wrongs life had thrown in Jacob's way, she would be satisfied with that. She was never letting him out of her sight again. "You're here now, Jacob. I'll take care of you."

He offered her a curt nod. Like believing the world was a good place and someone was prepared to make his life a better one couldn't possibly be true.

They shared a history. He had to know he could trust her. As soon as she was in front of her laptop again, she would request his complete file. This was something she did with all the kids, but she would pore over Jacob's and read between the lines if she had to. "Have you got all your gear out?"

"Yeah," he croaked, his emotions catching. "I don't have much anyway."

This would break her. She bit down on her lip, patting him on the back and directing him to the homestead's front steps. "Flora has morning tea for you all. You're safe now, Jacob. I promise."

He blinked rapidly, his knuckles shining white as he clenched the shoulder straps of his backpack. Then he gave her another nod and wandered off.

Sally watched him walk away, a lump in her throat, tears still blurring her vision. He looked back once, and she forced a smile. Enough for her to witness a smidgen of relief to pass over his face.

All she wanted to do was rage and throw things. Rally and rant at the injustices of the world that some kids found themselves in. She'd made a promise to keep him safe and she would. New determination found a home and surrounded her. A new strength of will. This ... she didn't know what to call it. It must be what normal, loving parents felt towards their children. The mothering instinct. Nothing would dampen it. Never! She just had to convince Jacob she meant it.

This was one promise she would *never* break.

# Chapter 21

*C*rash!

The sound of the ceramic mug hitting the floor echoed throughout the homestead. Sally froze, then groaned at the sound of footsteps. How was she so careless? Again?

A morning cup of coffee. One flaming cup of beverage to help her get through the coming day after sleep had evaded her all night.

"Sally? Everything okay?" Flora bustled in, followed closely by a sleepy Ben rubbing his eyes.

"I'm sorry, Flora. I didn't mean to wake you." She did her best to keep her voice hushed.

Flora tutted while Ben took her in his arms. "Are you okay?"

She hadn't gone to his bed last night. Too consumed with Jacob's arrival, her head was all over the place. Her priority had been to source all the information she could on Jacob from the department and delve into why he'd turned up in this program. After that, there was Buckley's chance of falling asleep. She'd tossed and turned all night.

She shook her head. There was no hiding it from Flora who would assist with the counselling. There was no hiding it from Ben because it would eat her from the inside out if she didn't share it with him.

The anger, the frustration, the disbelief that this could happen to a child and his younger sibling tore her to shreds. She'd held herself together all night, fury keeping her tears at bay, but now they made their escape, flowing past her eyelids in a steady stream. She shrugged out of Ben's hold, crouching to pick up the scattered pieces of the mug through blurred vision.

"I'll do it," Flora said. "Take her away, Ben. I'll bring you coffees in a minute."

Blinded by her tears, she didn't fight Ben when he helped her rise and steered her outside. Apart from the rustic logs screwed together on the homestead verandah, there were no outdoor settings they could use. Only a dozen or so hefty tree trunks scattered around.

She shivered as the crisp morning air brushed her skin through her cotton pyjamas. A thin haze of light beginning to rise above the horizon was the only hint that dawn was approaching. It was probably close to five am, seeing she'd last spied the time on her phone at four-thirty. It was at this point she'd thrown off the covers and gone in search of a coffee.

Ben grabbed his Driza-Bone hanging off the hook at the front of the homestead and a rubber mat from a pile the boys used for weight training. He made for the largest acacia tree on the side of the homestead, furthest away from the bedrooms.

Ben sat with his back against the trunk and helped position her in front of his lap before wrapping the Driza-Bone over them to keep the chill out. The strong, musty smell of the oilskin filled her senses. She took a moment to calm down by concentrating on her breathing, wishing the product used on the iconic brand of outdoor coat was a drowsing drug. If bottled up, she could gulp it down straight.

It was still too dark to see much, except for some muffled kitchen light filtering past the window. Using her soft cotton pyjama, she wiped her face and snuggled in closer to Ben, seeking the comforting warmth of his body. She wanted to switch off from the world for a few moments. Forget everything she'd read on Jacob's file. Wanted to blot it from her memory for a couple of minutes. If only her brain would allow it.

Sitting beneath this tree was fast becoming one of her favourite spots in the afternoon when she allowed herself a little downtime. She drew strength from its strong girthed trunk which forked in three directions a couple of metres above; its sturdy branches and thick foliage provided valuable shade in the stifling afternoons. Ben's support and kindness gave her strength, too; she knew she would need it.

"What happened, Sal?"

Was she ready to talk? Lacking sleep, a good solid cry was what she wanted, but there would be many nights when she could do that. She needed to get this off her chest now! Stewing over it all night and deciding how to approach Jacob with it all, tormented her.

Not even Donna, the second teacher, was privy to this information. Donna's notes after having him for four weeks indicated he was a troubled and aloof kid, prone to temper tantrums. He struggled with emotional management and didn't interact well with the other boys. No bloody wonder!

The chilly morning air filled her lungs, clearing her fuzzy head. With so many thoughts zooming around in her head, she doubted even a good sleep would settle it. Releasing the breath in slow, measured puffs, she interlocked her fingers with Ben's, resting them on her stomach. She needed all the support she could muster to repeat the words she'd read.

"Jacob's mum died at the hands of her violent husband. He's now in prison."

"Oh, fuck." Ben hissed, tucking her in closer beneath his chin, the rise and fall of his chest mirroring her anger.

"The report says that Jacob and his sister took off for the neighbours to get help. The neighbours kept the children with them, thank goodness, because when the police arrived, the mother was deceased from knife wounds and the father had disappeared. It took the police two weeks to find him. In the meantime, authorities placed the kids into protective care." A small sob broke past her defences, and more tears trickled down her cheeks. "Oh, Ben, the medical report and assessment done on Jacob and his sister is horrifying."

"Shh," Ben comforted, "don't rush it. If there's any positives to this, Jacob and his sister didn't witness the murder."

"But am I too late to save Jacob?"

"Never, Sal. He's only twelve. If anyone can help him, it's you."

"He was such a different kid when I last saw him. Why is life so cruel?" She made a superhuman effort to stem the flow, clamping down on her jaw. Crying could happen later in the privacy of her room. Today, she needed to be strong and come up with a solution for Jacob's welfare. She wiped her face dry again, sniffling once more. When she looked up at the crunch of footsteps, Flora appeared with two steaming mugs of coffee.

"Here you go," Flora announced, holding out the mugs.

Sally loosened her hold on Ben and took one, then wriggled away from Ben so he could take his. "Thanks, Flora, and sorry about the mess I made."

Ben snorted quietly beside her. "She's a tyrant around mugs. I've seen a couple end their life around her."

Flora harrumphed. "Sometimes a woman's gotta slam that mug against a brick wall to get everything out. It's only a mug, after all."

She managed a lopsided smile at Flora's metaphor despite everything spinning around her head. "Does letting it slip from your fingers unintentionally mean the same thing?"

A little lightness to start her day after the terrible night was exactly what she needed. She took a generous sip of the warm, milky coffee, sighing with pleasure. "Thanks, Flora. It's been a rough night. I'll fill you in later."

"We'll sort it out whatever is troubling you, girl. Now, I don't know about you pair, but I reckon I could sneak in another hour of sleep."

"Thanks for everything, Flora."

Flora flicked them a quick wave before turning around and scurrying back to the homestead.

"Are you warm enough?" Ben asked the moment Flora left.

Sally carefully shuffled closer to Ben again, greedily wanting more of his body warmth. Ben adjusted the Driza-Bone around them as she tucked her knees up to her chest, cradling the mug in both hands. She nodded, looking up as a slight breeze fluttered through the foliage. A couple of leaves dropped on her head and arms. She blinked away debris caught on her eyelash and sighed, comfortable with how the quiet of the early morning surrounded them both, a peacefulness descending over them. A far cry from the state of her mind less than an hour ago.

On this patch of new lawn that she and the boys had tended, Ben must have sensed words weren't necessary. They drank their coffees in companionable silence. It didn't take her long to drain her mug. When Ben placed her empty mug on the ground beside his, a sense of gratitude swept over her. A reminder of how lucky she was to have crossed paths with this man. This program might have been steered in a different direction. With incompatible people. A failed project from the start. She shook her head. She was just thankful she'd made all the decisions that led to where they were. "Thanks for being here, Ben."

Ben wrapped his arms securely around her waist, drawing her close against his chest. "Sometimes, that's all a person needs. This isn't the time nor the place to discuss Jacob's file, but we can go through it later this afternoon. With Flora's help, we can work out a path forward for the boy."

She nodded, looking across to the horizon where the faint white line slowly stretched with the coming dawn. "I want a chance to speak to Jacob privately. I'd like to get his take on what happened. Two years ago, when we last saw each other, he was an open and optimistic kid. I know so much has happened to him since, but I want the chance to rebuild the relationship we once had."

"Good idea." Ben tucked her head under his chin where his warm breath fanned the top of her hair.

"Thanks for being so understanding. I feel I owe it to him. Maybe if I'd done things differently back—"

"Don't, Sal," Ben cut in. "Don't beat yourself up. Some things happen for a reason. Trust me, I know."

"And one day, we'll take the time out to talk about it?" Sal whispered.

She twisted around, allowing Ben to steal a kiss. "When we're not having hot, out-of-this-world sex."

Sally let out a quiet chuckle. Despite how bad her night had turned out, that Ben could make her smile and laugh was proof of how special he was.

"I missed you last night." Gone was his jovial tone. He was back to all seriousness as he whispered the words close to her ear, sending shivers down her spine.

It was hard to ignore his reaction to having her in his arms. His erection prodded her back like an engine piston. Strong. Insatiable. For the first time since Jacob's arrival, she was able to switch off.

Cocooned and not so strangled by her thoughts, she could use some relief from the torturous thoughts that had bombarded her for hours.

Her body was already taking that road without her mind's consent. She shouldn't want to divulge in sex, but being around Ben was like taking an addictive drug. There was never a time when she had enough.

Even after learning terrible things about what adult humans did to small humans, unfathomable in her mind, she couldn't avoid this thing with Ben. She berated herself for letting her work get between them, but then she softened her chastising by claiming that taking care of Jacob would never be slotted into the 'work' category.

"We have exactly thirty-three minutes before anyone shows up," Ben prompted, jolting her back to the present and the unpleasantness of the night gone by.

"Do you want to head back to my room?" she asked.

"We'll have to." Ben made to rise when he quietly chuckled. "Hang on a minute." He pulled the jacket away from her. She shivered at the loss of its warmth. "I think I put a couple of extras in this inside pocket the night we stole out to the digging site."

"I hope so because I'm freezing," she whispered, allowing herself to blot everything out except for the here and now. If only she could stop shivering.

She heard the crinkle of the package before Ben whispered, "Oh, my God, I have one here."

"No way!"

"Yes! This is a win in my books."

She snorted and Ben shushed her. "No noise, Sally. Absolutely not a sound, okay? You've already woken enough of us this morning."

"It wasn't my fault I broke the mug."

"You probably say that every time you break one."

Sally harrumphed, shaking her head. *She* couldn't believe she'd broken it.

"Now, can you do this quietly?"

"How is that going to happen?" she whisper-hissed. "I bet *you* won't be able to keep quiet."

"Just watch me!" Ben tore the foil package apart and pulled his loose cotton pyjamas down enough to sheathe himself. Taking her with him, he laid down on his back, making her comfortable on top. Then he adjusted the Driza-Bone over their coupled bodies before beginning his magic with both hands and mouth. With loosely fitted pyjamas, there was no need for Sally to remove any clothing. Everything could be easily stretched and reached how they were. Ben didn't hesitate to touch her in all the right places, going straight for the warmth between her legs as she wriggled on top of him.

Unexpectedly, she giggled.

"Shh, Sally," Ben hissed, directing his erection to her wetness so she could slide over it and settle comfortably along its perfect fit.

Oh, she wanted so badly to moan out loud. She soon forgot how chilly her exposed feet were at the bottom of the Driza-Bone. It didn't take long for heat to generate between them as they rocked and ground against each other in a rhythmic pattern as old as time.

There was no taking this slow. There was no holding back. The risk of being caught took a back seat because nothing would hold them back from this point. This risk-taking sent a delicious shiver along her skin. The new Sally was bold and audacious, taking what she wanted whenever she could. There was no going back to the old Sally.

Tangled with her cotton pants, Ben clasped her backside and pressed her closer, drawing her fully over his erection. Oh, this was so good; her moisture reduced any friction as she continued to ground against Ben. This raw need obliterated everything, including the sleepless night. She needed this badly.

"Remember, no noise," Ben reminded her, his whispered voice catching on a moan.

"I can't promise that," she retorted, wanting like all goddesses to howl like a lioness who'd caught her male king. Holding back almost killed her.

They began the rapid climb to the top. Mount Everest was suddenly very close. Ben sought a nipple underneath her top and took it between his teeth, sending her mind into a delirious spin before claiming her mouth again, his tongue darting in, warming her from the inside out. A hot, delicious, burning kiss that carried through right to the tips of her exposed toes, making a mockery of the chilly morning temperature.

She snagged, caught sight of the top, and reached it seconds later. Shards of light splintered and shattered behind her eyelids, while Ben reached that space of intense pleasure too, as his body spasmed underneath hers.

As Sally came back down to earth, only their loud breathing disturbed the early quiet, together with the gentle rise and fall of their chests.

"Feel better?" Ben asked in between a laboured breath.

"You bet. Now, I guess we better sneak back inside without getting caught."

Ben chuckled quietly. "What have I started here? I feel fifteen again, sneaking out to the stargazer's lounge, hoping to snag the attention of a twenty-something jillaroo."

"What, you did that?"

"Maybe. Once," Ben admitted, rolling her gently off his length so he could rise. Then he helped her up, being sure to keep the warm Driza-Bone wrapped around her. "Where are your shoes?"

"They can't be too far." They'd long flung off her feet when Ben had taken her down with him.

"Here they are." Ben spotted them on the grass.

She slipped her feet into them, their coolness sending a rush up her warm legs.

"Ready?" he asked, collecting the empty mugs and rubber mat.

She nodded.

"Okay, I'll go clean up. See you at breakfast."

Sally grabbed his arm before he rushed off, giving it a squeeze. "Thank you, Ben."

"Thank *you*," he replied. Tucking the mat under his arm, he gave her a good, long hug with his free arm. "Can you believe it, Sal? We're wrapping up Penny's second fin today. We are doing so damn well at the grid; it's too good to be true."

Sally smiled. Ben's adrenaline was infectious, and his mind was already on the day's tasks to complete. She was more than fine with that. Nothing could tamper the excitement of what Penny was turning out to be.

Hand in hand, they walked together towards the homestead, the sun just peeking over the horizon. This was an extra incentive for Sally to make Penny a star. A giving star to a small community that could use anything to keep it alive, prosperous, and firmly on the Queensland map.

# Chapter 22

"**I** was going to get a knife and stab my father to death."

"Oh, Jacob." Sally wept inside for the anguish Jacob suffered barely a year ago.

With the other five boys following Ben towards the digging grid, Sally had encouraged Jacob to follow her as they turned left towards the river.

"Instead, the bastard did it first to Mum before I could get to him."

Spoken with such venom, like someone twice his age, Jacob's features hardened. He would probably carry the guilt of not saving his mum forever.

This sort of trauma was beyond Sally's experience. She only wanted to re-establish their friendship of two years ago. This admission by Jacob grabbed at her jugular and tightened its hold. A pain she couldn't fathom ever understanding.

They sat on the sandy bank of the slow-flowing river, where it looked shades of green or brown, depending on how much sun shone through the thick expanse of gum trees. Enormous granite boulders lay jumbled along parts of the riverbank too, where the sun's rays glistened off the millions of little specs of granite, resembling shiny jewels. The gum trees lining the bank provided mottled shade, the shadows moving across Jacob's serious face in time with the lazy breeze rustling the foliage.

"This is an awful burden for you to carry, Jacob, and I'm thankful you trusted me enough to share. Talking is what will help you through this terrible ordeal, and I'm so glad you found your way to my program. I am so, so happy you're here." She wrapped an arm around his shoulder. Jacob didn't budge but continued to stare at the river. She doubted he even saw it. Sally hoped, though, that the visions flickering behind his eyes might one day be soothed by such simple things as water flowing down a river or a canopy of trees moving with gentle breezes.

"Were you still living in the north?" Sally removed her arm from around his shoulder and settled it in her lap.

Jacob dragged his blank stare away from the water, blinking a few times before focusing on her. "He took us to Toowoomba in the middle of winter. It was freezing, and we didn't have heating in the house or enough warm clothes. I was always so cold."

"Oh, Jacob, I'm sorry I wasn't there to help you." She blinked furiously. Now was not the time to break down. She could do so in the quiet of the night when she was alone or with Ben.

"I wish you'd been closer too." He hung his head, his small round shoulders slumping with defeat and sadness. No wonder he never smiled. Sally didn't know how someone so young and traumatised could come back from this.

Jacob's medical assessment, conducted after the siblings entered care, revealed cigarette burns on both him and his younger sister, Maddison. There was evidence of extensive bruising, both new and old. Blood tests revealed rat bait in their digestive systems. What sort of monster did this to his children?

Agitated, Jacob rose and paced the soft sand. "It's too late for Mum. It's Maddy I have to worry about. I promised her I'd look after her." He spun around to face Sally, and she swallowed, wanting to die with the look of anguish he wore. "She's only eight, Miss Barkworth, and she'll be so scared. I don't know where they took her. I can't find her. Nobody will tell me anything."

Sometimes the system sucked. Badly. Siblings were meant to be kept together. "Why wouldn't they tell you where she was?" Her heart broke, piece by piece.

Jacob's knees buckled, and he fell backwards to his backside. With both hands, he clutched at his head, roughly running them through his short-cropped brown hair. "I said all the wrong things, Miss. I'd already told them about wanting to kill my father. And I threatened to stab them, too, if they didn't let Maddy stay with me. I was so angry. Why couldn't Maddy stay with me? I would never hurt her."

Sally wasn't expecting this hardened kid to show any emotion, but something broke inside him as he crumbled inwards, followed by loud, ugly sobbing. A dam bursting, and probably something Jacob had held on to for many, many months. "I didn't mean any of it. I just wanted us to stay together. But they dragged her away crying and screaming." Overdue tears gushed down his cheeks, and his shoulders shook with his anguish.

Did she hold him? Did she make promises she wasn't sure she could keep? God help her; he was a twelve-year-old boy who'd seen too much and who desperately needed the love of a family.

Her mind whirred and clicked, thinking through the thousand and one possibilities of what to do. What she and Ben could do as a united front. The channels she could pursue with her connections and training. Then her mind blanked, and she did what felt natural. She got up, sat beside Jacob and took him in her arms, holding him while he cried his heart out.

If this was the wrong thing to do, she would bear the heavy weight of her actions. For now, she wanted to be the mother he no longer had and curse the father who never deserved such an amazing kid. For a split second, a vision of her stabbing this cruel man took centre stage in her mind, and she hardened that little bit too.

If it was the last thing she ever did, she would find his sister and reunite her with Jacob. They were family. They were meant to stay together. Her arms tightened around Jacob as her resolve to fix this for him grew stronger.

Ben lay awake on his back, Sally sound asleep tucked in beside him. There was a niggle he couldn't capture that had woken him up. It was pitch black outside, and he didn't want to move to check on the time in case he woke her. Whatever was concerning him was wedging its way inside his mind like a persistent, buzzing fly, insistent on getting its message across. If only he knew what.

"What's up, Ben?" Sally whispered in the darkness. Although the homestead had thick, sturdy walls, noise still carried easily in the quiet of the night.

Ben rolled towards her, wrapping her in his arms. "Sorry, Sal, I didn't mean to wake you. Something is nagging me. I have no idea what, and it won't let me relax." Ben spoke in hushed tones, too.

He sensed her coming more awake. Sally did her usual comforting thing, smoothing his right eyebrow towards his temple with her fingertip. Even in pitch black, she had a knack for finding the spot. He closed his eyes, her soothing doing its magic. He couldn't believe how something so simple had such a cathartic effect on him.

"Take a minute and see if it comes to you. I'm right here."

Ben smiled in the dark at her no-nonsense approach. He took a moment to sift through what they'd talked about that afternoon. Together with Flora, the three of them went through Jacob's file and discussed locating his sister. Jacob's welfare would consume Sally until the little girl was located, but he dismissed this as the cause of his worries. Sally had her finger on the pulse and the ability to seek help from the department internally, and she would find the girl soon enough.

"I've been thinking of something else too, Ben." Her breath was warm against his chest as she spoke.

"Hmm?" He nuzzled his face over her hair, filling up with the scent of their heated bodies.

"I really want to look at the long-term guardianship of Jacob and Maddy. I know how it works."

"Like adoption?" Ben asked.

"Adoption is not likely as the father is still alive. While adoption is done through an agency, long-term guardianship is done through the Department of Child Safety. They advocate for these children and take care of them. If we remain a couple, we'd each have to submit a statement as to why we want to become a 'special person'."

"What does that mean?"

"Well, we apply to become a foster carer first. Receive training, especially in trauma, and then they unpack your entire life."

Ben's body stiffened. He bit down on his lip to keep the groan contained, remembering others slept in the homestead. But he was already shaking his head, shuffling away from the centre of the bed. "I can't, Sally. I'm sorry," he whispered.

"Ben, we're only discussing it now. It doesn't happen overnight."

"But you want it to?"

"Yes, of course I do. Until I know Jacob and Maddy are taken care of, I'll never be able to sleep another night. I'm the best person for it. I'—she scooted over to where he'd escaped—'ah ... thought we might be the best people for it. Am I wrong about that?"

Ben quietly moaned when he should've been reassuring her she was definitely the best person for it. Compassionate, amazing and resilient. Everything he'd hoped to find in a soulmate after Rhylee. "You haven't searched for the sister yet?" God, he needed to buy time. Drag this out until he had his head sorted and told Sally about his past so she understood the predicament this would put them in.

"We both know in my position, it won't be hard."

That was true. They could have Maddy's location sorted in a matter of days, leading the way to exposing the real reason the idea of guardianship alarmed him. His black box of hell would need to be revisited. Put under the department's scrutiny. Someone would read the reports completed by the psychologist. There was a thick folder with his name on it. He'd spied it towards the end of his counselling days. Hoped to never lay eyes on it again.

Once an interrogation of his past was complete, they would never allow him guardianship rights. His entire past few years were a hotbed of potential triggers. If he couldn't take care of himself, how was he expected to look after traumatised kids? He was setting Sally up for disappointment if he didn't nip this in the bud now.

"Ben, I don't want to upset you. I'm sorry, but I told you once that I would always be open with you. It's what you wanted, if you remember."

There it was. The biggest stab to his chest. A reminder of the plea he'd asked of her to tell him things along the way. Not keep it locked inside until it blew up.

He should be telling her about those years and warning her. They hadn't even come close to discussing what went wrong with Rhylee or the time after. How did he start now? They would never be granted permission to take on guardianship of Jacob and Maddy, and all because of his past. If Sally was hellbent on fostering the two children, she would have to choose between him or them. Just when he'd spied some hope, a small ray of light at the end of the tunnel, now this. Another setback.

"You can't just come out and make this announcement." He didn't want this to become a slinging match with raised voices, but being forced to talk quietly was killing him.

"I am trying to discuss it now. I didn't plan for it to be in the middle of the night, but we're both awake and, for a change, with nothing to distract either of us."

He rolled towards the bedside table and switched on the old-fashioned lampshade he'd found at his mum's, squinting in the bright light.

With a sigh, he rolled back to the middle of the bed, his gaze resting on Sally. Her hair was mussed, and worry lines etched her forehead. The muscles around his chest clenched into a tight knot. This woman had awakened so much in him. Why did he have to deal with this complication?

"I'm sorry I brought it up, Ben. I didn't realise you would be so opposed to the idea without discussing it first. Because honestly, that was all I was proposing now. As I said, there's a process, and it doesn't happen overnight. We've never discussed us, I know, and I'm giving you time to get yourself together. I certainly wasn't putting any pressure on you to do more than that. I'm happy to carry on as we are. But this has happened, and I can't walk away from it. Our chances of achieving this will be better, working together—that's all. I'm sorry you don't feel the same way. I respect that, but I will go it alone if I have to and put Jacob and Maddy in a safe place."

At a time when he finally thought he'd laid his past to rest, it was important he saved this relationship because it meant a lot to him. When he tried to take her hand, Sally shuffled to the other side of the bed, out of reach. She closed her eyes and lay like a statue, the tension in her body palpable. He tried to calm his breathing as his heart rate spiked at all the remembered anxiety. Suddenly, there was an impenetrable gulf between them, and it was his fault.

He closed his eyes, trying to think of a way past this. As the minutes ticked by and neither spoke, a wall of awkward silence built up around them. Had he broken them? All because he hadn't opened up to her about his past?

Words flittered through his brain, remembered segments of their discussions this afternoon. He was looking for anything that would give him the courage to overcome his fears.

It slammed all at once against his chest. He spasmed, that niggle finally coming to light. "Sally!" he hissed quietly, shaking her to make sure she was awake. "Sally, are you awake?"

Her eyes shot open at his hostility. "Of course I am. Do you honestly think I would be able to sleep when the man who has turned my life upside down won't even consider discussing something important with me?"

Ben gritted his teeth. "Sally, listen. Repeat to me what the report said about the side effects of the kids being fed the rat bait."

"Huh?" Sally rubbed her eyes like she was being confronted by the strangest of sights. What she should've been doing was rubbing her ears in case she thought she was hearing things. Ben got it; he couldn't believe it himself.

"The report. What did it say about the rat bait poisoning? How was the father doing it?"

"What the heck? Why is this important now?"

"Tell me!" Ben hissed quietly, wanting instead to shout the command out at the top of his lungs.

"Go to sleep, Ben. We'll discuss this during the daylight when we're not so tired." Sally huffed, rolling to her side and facing the other way.

Ben scrambled out of bed. "I'm leaving. I'm driving to Malanda, now!"

"Are you nuts?" Sally shot up in bed, doing her best to keep her voice low.

"Then tell me, damn it! Why won't you answer me?" Ben hissed again, his leg catching as he struggled to get his jeans on. He nearly tripped and landed on his backside but caught himself in time.

"Because it's painful to bring up, that's why!" Sally retaliated, getting out of bed and facing him. "That monster was hiding it in the gravy of their nighttime meals when Jacob and his sister probably thought they were lucky to get a meal. The bastard was slowly trying to kill his children. Jacob hasn't been told about the poisoning. The blood tests revealed its presence, and when they interviewed Jacob, his responses were consistent with some of the side effects: diarrhoea, stomach pains, chest pains, weakness and loss of appetite. Of course, kids don't realise what else happens when they're given this stuff, but warfarin works on blood clotting and reduces vitamin K, so it makes bleeding easier."

"Oh, my God, all this bloody time," Ben whisper-hissed, pacing around the bedroom, knocking his head with his knuckles. Blaming himself, of course, for not picking it up sooner. He found a pair of socks and slipped them on before shoving his feet into his dusty, worn riding boots.

He located his wallet, phone and charger and shoved them into his old duffel bag, along with a change of clothes.

"What are you going on about?" Sally glared at him.

"I'm leaving."

"All because I suggested guardianship for Jacob and Maddy? Honestly, Ben, I don't need you to do anything. I can do this alone. I won't bother you again with it."

Ben was looking for the keys of his utility as Sally's words knifed him in the back. They'd fallen to the floor. He bent down to pick them up. Shoving them in the pocket of his jeans, he straightened and spun around. Her mouth was a straight line, her arms crossed against her chest, creating another physical barrier between them. He didn't have the headspace to explain it all. An excruciating eight-hour drive was his first and only job to do. He couldn't go anywhere else or give her hope where there might be none. With so much on his plate already, he couldn't spread himself any thinner. For now, only one thing dominated his thoughts. He had to save his grandfather. He was so sure this was the cause of the niggle that woke him in the first place.

His grip tightened on the strap of his duffel bag, his chest heaving. His heart already lamented the damage he was going to create by racing out the door in a rush.

If he didn't leave now, he'd never forgive himself.

If he stayed and explained, he'd ruin everything anyway.

He shook his head, cursing how life had thrown him another curveball. "I'm sorry, Sally, but I can't consider anything at the moment." No way would he utter a word about his fears without proof.

He rushed out the door, urgently needing to breathe in a lung full of fresh nighttime air. Knowing he'd have to call Lucy to explain his absence. Ring his parents and explain why he was rushing to Malanda. Save everything between himself and Sally once he made it back mentally in one piece.

But not until he held the evidence in his hands.

# Chapter 23

Ben's grip tightened on the steering wheel as he negotiated Grandad's driveway. The wipers flicked back and forth, the heavy downpour finally dropping from the black clouds building up for the last hour of the drive.

Grandad wasn't expecting him. No one knew his reason for arriving unannounced. Not a soul suspected anything was amiss.

He was tired. Bone tired. He'd phoned his mum and Lucy on the way, explaining he'd be absent from the homestead for a day or two. His mum didn't buy it but knew better than to prise it out of him.

"Let me know when you get there safely," were her parting words before he disconnected the call.

Parked underneath the shadows of the towering rainforest bordering the property, he sat, deciding to wait out the storm until the worst was over.

He couldn't explain why nerves churned in his stomach. Impatience gnawed at him. His timing of arrival was all off. It was just after lunch. He would have to get through the afternoon, dinner, and hopefully, a decent sleep because he wasn't driving again until the next morning. This meant an excruciating wait. Knowing. Watching. Not giving anything away until he begged his grandfather to come with him. There was no way he would leave without him, and he would use any subterfuge to get him to agree.

He picked up his phone, which lay on the passenger seat, and tapped a message to let his mum know that he'd arrived. Nothing else. Not yet.

When he looked up, Grandad was hobbling towards him with a giant umbrella. *Oh, fuck!* Were his suspicions correct? Had he worked out the reason his grandfather looked haggard and old before his time?

If he was wrong, he'd upset his family and risk his grandfather's health even more by dragging him away. Shaking his head to dislodge the fatigue, he opened the door and got out quickly, shutting it after him.

"Hello, my boy. This is a surprise," Grandad said over the noise of the drenching rain.

Ben worked his hardest to paste a smile on his face as he grabbed hold of the umbrella and wrapped an arm around Grandad's thin shoulders, steadying him. "Hello, Grandad. Now let's get you back inside, you crazy man." Ben found a chuckle from deep within. He loved this man so much, his heart clenched with pain. How had conniving Gwen fooled them for this long?

With a firm hold on his grandfather, they steadily walked back towards the house. His boots sunk, squelching on the sodden lawn. The splattering rain sprayed dirt and water up the legs of his jeans.

Ben took a moment to breathe in the moist, wet air, hoping all this freshness would rejuvenate his tired mind and give him some headspace to work out his plan of driving away the next morning—with his grandfather in tow.

✦

Ben woke to the sound of drizzle. He opened his eyes and turned his face towards the window and the grey dawn. The splatter of heavy drops on the glass blurred the outline of branches gently swaying against it. He blinked a couple of times before rolling over to grab his phone and check the time. Seven am. He put the phone down, closing his eyes again. He'd switched off notifications before going to bed and wasn't game enough to check if any messages waited for him. This was the calm before the storm.

He inhaled deeply, slowing his racing heart and pushing away the anxious thoughts.

Forcing his mind away from his grandfather, he dissected again how badly he'd treated Sally when he rushed out of the homestead. An eight-hour drive was a long time to dwell on matters. His thoughts had circled round and round. How to find an option to work past his anxiety and fears? How to deal with Sally's reaction when she learnt how badly, for a time, he'd skidded off the rails? How it would crush her when she realised his past would jeopardise her hopes of one day fostering Jacob and his sister?

He arrived yesterday drained, and by the time he'd gone to sleep, his body had been beyond exhausted. While a good sleep put everything in a better light, it still eluded him how he was going to find a solution to fix it for Sally. But he had to find a way. If anything brought it home for him, it was that Sally was fast becoming the soulmate he'd been searching for all his life. Or was it too early to know?

He sighed, cushioning his face deeper into the soft pillow and groaning. With reluctance, he pushed the matter of Sally aside. Today, he would tackle a much greater problem. He needed every ounce of strength, patience and stamina to get through the day—if he didn't estrange himself from his family first.

Over dinner the previous night, he had ground his teeth until his jaw hurt. Watched in horror as Gwen served the lamb chops and trickled Grandad's gravy over his serving. Always the helpful wife. How lucky he was to have her. Wholesome and healthy meals prepared every day. Nothing out of a packet for her. On and on it went. The drone of her constant reminders of how much she did for Grandad had him wanting to run outside screaming, tear his hair out, and shout out into the forest while he pummelled his chest.

Gwen then placed a separate pitcher of gravy in the middle of the dinner table. Was this how the help pages on the internet advised you to do it? His memory whirred with how many times he'd witnessed this.

Milk poured over Grandad's breakfast cereal for him because he was always feeling unwell. Gravy, always gravy on his dinner.

Was she feeling clever about it all?

His resolve hardened. It was time to follow through with his concerns. He'd bided his time since arriving. Too wet to help Grandad with any chores outside, they'd played board games and cards in between naps when Grandad's fatigued body needed to rest in short bursts to keep him awake until dinner time.

Relieved that both his grandfather and Gwen went to bed early, Ben hadn't lasted much longer. When exhaustion finally won out, he sent one message to Sally saying **_I miss you_** before closing his eyes and falling into a deep sleep.

He stretched his legs, pulling the covers up to his chin, wishing for all the world that Sally was lying with him now. This was the sort of morning where you slept in later than usual, snuggled up to the person you loved, touched them in all the right places. Created magic. With Sally at the forefront of his mind, it was enough for his erection to strengthen. He missed her. Couldn't bring himself to check his messages. If there was nothing there, he risked taking a step back towards that black hole. He didn't want to go there this morning. Wouldn't tempt fate. He had a mission to complete first.

With that grim thought, he stripped the blankets back and sat up. The morning dampness was enough to douse his hard-on. Exactly what he needed. He scrubbed both hands over his face, rubbing his skin, ironing out the kinks from sleep, massaging his eyes until he was certain he was fully awake. It was time to ready the bed for the next visitor and pack his few belongings.

Ben closed the door to his room and slung his duffel bag over his shoulder as he walked down the internal stairs to the living area. There were no sprinklers turned on this morning. With enough moisture drifting in from the outside, all of Grandad's plants looked healthy and green. His chest expanded as he filled it with all the forest scents encapsulating this house. Grandad would miss his plants because if Ben got his way, his grandfather wouldn't be coming back until Gwen was gone.

A clatter echoed from the kitchen. He put his bag down and headed in that direction. Grandad was already seated at the small island bench where they sometimes ate their breakfast.

"Good morning, Ben. Did you sleep well?"

"Good morning, Grandad. Like the dead."

Grandad chuckled before taking another mouthful of cereal. Ben's stomach cramped with knots, the overfilled bowl of milk soaking Grandad's cereal.

Ben did his usual breakfast preparations by going to the small pantry tucked in beside the kitchen. There was no sign of the rat bait in the pantry, which only sky-rocketed his anxiety. Did he have this all wrong? His stomach roiled with uncertainty. He wasn't sure he could eat anything, but had to try. With a long day ahead, he would need every bit of sustenance to get him through.

Ben sat beside his grandfather as they faced the back kitchen door. It was closed this morning with it being so wet outside, which was a pity. Ben wouldn't have minded a stray cassowary to pop its head inside for some distraction. It wouldn't be the first time.

"What's your plan for today?" Grandad asked, spilling milk from his spoon onto the bench. "Oh, bugger. I'm such an untidy brute."

Ben chuckled. "Give me a sec. I'll grab some paper towel to mop that up."

"Thanks, my boy. I think Gwen keeps it in that top right-hand cupboard," he said, pointing for Ben's benefit.

Gwen was no longer in the kitchen, and Ben heard her shuffling around in the laundry. He rose and went to get it. The paper towel was sitting at the front. He grabbed the full roll, stumbling back when it revealed the same rat bait he'd spied in the pantry all those weeks ago and an open packet of a second brand, too.

Heart hammering against his ribs, he tore off a few sheets of the paper towel and returned the roll to its spot. He quickly mopped up Grandad's spill, scrunching the paper towel into a tight ball and disposing it under other rubbish in the kitchen bin.

Seated again, his hand tightened around his spoon, his knuckles showing white. "Grandad, I need your help."

Grandad stopped eating with his spoon frozen midair, a look of concern crossing his face. "What's up? I knew there was something going on when you turned up unannounced yesterday."

"I need you to come with me for a drive. As far as Atherton, for starters."

Grandad finished his spoonful of cereal and placed it down beside his bowl. "Is there something wrong?"

"I hope not, but"—Ben tapped his head with his knuckles—"it won't leave me. Until I check it out, I can't move forward. I'm sorry, Grandad, I don't want to worry you, but I need your help here."

"Of course, I'll do anything you want. Does anyone else know about this?" The wrinkles on his tired, old face gathered at the corners of his mouth as it turned down into a frown.

He shook his head. "Can you bring a change of clothes and maybe your toothbrush, just in case?"

His grandfather's frown intensified. This was the crunch. Talk of taking him away from his home for any length of time was where he might baulk at the idea of helping. And this was only the start. There was the blood test next, which Grandad wouldn't know about until the last minute.

Frozen until his grandfather processed what he was asking, Ben couldn't move an inch. Their breakfasts got soggier the longer they sat, and Ben held his breath, waiting for Grandad's response.

"Is that what you want me to do?" Grandad finally asked. It was as though the cogs in his usually sharp brain faulted for a moment before finally turning another notch.

Ben nodded, not game enough to speak, the wad of emotion stuck in his throat refusing to budge.

"I'm a bit confused about the spare clothes"—Grandad reached across and squeezed his arm—"and even if Gwenny complains about me leaving, I'm here for you, okay?"

His grandfather ignored his breakfast and sat assessing him. Ben looked across, eyeing his grandfather's genuine concern. "I have to admit, I'm surprised about this. I honestly thought you looked happier the last time you were here with Sally. I liked her a lot. Seeing you together, it looked like you'd finally turned a corner and were on the home stretch."

*Oh, Grandad, if only it was a 'me' problem.*

Ben sat a little straighter, hating not being able to tell his grandfather the truth. To utter Atherton Hospital would invite more questions, hesitation, until Ben would have to tell him the truth. He wouldn't outright lie to him but word it in a way and put the onus on his problems, not his grandfather's. For now.

They had to get moving, but it would take time for his grandfather to finish his breakfast, brush his teeth and pack an overnight bag.

Something furry rubbed against his ankle. When Ben looked down, Moby rubbed against his leg and began a keen meowing as if he sensed something too. Ben picked him up and put him on his lap before taking his spoon again for more breakfast.

"I can't leave Moby behind." Grandad perked up, scratching Moby between his ears.

Moby looked up at Ben with inquisitive eyes. "How about we take him with us?"

"That will make it easier for Gwen. She often forgets to feed Moby."

*And a good thing too.* What if she tainted Moby's milk? Except now there was the added concern of logistically carrying a cat all the way back to Richmond. "Okay, Grandad. You finish your breakfast and get ready to leave. I'll organise the travel cage for Moby and some food, so we can make him as comfortable as possible."

His mind was agog with worry that this could all fall flat on its face. The responsibility of taking care of a sick man and a cat weighed down on his shoulders. He held onto the hope that the results would mean his grandfather's health returned to where it should be for a man of his age.

As for what happened to Gwen, well, he wasn't going there.

# Chapter 24

*I'm sorry, Sally, but I can't consider anything at the moment.*

Then one lousy message about missing her. Nothing else. What the hell was going on?

Sally had nothing. Nothing to offer Lucy either, except for some weird random stuff about rat bait, which she had no idea what it meant, so she said nothing.

God, it was hard to concentrate on the program. The boys needed her attention. Flora kept giving her looks like she might know something, but she didn't know a thing about Ben and his past. She squared her shoulders, carrying the burden of misery quietly. When all she really wanted to do was curl up in a ball and cry until she couldn't anymore.

Was the traumatic event in his past to blame? If she knew all the details, it might help her understand how he was suffering. It still didn't mean he could just walk away without considering what it meant to her to keep the siblings safe.

This cut the deepest, but the program would continue because this was her baby and she would see it through until the end. Then she would push for another round, regardless of whether Ben stayed or not. In the Richmond area, or not. She would rally to keep the bones in Richmond because that's what she did. She didn't break promises, and so help her, she didn't need a man by her side to get things done either.

After drowning in paperwork and letters to the councillors, she tidied up the small desk in her room, shoving pens into an old Vegemite jar. When everything was piled neatly in the correct order of what needed doing the next night, she took a moment to still her unsteady heart, absentmindedly trailing her finger over the deeply etched engravings 'Abbey loves Jamie' on the old school desk. It probably sat in this room for decades. So eloquently carved in old-style cursive writing, tears blurred her vision for a moment. She blinked them back. Had Abbey and Jamie's love made it to adulthood? Survived the decades? She couldn't manage a few months and here she was, for the first time, believing she might have met the one who was her destiny.

It was time for bed. With a sigh, she tried to straighten her aching shoulders, the weight of the day pressing down on her. How was she going to shut off and sleep? If he damn well missed her, why hadn't he called? Even once. She should've been heartbroken; instead, she was annoyed. More with herself. She'd let good sex get in the way. Had missed something vital about Ben.

Just what? She had no idea.

She gathered her toothbrush and a cup of water and went outside. The homestead was quiet for a change; even the boys were too tired for games. She'd made good progress in her attempts at locating Maddison, and her contacts at the department were certain they could give her an answer as to where she was by the next day. She promised Jacob she would find her, and she was one step closer. Then, she would relocate her to the program or, if not permissible, begin the fostering process in the interim. If she had to use every contact available to her, she would. Ben's rejection of the idea only strengthened her resolve. Nothing would stop her now.

She sat on the front homestead step, brushing her teeth. When she was done, she got up and walked to the edge of the front yard, rinsing her mouth and spitting out the water. In an instant, a rush of wonderful memories of camping with her family as a young girl came flooding back where teeth-brushing was done this way. Weirdly, this brought out a few stray tears. She blinked them back, refusing to let them take over, trying to stay strong.

No way would she glance towards the dark shadow of the large acacia tree looming over her, where she and Ben made love wrapped in his oil-smelling Driza-Bone. She averted her face, finding her way back towards the front homestead steps by the light of the stars. Her ears pricked at the sound of the front door opening.

"Hey, Sally." Flora held two steaming mugs. "Here." She passed one over.

"Oh, Flora, thank you, but I just brushed my teeth."

"Well, brush them again."

Sally smiled in the dark. This was Flora's way. "What is it?" Didn't smell like coffee, which was a good thing; otherwise, she'd never sleep a wink.

"Camomile tea. It'll do you good."

Sally winced quietly. She wasn't a great lover of its taste but knew it was supposed to be a calming drink. She took the offered mug, the first sip tainted with toothpaste.

"Then tell me what happened. Even I'm confused." Flora sat on a rustic seat on the homestead verandah, motioning for her to join.

Sally groaned, sitting beside her. Flora meant well and cared about them all, Ben included, but how was she going to explain how she sent Ben running? She took another sip, gradually accepting the taste of the herbal drink, and started talking. Explained what happened between her and Jacob and why it was important to her to reunite the siblings and keep them together permanently. The suggestion she'd made to Ben. His immediate rejection of it. Her suspicions that it had something to do with his late wife. Her fear that Ben was carrying more baggage than she could handle.

Flora sighed beside her. "You're a good soul, Sally, but there's something more here I don't understand. Ben *was* finally coming good, so whatever it is, there must be a valid reason. I guess we'll have to wait until he returns to find out. How about you call it a night and try and get some sleep?" Flora patted her hand and rose.

Surprised she'd finished her tea, she passed the cup over, rising too. "Thanks, Flora. Thanks for listening." She did feel better after offloading. Her shoulders weren't so tense as she released a giant yawn. A good sign her body was ready for sleep.

"Come on, let's get you to bed. Don't forget to brush your teeth again."

Sally chuckled. "Yes, Mum." She wound her arm around Flora, holding her close.

"And you wait and see, everything will work out. Stick to your path; don't veer from it; otherwise, you'll always have regrets. Ben will sort himself out, whatever it is. I know it."

"I hope so, Flora. I really do."

"Me too."

She missed him so much already, and he'd only driven away early that morning.

⁕

"What are we doing here, my boy? Is this the new hospital? I haven't seen it yet?"

Outside the new Atherton Hospital emergency department, Ben helped Grandad down from his ute, doing his best to hide his fury. "Yeah, Grandad, it is." If his grandfather had never seen the new hospital renovations, officially opened about twelve months ago, at what stage had he come into town to go to a doctor? It was hard to miss the recent additions—shiny buildings with beautifully landscaped gardens. Was Gwen roleplaying doctor, nurse, and emergency department all in one? "I'll help you inside, then I'll come back and move the ute to a shady spot. I'll put some food and water out for Moby, too, in case it takes us a little while to get sorted."

"What's going on, Ben?"

They trudged along the concrete path. Huge rocks tumbled inside Ben's stomach. Somehow, he'd gotten this far. Had even placated Gwen when she protested about Grandad's absence not being good for his fragile health and that Ben should return him home as soon as his business in Atherton was done.

Too late to stop now. Outside the glass sliding doors, Ben stopped, turning to face his grandfather. "Do you trust me, Grandad?"

"Of course, my boy."

"All I'm asking you to do is have a blood test. I organised a pathology request yesterday at the Richmond Health Centre where your details are still on record. They've emailed me the information, so all the hospital has to do is scan my phone, and they'll have all the details. Please, do it for me if not for yourself. You took care of me when I needed you. Now, I want to do the same for you."

Grandad's head bobbed up and down, absorbing the words. "You're really worried about me, aren't you?"

*Christ!* He had no idea. "I am, and if I don't do this now and something happens to you, I'll always regret it. Please, Grandad, can you humour me this once?"

"What are they going to test for? You think there's something going on in this old body, don't you?"

"There's a string of things they test for. I want them to do an overall check on your blood first. Then we can decide if there's anything else that needs attention."

Grandad chuckled but turned and continued walking. "Okay, we can do a simple blood test."

Ben released the breath initially trapped in his lungs as the automatic doors slid open. A rush of cool air sent a shiver along his arms, more of a premonition. He may have won this initial step, but there was still a road to go. Literally. He had every intention of driving out of Atherton and onto the highway leading to Richmond after the blood tests.

One step at a time. With his grandfather seated comfortably in the chairs provided, Ben left him to shift the utility and make Moby comfortable.

The first hurdle had been explaining to long-time family friend and nurse, Lee-Anne at the Richmond Health Centre what needed testing. What if his thinking was completely skewed? He rubbed his arm when he reached his utility. His gut was telling him otherwise.

Lee-Anne was flagging the bloods as urgent. With one overnight stop along the way, the results would be waiting for them when they arrived. There was a tough couple of days ahead for him. A long drive would knock his grandfather around. Added to that was the complication of travelling with Moby.

But no regrets.

The cat would give his grandfather comfort when the time came to reveal Ben's worst suspicions.

He shook his head as he got in the ute and turned the ignition key. Seeking shade, he found a parking spot on the tree-lined side street. Indicating, he steered into the morning traffic, turning right.

How would he tell the family? His parents and brothers? He winced, getting out of the utility to sort out Moby. This would be the hardest complication to deal with. It would crush his parents, especially his dad, who'd idolised his father forever. His breath whooshed out in a noisy rush, his heart thumping as he was met with a sleepy-eyed cat who didn't mind going for drives.

Was there one tiny chance he was wrong?

# Chapter 25

They'd left Atherton after a quick morning tea and toilet stop. Grandad seemed resigned to his fate and argued little when Ben told him they were heading west.

"What about leaving Gwenny on her own?" was the only question he'd asked.

"We can phone her along the way. That way, she won't worry so much," Ben had replied.

The ease with which his grandfather agreed concerned Ben. Was he already too ill to care? Surely, after the blood test, he must suspect something? But nope! Nothing! Or was his brain too muddled from the poisoning, and he knew no better?

Ben kept glancing over at his grandfather, who dozed on and off. There was no music blaring on this drive. No off-key singing, no chance of stopping halfway for mind-blowing sex. Just eerie silence inside the cab, which allowed for too much thinking, a bucketful of concerns if he got this wrong, and a niggle that his life would side track again.

Less than half an hour of driving would see them at the Lynd Junction, a meeting point of four major routes in northern Queensland and miles from nowhere. Ben had already phoned ahead to book a room each at the Oasis Roadhouse. There was nothing else at this isolated junction, but it was a critical refreshing stop nearly halfway to Richmond.

Despite all his anxieties, Ben managed a lopsided smile. His fingers tapped the steering wheel to an imaginary song while memories of passing through Lynd Junction resurfaced aplenty. You couldn't miss all the signage around the roadhouse telling visitors the Oasis Roadhouse was Australia's smallest pub. Well, according to Google anyway. Ben shook his head. It was an outrageous way of getting your name on the map. A small dot in a vast country with all the necessities of civilisation. Including beer.

It'd been a long time since he'd shared this road with his grandfather and Ben would shout him a beer later. He gave him another glance, noting how his neck leant at an awkward angle. He should've brought a cushion and reprimanded his lack of planning.

He faced the road again, his back aching in new places. The strain of the drive caused fatigue to cloud his mind and worry dug its way onto his forehead. No doubt etching deep marks to remind him of what he'd taken on.

Which brought him back to Gwen. Ben had given away nothing, so there was no reason she should suspect anything about this trip. He'd told nobody, except for Lee-Anne at the Richmond Medical Centre who was sworn to secrecy. She'd done a lot for him during his darkest days. He trusted her with his life and knew she wouldn't utter a word. Especially if Ben had it all wrong.

In fact, he'd done everything possible since arriving unannounced in Malanda to draw attention to himself and away from his grandfather, so there was nothing for Gwen to be suspicious about.

But Gwen was a mistrustful woman, and Ben knew exactly what she hoped to gain. His grandfather was a wealthy man with enough cash deposits and investments to make a greedy woman want it the easy way. Securely married to Grandad, after his death, no one in the family would fight her for it.

Then, she would hand it over to her adult children without any misgivings. Her children were unsettled and usually unemployed, with no desire to make a life of their own. Gwen had greedily seen the potential a long time ago and sunk her claws into Grandad's life way before Grandma passed away.

A stealthy wariness of Gwen built up inside Ben's mind. More so during the time he recuperated at their home. Small things she'd done. Words spoken. How she spoke about money. This wasn't his imagination, and he hoped like blazes he was right.

Grandad snuffled in the passenger seat, shuffling and sat upright. Ben chanced a glance before looking ahead again. The road signs to slow down for the approach of the Lynd Junction flashed past his periphery. He tapped the brake lightly to disengage cruise control and bring the speed down to eighty kilometres per hour.

"You awake, Grandad? We'll have that beer I promised you soon."

"Are we there? Did I sleep the whole way."

Ben smiled. "Yep! Chilled beer is calling." He wouldn't have minded a sleep, too, along the way. Anything to distract his thoughts.

"Same here." Grandad chuckled, which was a good sign the drive wasn't tiring him too much.

A vehicle towing a caravan passed them, heading in the direction they'd come from. Ben gave them a wave and received a toot back.

Being early afternoon, it would be hellish hot outside. Ben would have to get Grandad sorted in his cabin with the air conditioner going.

When the Oasis Roadhouse came into view, Ben slowed down some more. He wanted nothing more than to stretch his legs and wind down. There was too much whizzing around his head. Now they'd arrived, all he wanted was a good meal, a couple of beers and the chance to relax. He would leave tomorrow's problems for then.

"Ben?"

"Yeah, Grandad," Ben said as he navigated the utility into the roadhouse's driveway, parking under the shade of the trees growing along the border fence. Reception was close, and he could get their keys sorted fast.

"Once we're organised, I want you to sit down and tell me what's going on. What's really going on, not some made-up story. Okay?"

Ben left the ute running, along with the air conditioner, unclicked his seatbelt and turned to his grandfather. "What do you mean?"

"My boy, I trust you with my life, with everything. You've always been by my side and done more for me than anyone else to prop me up when your darling grandma passed on." Grandad choked on his last words and, to Ben's dismay, Grandad's eyes watered. Losing his wife still cut him.

"It's Gwen, isn't it?" Grandad's voice was low and sure.

Ben froze. His grandfather wasn't so blind after all.

"What's she doing to me?" Grandad turned in his seat to look at Ben.

Ben tried to organise his tired thoughts. Plan the right words to say. Make the most of the opportunity now that Grandad brought it up.

"What if I'm wrong, Grandad?"

"You won't be. I know it. You wouldn't go to all this effort unless you were one hundred percent certain."

His grandfather had perked up. The sleep had done him wonders, but nerves roiled in Ben's stomach. It was now or never. What if he lost the trust and love of his grandfather?

"Spit it out, Ben."

A touch of his old grandfather shone through, and Ben swallowed back the nerves. "I've said nothing to anyone else, okay? Except for Lee-Anne at the medical centre, no one suspects a thing. So, it won't go past you and me if I have it wrong."

"Have what wrong?"

"What I think Gwen is doing."

"Come on, my boy. What is Gwen doing?" He joked nervously.

"I ... I think she's hiding rat bait in your food."

Grandad gasped, his hand clutching his chest, rubbing it slowly. Ben's skin tingled with alarm at the sound of Grandad's shallow breathing.

"That's why I want to check it out, once and for all. You haven't been to a doctor at all lately, have you?" Ben reached over, gently grasping his shoulder. "Grandad, look at me. If the blood test comes back negative, I'll take you back home. If you never want to talk to me again, I'll understand. But I couldn't stand back and do nothing. There were too many signs and open packets of rat bait in the cupboard for me to sit back and ignore it."

"Oh, Ben," Grandad hiccupped as tears slowly coursed down his wrinkled cheeks. "Why would Gwenny do this to me? I know I've been feeling off and wondering why."

Ben clamped his jaw tight, keeping his reasons to himself.

"You know, my boy, she was just there. After your grandma died, I half expected she would just stay on. She wasn't the same compassionate woman as your grandma. I got that. I just thought we could keep each other company and not get so lonely. But—"

Tears continued to trickle down his face, and Ben's heart cracked in half. It was hard to watch his grandfather cry. He reached across to the glove box and opened it. Scrummaging around for tissues, he found a packet, pulled one out and passed it to him.

"Nothing was ever the same without your grandma." Grandad dabbed at his eyes with the tissue. "Why would anyone do such a thing? Why would Gwenny do this?"

Grandad's shoulders trembled as the shock of what Ben told him penetrated further. Hurt more.

"I just want to be with my Lottie. I'm ready to go, my boy."

"No!" Ben spat, causing Grandad to raise his teary face and look across. "I need you, Grandad. I really do. Please. Grandma will be waiting patiently for you; I know it, but I still have so much I need to learn from you, to ask you. Like what to do now because I think I've stuffed things up with Sally. Please, can we get through this so I can have you back—like you used to be?"

Silence filled the cab. Grandad nodded, the cogs turning, his brain thinking, his mind mulling things over as he swivelled back and looked past the closed window. "Can a person recover from rat bait poisoning?"

Relief was rapid, and Ben's torso relaxed from the tension he'd been holding. "Lee-Anne mentioned something like activated charcoal will help. We can mix it with cocoa powder or moringa greens, and it'll help remove the toxins."

"What about Gwen? What will happen to her if she really did this?"

Ben hesitated, enough for Grandad to turn back from the window and look straight at him.

"Grandad, we'll sort that out once we have the results. How about we get our keys to our cabins? Then we'll have those beers and a good talk. What do you say?"

"I think I need to hold Moby. This news has shaken me up plenty."

Ben reached across. "I've got your back, Grandad."

A thin stream of tears began again while Grandad drew out a clean tissue. "Thanks, my boy. I also want you to sort out this Sally thing because I really like her."

"Me too, Grandad." Ben grimaced, opening his door.

*Me too.*

# Chapter 26

Another day passed and still nothing from Ben. No further messages, no phone call. Nothing. Not that she'd replied to his last message. She gulped back the dread trapped in her throat. After all they'd shared over these past weeks, it was hard to accept his last message was an excuse for him to hide from whatever troubled him.

There had to be more to it, and the stupid girl that she was, wanted to know why. Ben would return, of that she was certain, because his heart would always belong to the earth and this rich dinosaur country. She just might have to accept there wasn't enough space in his life for her. Or what troubled him was too big for the two of them to handle together.

Too bad he'd already wormed his way into her heart. Life without him was going to suck. Heck! The sex alone was off the charts. The best ever, and she was nowhere near close to closing off that chapter.

Her fingertips tapped the top of her desk, not far from where *Abbey loves Jamie* was scratched, as she re-read the emails received during the day. There was a lot going on, and she squared her shoulders. On paper, they all looked burdensome, but she would take on the challenges and see them through to the end.

One would change the course of her life, with or without Ben by her side. Maddison had been located and assessed. She lived in temporary foster care, and the possibility for Sally to reunite the siblings under her care looked promising. One step at a time was required, which she would follow to the letter of the law.

Guardianship was no easy road. It meant a lot of form filling, red tape, and training, but she would see it through. One thing she was certain of: taking care of children was her destiny—as a teacher, a leader of this program, and now with Jacob and Maddison.

She touched the spot between her breasts where her heart beat through the fabric of her shirt. As time ticked on, her desire to have children of her own sometimes reared its ugly head. The years folded into each other at warped speed. It wouldn't be long before her thirty-second birthday arrived. One day, she would wake up and find it was too late. Yes, there were other options she could use to achieve motherhood, but how hard was it to hold onto one man long enough to reach such fulfilment? Would this always be her private failure?

She grimaced, needing to stop this pity party. She had so much to offer other children. The need to remind herself that having her own children wasn't crucial to her life took centre stage in her mind. She held onto it for a moment, repeating the mantra.

*Okay, next email.* She pushed on, and this time, a smile lit up her face. Dean was coming to Richmond and was going to spend four weeks helping her with the program. Already, she pictured Dean's enthusiasm with the digging site and the boys. Like an older brother, he would take them under his wing in his patient and caring way. She couldn't wait.

Satisfied with the arrangements to get Dean out here and how to rearrange the sleeping areas, she opened the third email from the mayor. He endorsed the idea of a museum in the heart of Richmond. Warned her it wouldn't be an easy road but wanted to set up meetings in Brisbane with both Ben and Lucy in attendance.

If this discovery proved to be as unique as she was suggesting, they would need to begin the campaign for funds with the state government and Queensland Museum. He advised the council supported keeping the real fossil in Richmond, and they should advocate for world-standard facilities here in Richmond for the fossils to be showcased.

He went on to suggest all the possibilities for Richmond to become a hub in dinosaur country. Families would come for long weekends and school holidays and experience digging for bones in carefully managed dig sites, which the council would coordinate and provide on the outskirts of town. The mayor was confident Richmond was an attractive option for families wanting to experience the real outback. Lake Fred Tritton itself was a drawcard, like an oasis in a dry and dusty outback.

Sally wrote some notes, realising she and Ben would have to be on talking terms for this to go ahead. Stubborn as she was, though, she would accept a business relationship with Ben if it got the job done because that's how she rolled.

Yep, she slapped the top of the desk for good measure and kick-started her motivation. She worked solidly for the next hour, writing notes, filling in forms, replying to more emails, and setting up suggested times for appointments. Until her brain couldn't function for another minute, and she stifled a yawn.

She shut down her laptop and stared at the black screen. Her vision blurred, getting fuzzy around the edges. She stretched her arms above her head and ironed out the soreness from sitting hunched over.

With that done, she reached over for her phone, sitting on the edge of the desk. Tired as she was, it was time to take action. A relationship required two people. Communicating. She located Ben's last message and typed a reply.

***Where are you? Everything okay?***

She shoved the phone to the side, raking her hands down her face. Massaged the muscles of her cheeks and rubbed her fingers deeply into the sockets of her eyes. This thing between them couldn't end. They were so on the same page that, at times, it scared her silly. In a good way. And how was she going to erase the great sex from her mind? She couldn't. Not in this lifetime. Maybe when she was an eighty-year-old crazy cat lady looking back fondly on those weeks. Talking about it with fellow residents at the nursing home. Sharing a cup of tea and reminiscing about the good old days.

An idea popped into her head, and she straightened. Her heart tattooed a stronger beat. Could she be so bold? Force Ben to talk? Start the conversation? There was a hint of something deeper during a couple of their conversations. On the night of the wedding, he'd panicked. She'd seen it clearly. He'd asked her if she could wait until he got his shit together. Begged her to tell him things along the way. Not to keep it locked inside until it blew up. Not hesitating, she'd made the promise to always be open.

She scraped back her chair and rose. Now was the time to come good on it. If it didn't solve anything, she'd have no one to blame but herself. She'd gone into this with her eyes shut. She knew so little about Ben. Everything should've come out in the open way before they'd taken that blissful step on a drizzly Malanda morning at his grandfather's home. Only to be followed by the magic they'd created at that isolated stop halfway back to Richmond. Sex, not commonsense, had driven her actions since.

Tiredness suddenly overwhelmed her, and her shoulders drooped. All this wrangling didn't make her feel any better. Unable to hold back the longing and hurt at Ben's departure, and all the unanswered questions queueing inside her mind, she fell back onto the bed with her arms flung out wide, emitting a miserable, quiet groan. Allowed herself one minute—no, maybe two—to remember the way the sun had burnt down through the eucalyptus trees while they'd been on the sand. The trickling flow of water at the creek's edge where they'd done it all over again. Fast and furious, the heat of their bodies tempered by the coolness of the creek water.

Rolling to her side, Sally curled up into a tight ball, fisting her hands against her chest. She wasn't done with Benjamin Reginald Angwin just yet. Whatever distressed him, they'd work through it together. As she dug her nails deeper into her palms, she hated how wretchedness wrapped itself around her, sucking at her very life, threatening to kill her enthusiasm and drive. This was how easy it was to lose sight of everything she wanted to achieve on her long list of projects.

With a weary sigh, she relaxed her hands and dragged herself off the bed. It was time to get ready for sleep or she'd struggle to wake up the next morning in time for the digging session. While Ben's absence was sorely missed, Lucy and the assisting scientists could still create a hum of excitement over what they were meticulously digging out.

The shape of the dinosaur became more obvious each day, and the fact so few bones were missing was out of this world. The arrival of the second lot of boys hadn't required anything from Sally to drum up enthusiasm. They'd taken on board the excitement of the dinosaur discovery with gusto when they were told how special a find it was. Who wouldn't?

It was going to be the find of the century, and despite everything else going on, she wanted to be part of this. Preferably with Ben.

Ben pushed the cotton sheet off and sat up, sitting on the edge of the lumpy double bed. When his feet touched the coolness of the timber flooring in the roadhouse cabin, a chill ran up the length of his legs. He sat hunched over, rubbing the sleep from his eyes. He and Grandad shouldn't have drunk those couple of extra beers. It was going to be a late start for the remainder of the drive to Richmond. He almost cursed his stupidity, except the beers zonked him out and he'd slept soundly. *I think.* He wasn't convinced his body agreed with his head.

His grandfather slept in the cabin next door. Since he couldn't hear any noise, he hoped like blazes, beers aside, the damning discussion about Gwen hadn't kept him awake for too long after they'd retired.

After those extra beers, Ben hadn't held back. Hoping to take his grandfather's mind off Gwen, he'd spoken freely about Sally. Told him how they connected on so many levels, including how good the sex was, which got a smile out of Grandad.

Ben grimaced now at his boldness. A shaft of sunlight penetrating through the small window warmed a spot on his shoulder. The high position of the sun in the sky only reminded him how late it was. He had to get a move on. The kilometres wouldn't drive themselves. There was a solid four-hour drive ahead. He scrambled for his phone, still charging on the floor near the bed, wanting to check for any messages before they left the Oasis Roadhouse. Once out onto the desolated open road, they'd have limited reception.

Two messages flashed across his screen. The first was an urgent message from Lee-Anne at the Richmond Medical Centre.

**Hi Ben, you need to contact me urgently. The results are in and we have concerns.**

*Fuck!* Lee-Anne had already told him she'd mark the pathology request as urgent, so he wasn't surprised the results were quick. He wouldn't have minded one extra day, though, to get his head around everything he'd put in motion.

The second message from Sally had his chest constricting as his phone slipped from his fingers.

*Christ!* What a moment to receive her message. He wasn't okay. Not one iota. He rose and paced the small cabin, ploughed a hand through his ruffled morning hair and gritted his teeth. Could this mean Gwen was genuinely trying to poison his grandfather? This would involve the police. *Crap!* An unpleasant time for Grandad and their family. This was really happening. By chance, Gwen's evil nature was revealed.

Ben stopped pacing and took a moment to breathe deeply. Anything to relax his heart beating out of control. It was because of Sally he'd stumbled onto the unimaginable. He owed her a debt of gratitude. He should be moving heaven and earth to protect Jacob and Maddy. He wanted to. He really did. But nothing had changed his end. His medical history would make it next to impossible. Giving long-term guardianship to someone who'd been so medically unstable he had considered the unthinkable—numerous times—was, yeah, very unlikely.

*Think! Think harder!* He paced some more, clutching his hair and pulling on it.

An idea dropped. Would they? For him? Stumbling a step back, he sat down on the springy mattress. He picked up his phone with a trembling hand. It was a huge ask. The shock of what he had to tell them about Grandad would knock the wind out of them.

But if he explained everything, would they help him? The time had come to reveal the truth about those counselling sessions and how his grandfather had saved his life.

He made the call, waiting for the connection on the other end. Impatiently tapped his foot the longer it took. When his mum answered, he choked up and had difficulty speaking at first until his tirade began to flow and make sense. Leading him towards the biggest question of his life.

By the time he ended the call, a massive weight lifted from his shoulders. His mother promised to seriously consider it with his dad once they dealt with the shock of the poisoning news. As for his grandfather, he wouldn't utter a word about the results until Lee-Anne was there to explain it all.

Scrummaging around in his bag for a change of clothes, his face whipped up at the sound of a knock at his cabin door.

"Ben, my boy, are you awake?" his grandfather called from the other side.

He got up immediately, straightened his shoulders and filled his chest with much-needed stamina. "Sure am, Grandad," he said as he took two strides and swung the door open.

"Well, hurry up. I'm keen to get back to the station. I feel like I could ride a horse today."

Twenty-four hours without rat bait in his diet and already his grandfather looked perkier. Only just, but his eyes looked more alive than they had in a long time. "Have you already had breakfast?" Ben asked.

"Sure have. The best bacon and eggs I've eaten in a long time. Like the old days when Lottie cooked it."

Ben grinned, his heart at bursting point for this man. He hadn't thought it possible to resurrect his old grandfather of only a year ago, but suddenly, everything looked promising. "I'll be ready in ten minutes. Can you go order me the same? I'll wolf it down as fast as I can."

His grandfather hobbled off, and hope shone again. He would fix this for Grandad, for Jacob and his sister, and more importantly, for Sally. He would do everything in his power for things to go his way. Anything to prevent veering off course again.

# Chapter 27

Ben leant against the wall of the small consultation room. Sparse, really, with only a desk and laptop, a patient examination bed, a couple of chairs, a small cabinet, and some medical-related charts attached to the walls.

"Are you comfortable, Mr Angwin?" Lee-Anne fussed over Grandad, giving him a cup of tea and a comfy chair with a cushion.

Grandad smiled politely and accepted the hot drink. "I am, Lee-Anne. Now, can we cut to the chase? I've known you since you were born. Your grandparents were good people. What's going on here? Am I being poisoned or not?"

All the oomph deflated from the tall, robust mother of three teenagers, whom Ben had known all his life. She grimaced in Ben's direction before saying, "Let me take a seat so I can explain everything I need to before the doctor arrives."

Ben hadn't smiled much since arriving at Grandad's home barely two days ago. He almost did now but held it in. Two days without Gwen's cooking and another burst of the old Grandad he knew and loved shone through. The no-bullshit man who got the job done but with compassion and kindness. But this was a serious matter, one that could've easily cost him his life. For this reason, Ben kept the smile hidden and the bitterness alive. Gwen would pay, and he wouldn't stop until justice was served.

With Mum and Dad due to arrive any minute, it would be a long morning for Lee-Anne. She glanced in Ben's direction as she shuffled her chair close enough to Grandad's so the armrests touched.

"Mr Angwin, the doctor will give you the complete picture. Dr Pederson is aware our families go back a long way, and we have already discussed that I would give you a general outline of what your blood test revealed. There are definitely signs of rat bait in your blood. Ben has since given me the brands of the boxes he found in your home, and this is consistent with what the test revealed."

Grandad's shoulders shook as he placed his cup of tea down. Ben got it. It was a lot for an older man to take in. It would confuse him like hell. Ben came closer, crouching beside Grandad's chair. "I'm so sorry this is happening to you, Grandad. It makes no sense, but we're here to help you. Mum and Dad are on their way because the next stop is the police station."

Grandad's eyes widened. "Oh, really? I didn't think that far. What do you think will happen to Gwenny? She'll be worried about me."

Ben wanted to swear and say he didn't care what happened to Gwen. He hoped she was never okay again, but this wasn't the time or place. As for how worried she'd be, her hidden agenda was now out in the open. Let her worry, Ben wanted to shout. Her days were about to get a whole lot worse.

"How about we let the police do their job," Ben said. "She is totally unaware that we have discovered this information, so I'm sure when they turn up at the house, the shock will be great. Lee-Anne has suggested you stay at the medical centre for a few days so they can monitor you and do a full medical. Mum and Dad will stay here with you and then drive you out to the station. Depending on how you feel, once you're up to it, I'll come and get you for a day out at the old homestead. I bet you're keen to see what we've discovered. Remember how much fun it used to be?"

Ben did his best to distract Grandad, but despite his valiant attempts, nothing could hold back the thin trickle of tears sliding down his cheeks. "I shouldn't really be caring too much about what happens to Gwen, should I?"

Ben dropped his gaze to his grandfather's hand that gripped the armrest. Veins protruded on skin that was pocked and scaly. The skin of an aging man. A dying man slowly being poisoned for greed.

"I feel like such a fool, Ben. Such a stupid, old fool who should've seen it happen."

"Don't!" Ben hissed. "She's not worthy of your love and devotion, and especially not your home. You owe her nothing. Please, Grandad, don't blame yourself."

Grandad's face dropped, moisture dropping onto his jean. How had they, as a close family, not suspected anything sooner? "We'll need to ring her soon so she thinks I'm okay."

"I'll give her a call soon. Tell her I'm treating you to a short stay at Innot Hot Springs and the thermal pools. This should give us at least another day up our sleeve."

"Let's check some of your vitals, Mr Angwin," Lee-Anne suggested as she rose and rolled her chair beneath the desk. "That way, we're ready for when the doctor comes in. Ben, could you please go to the admin counter and fill in the admission forms for his stay here?"

Ben rose from his crouched position as Lee-Anne passed over a box of tissues. "I'll go make that phone call and be right back, okay?" Ben said to his grandfather.

Grandad nodded, dabbing his eyes with a clean tissue. "When did you say Paul was arriving?"

Ben pulled his phone out of his back pocket. "As soon as we were in reception range again, I told them we'd arrived. Just wait—"

A new message from Ellen appeared on his screen. "They've just driven into the car park now." Ben looked up. "I'll go meet them out the front and send them in."

A wisp of a smile tilted the edge of Grandad's mouth. He had a great relationship with his son and daughter-in-law. Having them here would be a huge morale booster. Already, he looked more relieved.

Ben pocketed his phone and left the small consultation room, his chest aching for the hurt his grandfather was suffering. At least there was a way back from this. Not without a lot of pain and heartache for the whole family, though. Attempted murder never sounded good for anyone, but the news would have to stay within this small circle for now until the police confronted Gwen and dealt with her first. His brothers would be the next to be told.

Despite his racing thoughts, the confirmation of this hideous crime was as good as winning the lotto. He'd won more than the lotto, though. He had his grandfather back. Not entirely yet, but Lee-Anne told him that with time, the body should repair the damage done.

Ben needed his mentor back—his biggest supporter—and in fighting spirit because Ben had a lot on his overfilled plate. It was time to begin eating away at it, so he didn't spill any.

When the doors to the medical centre slid open, he spotted his parents. "Mum, Dad!"

Ellen ran the last few steps, embracing Ben around the waist. Paul was only a step behind, throwing his arms around them both.

"How are you, son?" Paul asked, giving an extra strong squeeze before taking a step back.

With Grandad as his priority, and Moby a close second, Ben had kept it all in until now. A knot loosened inside his chest, and with it, the anguish he'd been holding onto tore a sob from his throat. Unexpected as it was, it felt good to unleash the tears. Ellen found a tissue in her handbag, and he gladly accepted it. "I'm sorry, guys, it's been a rough few days, that's all."

Ellen gave him another hug. "We'll never be able to thank you enough for being so vigilant. Oh, my God, how did this happen?"

"Shh," Ben said, making a valiant effort to stem the flow as he disentangled his arms. "I'll tell you how I worked it out when Grandad's napping. For now, he's waiting for you down the corridor, and Lee-Anne wants me to fill in his admission papers."

Ellen nodded in agreement, handing him another tissue.

"Good idea," Paul said.

"I'll join you as soon as I can."

Ben began striding away when Paul said, "Hey, son." Ben stopped and looked back at his dad. "We've got your back, okay?"

Ben nodded. There was only one other thing consuming his thoughts, and thinking about it brought on another spurt of tears. In amongst all the anguish, he managed a lopsided smile. How many tears could a grown man cry?

"Here, take the whole packet." Ellen slipped one tissue out for herself first, then passed him the travel pack of tissues, offering him an encouraging smile. "Thank you, Ben," she added, wiping her own eyes.

"We'll get through this, son," Paul said encouragingly, "and everything else. I promise. Now, you better go do the paperwork."

Unable to speak, Ben lifted a finger in salute and then turned towards the admin desk, leaving his parents to make their way to Grandad.

This was how it should be. For family to have your back when you needed it the most. Ben wanted to offer Sally the same sense of family and help for those in need. This was his next goal, and with this thought, he pulled his shoulders back. He had a plan, and he hoped like blazes Sally considered it because it could work. His grandfather would also play a role. With his grandfather back in the security of the family fold, it might help his recovery too.

It was also time to get back to the digging site. The update emails from Lucy were never enough. He wanted the dirt to slip through his fingers, the freshly unearthed million-year-old bones to sit in the palm of his hand. He wanted his breath to hitch every time Sally came into view.

Oh, boy, he wanted so much more from Sally. To touch, to hold, to sink into her depths. He wanted it all and was willing to give and give some more.

Was he mentally strong enough and ready?

And would Sally listen?

# Chapter 28

"**M**iss Barkworth! Miss Barkworth! Quick, Daniel has hurt himself real bad."

Sally's heart thumped against her ribcage as she dropped the laundry basket with the freshly washed clothes she was about to hang outside. "Liam, what happened? Where is he?" She'd left the six boys barely ten minutes ago with strict instructions to get out of the creek, dry off and walk back to the homestead. She was barely back inside the homestead herself. "Why are you all still at the creek?"

"He wanted one more jump from the tree. We told him not to."

*Bloody hell!* "Is he able to talk?" Daniel was, without a doubt, the risk-taker of the group.

"He's holding his arm and crying that it hurts a lot."

Some kids were destined to live dangerously, and she never tried to dampen their spirits. She did, though, try to direct their excess energies along the right path. But jumping out of trees? She shook her head, slipping her feet into her faithful boots.

"What's going on?" Flora came out of the kitchen wiping her hands on an apron just as Sally was about to dash out the front screen door of the homestead.

"Daniel's had an accident jumping out of a tree. Sounds like a broken bone. I hope that's all it is. Come on, Liam, let's go."

"I'll get hold of Lucy and send her over to give you a hand."

"Thanks, Flora." Sally pushed open the screen door, grabbed her hat off the front verandah rack and shoved it on. Only Lucy and the scientists remained at the digging site, with Lucy's husband and children returning home two days ago.

"I see the dust spiral of an approaching vehicle," Flora said, swinging open the screen door and stepping out onto the front verandah as Sally and Liam broke into a quick run down the steps.

"Huh?" Sally stopped for a moment. "Dean isn't due until tomorrow, but if he's arriving early, can you take care of him until I get back?" She hurried towards the edge of the front yard, making sure Flora heard her.

"Of course." Flora flapped a hand in the air, signalling she got the message and for Sally to get going.

That took care of Dean. There was a hurt child on her watch, and until she assessed how bad the situation was, there was no room for much else.

A broken bone meant someone had to drive Daniel to the main homestead so the Royal Flying Doctor Service could land safely. Concussion or something worse, well, she had no idea how to proceed. If Ben was around, he'd know what to do. But he wasn't. Gone for days. Almost a week. Damn him! He was part of this program too and should've been here for the boys. Sudden fury at his absence lent her energy she didn't believe she could conjure on a hot, late afternoon as she and Liam sped the distance from the homestead to the creek bed.

She knew her anger was misdirected and that Ben had issues he was dealing with, but it wasn't helping her now when she could've used his outback experience; she'd have to make do with Flora's knowledge instead.

At the creek bed, Jacob was sitting against the wilting bark of a eucalypt tree, its gnarly roots exposed as they sought life within the dirt, sand and rocks on which it was perched. He held a teary Daniel in his arms. The other three boys hovered.

Sally dropped to her knees on the exposed grainy rock. "Daniel, look at me."

His eyes were awash with tears, but she needed to check if he had a concussion. "Look at me, Daniel, then close your eyes. I'll tell you when to open them again."

Daniel closed his eyes but continued to wail. "Oh, Miss Barkworth, it hurts so much."

"Where does it hurt?"

"My arm," he said with a sob. There was swelling around the elbow and an unsavoury lump pushing against the skin between the elbow and wrist. Eek! She gulped back the concern that this was where the fracture was.

Sally squeezed Jacob's shoulder and mouthed a thank you. He reciprocated with a slight nod. "I think he's broken his arm, Miss Barkworth. It happened to Maddison once when she was pushed against a cupboard. It looked just like Daniel's does now."

Sally flicked her gaze back to Jacob and was hit with a blanket of sadness. Enough to tell her the push to Maddison was no accident. Sally bit down on her lip to stop herself from swearing and turned back to Daniel. Another small window into the horrors of how Jacob and his sister had suffered.

"Okay, Daniel, I want you to tilt your face upwards like this"—she gently moved his face so she could see his eyes better—"and open your eyes." Immediately, his pupils contracted, and she heaved a sigh of relief. "Okay, that's a good sign, Daniel."

"What do you mean?"

"I'm checking to see if you have any concussion. Liam tells me you were jumping out of the tree. What happened?"

"He slipped off before he could climb high enough to jump in the water," Liam said. "And landed on those rocks instead." He pointed to the pile of white granite rocks jumbled along the edge of the creek.

"Looks like we'll have to get you to Richmond so they can look at your arm. Might mean a trip in an airplane. I'll have to check with Flora and Lucy how we do this."

"Really? A plane." Daniel's pained look ceased for a nanosecond as he contemplated this.

"Yep. Do you think you can stand up and we'll help you walk back to the homestead?"

"Yes, Miss."

Jacob slid out from behind Daniel and helped him to his feet.

"Boys, can you make sure all the towels are collected and brought back with us? We don't want to upset Flora."

The boys collectively chuckled. Nothing they did ever upset Flora and they knew it.

"Hey, look who's back. Hello, Mr Angwin," Liam shouted, a thread of joy in his voice.

Sally's knees wobbled as she and Jacob held onto Daniel and awkwardly turned to face the track. A heavily sweating and panting Ben stood in their way.

"Here, let me take over," Ben puffed.

Sally refused to move aside. At least his appearance answered the mystery spiral of dust. "Jacob and I will be fine," she snipped. "Why don't you go for a swim and cool down?" She tried to sound normal despite her thumping heart. She hated her betraying body when all it took was for Ben to reappear and be close by. But she didn't care. She'd look after Daniel and do it without Ben's assistance.

"Okay, let's keep going, boys." She put some chirpiness back in her voice so no one suspected how being close to Ben brought on both dizziness and a spurt of anger, all mixed into one hot mess.

She kept her gaze averted towards the track leading back to the homestead but chanced a glance at Ben.

He frowned. Hopefully, the message got through loud and clear that she didn't need him or his help. If he suspected she was peeved, well, she was. She ground her jaw tight, needing to hold back from saying too much and keep everything in check in front of the boys.

"Don't be ridiculous, Sally. Move aside and let me help."

She *was* being stubborn. The signs were all there when she stiffened beside Ben as he muscled in and took over from her, with Jacob still carrying Daniel's weight on the other side.

"Now, tell me, boys, what exactly happened?" Ben asked as he shouldered most of the weight and began the walk back to the homestead.

Just like that! Like he hadn't gone AWOL for a week. Nothing to say for that time except for one lousy text to say he missed her. Why had he bothered to send it and then ghost her?

She stomped behind the group, holding her hat as an afternoon gust of wind picked up leaves and dust along the track. Sally shut her mouth and shoved the flap of her hat over her eyes as the small whirlwind finished just as quickly as it started. The grit and dust weren't the only reason she zipped her mouth shut. God almighty, she had a lot to say, but now was not the time or place.

Would this be her life if she stuck around? Ben disappearing whenever things got too much? Yes, she promised to give him time to sort his shit, but Daniel's accident just went to show how Ben's absence had slowly wound her up. Today was one of those days she didn't want to make any promises. If she sounded ungrateful and was acting the real bitch, she'd live with it.

"Everything okay, Ben?" Lucy rushed from the direction of the dig site and met them at the junction. "What happened? What can I do?"

"Can you ring Mum so she can coordinate for the flying doctor to meet us at the homestead in about an hour?"

"Onto it, and good to have you back." Lucy sent Ben a dazzling smile. Ben managed a tight smile in return, but still, they were comfortable and at ease with each other.

Why hadn't he asked Sally to phone Ellen?

"How are you feeling, Daniel?" Lucy asked as the group kept walking towards the homestead.

"My arm really hurts."

"Hmm, looks like you did a real number on it. We'll get you looked at real soon. Ben will strap your arm to your chest so it doesn't move much on the drive out. Okay, mate?" Lucy reassured the young boy with a quick hair ruffle.

It wasn't long before the homestead came into view. Ben was very nearly carrying Daniel. No wonder the walk back seemed to fly by.

Doubts crowded Sally's mind. Why didn't she think to ring Ellen? It wouldn't surprise her if Flora had already made the phone call and Ellen was on standby.

Maybe she wasn't cut out to live in the outback. Let alone fostering one or two traumatised siblings. Could she handle the isolation and lack of medical care? A place you needed to have your wits about you just to survive? She would need to do better if she wanted to contemplate a life around Ben.

But who was she kidding? She didn't want Ben in her life. If he was the sort of person who needed to disappear for a week without a trace, why would she encourage such a relationship? In her books, it was better to move on and go it alone.

But heck, she'd enabled this situation. Given Ben the best of both worlds and she was the fool who'd fallen for it. Hook, line and great sex. That part hurt the most.

Flora met them on the front lawn looking frazzled. "How bad is it?"

"It'll need to be plastered," Ben said.

"I'll go make the phone call." Lucy walked away from the group, retrieving her phone from her jeans pocket.

"Already done, Lucy. Ellen just needs to know when you're leaving so she can make the arrangements. I'll get a few of Daniel's belongings ready for you to take." Flora was about to walk back inside when she turned back. "Sally, you get yourself a change of clothes too. You can sit with Daniel for the drive out."

Huh? Stuck in a vehicle with Ben? She wasn't sure she was the best person for the job, but the need to push aside everything between them and concentrate on Daniel had to be her priority.

"Okay, mate. Let's get you sitting here." Ben and Jacob walked Daniel up the verandah steps and sat him on the crudely made seat in the shade. The other boys were oddly quiet. Milling around, uncertain of what to do. Taking in all the drama of the accident.

Flora was back in a flash with a clean towel, a carryall with some of Daniel's belongings, and a first-aid kit tucked under one arm. In her other hand, she held a jug of cool water and some plastic cups. "You'll all be thirsty. Get through this jug, and then I'll go get another one."

What a formidable woman! Did you have to be born into this life to think of everything required in an emergency?

Sally kept walking towards the homestead steps so she could pack a small bag, as Flora suggested. Everyone knew their role. Their place. How things were done in the outback, and she loathed feeling like a fish out of water. All it took was for one man to turn her life upside down, and it rendered her useless.

*Move on, girlfriend.*

Yes, this was what she needed to do. Forget about him; he was too complicated. She pulled her shoulders back, determined to find the Sally she was before she met Ben. Revert, reassess and get back on track. She'd live without the sex. Right?

No! She didn't want to. Gritting her teeth, she kept in check the guttural groan wanting to be released.

"Miss Barkworth?"

A teary Daniel halted her progress after she'd climbed the steps to go inside. "Yes, Daniel?"

"Can ... can you please sit beside me while they strap my arm? Please."

Sally swallowed back the lump stuck in her throat. Her heart clenched with love for these kids. That's all they were. Young kids who needed nurturing. "Of course." She chanced a glance at Ben, who had already grabbed the roll of stretchy medical tape out of the first-aid kit and was about to begin. Vivid green eyes collided with hers. Not with anger. Not with uncertainty, but possibly an apologetic look, if that's what it was and if she was reading him right.

But she wasn't buying it. In her books, he wasn't doing such a great job of showing her how sorry he was or if he'd missed her. All the modern technology in the world wasn't enough for him to use it to send messages. Instead, the fallout left her hurt, annoyed and frustrated.

Sally looked away as Daniel snuggled into her side, making it tricky for Ben to wind the strapping around his arm and torso. She was doing her best to avoid skin contact with Ben, which was impossible under the circumstances, but no way would she allow herself to feel anything. Those days were done.

"Okay, are we ready to go?" Ben was all authoritarian as he rose from his crouched position and looked for the adults. "Flora, Lucy, is everything in place?"

Flora nodded. "Here, Sally, let me take over while you go pack yourself those few things to take with you." Flora embraced her, giving her a look of compassion. It was like she saw right through her.

Sally swung open the screen door and sped past the kitchen where Lucy had the other boys sitting around the table eating cake.

With the basics piled into a small travel bag, Sally emerged from her room and was met by Lucy. "I've thrown a few snacks together for later. Ellen and Paul are still in Richmond, so they won't be there to meet you."

"Thanks, Lucy, I appreciate it."

"And hey, please try and go easy on him."

Sally's mouth opened, and then she closed it on a silent groan. What she really wanted to do was swear out loud. With her lips in a straight line, she hissed, "Pigs arse. Where has he been this past week? Did he tell you?"

Lucy spoke for her ears only. "I don't know, okay, and no, he didn't, but there'll be a good reason."

Sally backed off. If Lucy was ganging up on her, she was over it. "I bet you outback women always say that to protect your own."

"Ask him," Lucy pleaded. "I've known him for a long time and he wouldn't just vanish from a dig without a damn good reason."

"Sally, are you ready?" She spun around when Ben's shadow darkened the doorway leading from the hallway to the kitchen.

Sally ignored Lucy's final imploring look, hugging her bag close to her chest. Being confined with Ben was going to be a mental challenge. She could hold onto this foul mood for days, weeks even. Sally glanced back, spying Lucy shrugging at Ben.

Yep, there was something she wasn't being told.

# Chapter 29

It was a blessing Ellen and Paul were still in Richmond. Sally could shake off her concerns for Daniel as she watched the flying doctor rise in the sky with him slightly sedated.

The professional duo of doctor and nurse were a balm to her already frayed nerves. They did everything possible to make their little patient feel safe and comfortable. For this, Sally was grateful.

Daniel would return to the main homestead with Ellen and Paul, if not tomorrow, then the next day. She and Ben had played the model coordinators of the program, putting Daniel first in all their communications.

With the plane now airborne, there was nothing left to say to each other. Or so it felt.

Sally rubbed at her temple where the mother of all headaches pulsed a strong beat. Now what? She was stuck here, with Ben as her only means of transport back to the digging site. Her earlier frustrations of being the odd one out had abated. Now, she wasn't sure if she even cared. If anything, she was just plain, bone-deep tired, her muscles heavy with exhaustion.

A ute drove through the main homestead gate, tooting its horn as it veered towards the station accommodation. It raised a spiral of dust which blew their way with the gentle breeze. Beside her, Ben raised a hand in greeting, a smile on his lips as he acknowledged the occupant. Like any working station, there was constant activity. Just because Paul and Ellen weren't there didn't mean the place shut down. Sally got that, but it was one of those moments when she wanted Ellen in Richmond to take care of Daniel but also wanted her here to break the awkwardness of being around Ben. She liked Ellen a lot. Might have been able to ask her some questions since Ben had no intention of telling her anything. Her big plans of starting a discussion seemed like a distant dream. One where she'd been pumped enough to work through this thing between them. She didn't think she could drum up the energy anymore.

She blinked and closed her eyelids for a moment to prevent any further dust from getting past them. The darkness was a momentary reprieve from the glaring sun.

"I'll cook us some dinner. We'll stay the night, then leave at first light," Ben said once the ute was out of sight.

"I'm not hungry." Sally stalked off towards the stargazer's lounge. She didn't know where else to go.

"For fuck's sake, will you give it a break?" Ben latched onto her arm and swung her around.

With a sharp shake, Sally flung his hand off and crossed her arms. "I've given you an entire week's break. You want to disappear and say nothing, that's fine. Just don't expect me to wait around like the dutiful woman I've been, keeping your bed warm."

Ben hissed, ploughing a hand through his hair, causing his curls to spring up in unruly waves. "Oh, Sally." For a moment, he looked a little lost, but she ground her jaw. She wasn't falling for that.

"Just as I thought. Keep Sally in the dark. She won't mind." Yep, this would get things sorted between them—not!

This time, he didn't try to stop her as she stormed off, her headache a full-blown and agonising pulse. A swirl of smoke lifted above the building surrounding the fire pit and general chatter filled the twilight hour as she drew closer to the stargazer's lounge. The sun had slipped past the horizon, and a dusky lavender hue covered the sky. Oh, how she needed strong arms wrapped around her. She grimaced, looking up as one by one the stars popped into view, hoping their appearance would calm her.

She would sit amongst the jackaroos and jillaroos, say little and pass the time. Remembering the blanket box, she decided to sleep the night out there and ignore the hunger grumbles coming from her stomach.

Ben watched as Sally marched away, fury radiating. He knew the time to tell her everything was drawing closer. That would mean talking about his grandfather, but the police were adamant it remained quiet until they dealt with Gwen. *Come on, Sally, give me a break.*

Once they got the green light, they would share the news with his brothers and Sally, of course. It would rock their family's very core. All the more reason to have Sally by his side.

This entire poisoning saga meant delays in sorting out the other matter. The one closest to Sally's heart. There'd been no time to discuss anything with his parents because his grandfather was at the forefront of their minds.

He massaged the weariness from his eyes. His days kept getting longer and longer. The last thing he expected when he'd arrived at the old homestead was an emergency. He'd practically thrust Moby at Flora before he dashed off to the creek bed. God, he hoped Moby was okay.

He needed a shower but didn't have the stamina to move. As for eating, he'd lost all appetite despite his grumbling stomach from earlier. This was his fault. He got this.

Reluctantly, he trudged towards the stargazer's lounge. Took the time to look up as the stars appeared one by one into their canvas of magnificence. Eight people were at the lounge, plus Sally. She sat a little distanced from the group as they laughed, joked and played country music.

"Hey, boss," one of the youngsters called out, holding up a can of soft drink in greeting.

Ben raised his hand in acknowledgement and tried to show a semblance of a smile. This young jackaroo was a true larrikin, gathering in all the others and making them feel like they were at home. Ben liked him a lot.

Ben dragged one of the older deck chairs, pushing it alongside the one Sally was on, and sat. Didn't utter a word, just let time slip by as he watched the antics of the others. It was a work night, and they all had an early start in the morning. Ben didn't expect them to stay up too late. They knew the rules and understood it wasn't worth losing their job over.

A half hour easily slipped by when one of the older jackaroos called out, "Last drinks, everyone, before I shut down the music."

"Then put a slow number on, old man," a young jackaroo said.

Others chuckled, including Sally beside him, and Ben smiled as the light from the flames flickered across her face. This jackaroo was in an obvious new relationship with a young jillaroo who'd not long started working for them. No different from how his mum and dad met. Ben remembered the headiness of a first time. There was something special about it.

With the pluck of the first guitar chord in Rascal Flatts 'Bless The Broken Road', something inside Ben's chest tightened. He knew this song well and had listened to its lyrics many times over the years. The words covered him like a warm blanket on a chilly night, their meaning resembling a horoscope of his life. How many lost dreams had he experienced over the years? How many broken roads had he travelled only to find one that finally led him to Sally? Rhylee, who'd broken him completely, was really his northern star. Pointing him to Sally's loving arms.

As the heartfelt lyrics pushed and nudged around his heart, sometimes he despaired of ever finding true love along his broken road. Yes, he'd gotten lost a time or two, but he wiped his brow and kept pushing through. This had been his life for a long time, until it finally dawned on him that every sign, every day of sadness, pointed him straight to Sally.

The young working couple danced slow steps in time to the music under the splendour of a star-studded sky. Regardless of where this couple's future lay, Ben was certain they would never forget the simplicity of this night. If anything, it could cement their future together. Such was the power of the setting.

As the song repeated its chorus for the last time, one which spoke of God blessing the broken road and of rolling home into his lover's arms, Ben sat up and turned towards Sally. There was only enough room for his legs between both chairs. His mouth opened on silent words, only adding to his pain as tears trickled down her cheeks.

*Oh, Sally.*

She looked across, not hiding anything. Looking deep into his eyes and expressing all the hurt he'd laid at her feet.

"Can we talk?" he asked quietly as the music ended and the others tidied up before ambling off with goodnights and waves.

Sally shrugged, turned away from his probing gaze and looked towards the ink sky again. The outline of her throat bobbed as she swallowed back emotion. Something he'd caused. She hadn't said no to his question.

Ben waited until the lounge area was quiet and there were just the two of them. He had to take a chance or risk losing everything.

He rose from the chair and held out his hand. "Will you come with me?"

She took agonising seconds to decide. When she lifted her hand and fit it snuggly in his, he could draw breath again. She got up, giving her recliner a short shove with her foot so there was standing room for them both. He circled her waist and held her close. Touched his forehead to hers and closed his eyes. Needing a moment to take in everything that was Sally and sacred to him.

It was time to walk her back to the main homestead, ply her with food and start telling his story. He gulped back nerves as they walked back silently together, his fingers clutching hers. Somehow, he had to find a way to break through the barrier she'd put up around herself. It was still there, and she certainly hadn't forgiven him.

Yet.

# Chapter 30

Sally showered while Ben cooked a simple, yet filling, meal of spaghetti using a rich, red sauce Ellen kept frozen, ready to use at a moment's notice. Bless her. Ellen was a true outback woman, made from the same ilk as Flora.

When it was Ben's turn to shower, he went back to his donga while she cleaned up the kitchen. Using a washcloth, she wiped the kitchen bench and stove before rinsing it out and spreading it over the dish rack to dry. Would she ever be a match for the women in Ben's life?

They'd spoken few words while they ate. Fatigued, weary, heartsore. It didn't matter what you called it; she was out of sorts.

With the kitchen sorted, Sally went into the lounge room and eyed the comfy leather sofa. She rubbed her tired eyes, certain she could sleep for a year if she would just close them. But Ben promised to talk, and she would stay awake for eternity if it meant he would finally explain where he'd been and why his life was such a mixed up mess.

She browsed the photos tastefully arranged on a shelf running the length of the room. There were many of Ben with his brothers and other family members. As she casually strolled past them, Ben's rascally smile shone in most of them.

Sally slowly turned three-sixty degrees. She hadn't spent too much time in this room and was impressed with Ellen's good taste in how she combined solid timber dressers of yesteryear, full of special glassware and trinkets, with the newness of the three-piece dark grey sofa. The photos and a sense of homeliness added to the simplistic yet elegant room that welcomed her with wide open arms.

She grabbed a couple of cushions resting on a single matching recliner and laid down. Before she had time to sink into its softness, Ben entered. Oh, God, he smelt clean and earthy. She could do with dirtying him up somewhat. Her body ached for his touch.

"Feeling better?" he asked, looking down at her.

She nodded, wishing this discussion was over so they could make up and get on with life like it was a week ago.

He looked just as tired as she felt. "Where do you want me to start?"

She sat up, rubbing her eyes. Ben towered over her, and she beckoned to the spot beside her. When he didn't take up the offered seat, she got straight to the point. "Why not start with why you rushed away a week ago."

Instead of sitting, Ben paced the lounge room with restless steps and a stiff back. When he eventually stopped in front of her, he looked grim. "Okay, but I need you to understand that what I have to tell you is extremely sensitive and cannot leave this room."

It stung that he even had to ask. Why hadn't he said so days ago? "You disappeared without a trace because you weren't sure about trusting me? Really? After everything we've done together?"

"It's not like that."

"Then what is it like? Two people as intimate as we've been should be able to trust each other."

"I do, but I need to make absolutely sure."

Sally rose, unease settling inside her chest, along with irritation. "Maybe you shouldn't say anything. If you can leave me hanging for a week, who cares about trust?"

Ben huffed. "Will you quit this?"

"Quit what? You can't see that this entire debacle has upset me?"

"Look, I'm going to tell you why I rushed out, okay? This thing between us is getting complex, and the air needs to be cleared."

"Complex? I thought it was very much the opposite. No commitment, no pressure, sex on demand. Nothing much else." Oh, she was getting fired up now.

"Is that all it is to you?" Ben asked, clipping each word.

"If I was disappearing for a week, I'd at least say something. You obviously couldn't be bothered."

Ben took a moment to breathe in deep, his chest rising and deflating with the slow release of air. Was she being too immature? Would another woman look past the hurt and accept it? Her heart started beating faster, her mind a turmoiled mess. She'd promised to give him time to sort things out and hated that she'd put them in this angry moment. All she wanted was for Ben to take her in his arms and hold her tight.

But he'd hurt her.

Badly.

Forgiveness would have to be earned.

Massaging his temple, Ben finally spoke. "Jacob's report triggered something for me."

She shook her head, trying to clear it of the fuzziness caused by fatigue. "Huh? What's the report got to do with anything?"

"Shush. Will you just listen?" He held up both hands, palms open, a silent plea in his wide eyes.

Chastised, she dropped back into the softness of the couch, her fingernails digging into her palms, and waited.

"You know I've been concerned about my grandfather. Something wasn't right, and I couldn't quite pin it down. Whatever it was, I knew it involved Gwen. When you said the report diagnosed possible rat bait poisoning, this was the catalyst I needed to put everything together. All the signs were there for me to see, but I was blind for too long. I drove to Malanda, picked up my grandfather and got him to have a blood test before we left Atherton, all without Gwen's knowledge. Not even my grandfather knew what I was up to until we were halfway back to Richmond. I approached it in a way that it was about me, not him. The only person who had any idea of what I was trying to do was the nurse in Richmond. I risked everything familywise by taking Grandad away and raising this ugly subject. Because—"

Sally waited with bated breath, her thoughts scrambling to catch up with what Ben was saying.

"Because ... what if I was wrong?"

Sally's eyes widened as she absorbed the horrible news for Ben and his family. *Why didn't he trust me with this?* "Why didn't you say so? That it wasn't about me, that it was about your grandfather, and you'd explain when you got back? One quick call, Ben, that's all I needed. Oh, my God—"

"I couldn't. Honestly, it felt like I was functioning on one brain cell. I had no room for anything else. Can you try and understand how desperate I was and the urgency of what I needed to do."

Sally wanted to melt. Crumble. Fall in a heap, then say it was okay. Forgive him. She got there were things that happened in his past that she didn't understand. The gravity of what Ben discovered about his grandfather was truly horrible, but would this be the norm in their relationship? Ben disappearing when things got tough? Ben not sharing his thoughts and emotions when things were against him?

She wasn't equipped for this and had no idea how to move forward. "For an entire week, I assumed it was my fault you disappeared. That's a long time to be in that headspace, to carry that burden, Ben." She shook her head, looking deep into his sorrowful eyes. "I'm not sure I can do this." Was it time to walk away? Make a clean break? How would the program look without Ben and the station?

She rose on trembling legs, walking a crooked path from one end of the room to the other, pressing her palm against her forehead where her headache, which had eased over dinner, was re-awakening with a vengeance.

"What the heck?" Ben grabbed her by the waist and held her close when she tried to walk past him. "This wasn't about you."

She jerked to a halt. "I know that. *Now.* I understand you've had an incredibly tough week. But we're supposed to be a team. A team talks to each other, helps the other out. But you left in the middle of a discussion without telling me anything. For one entire week!"

"I know, and I'm sorry." He looked apologetic but it still wasn't enough.

"One phone call would've eased all my doubts. I would've rallied for you, not against you. And I would have guarded your secret with my life. But—" She flapped her hands, not sure what to do. Fresh air. She needed to get outside. "I need to leave."

"You're staying put, especially while you're in this state," Ben all but yelled.

"Whatever state I'm in, you put me there."

With her head pounding, her mind overwrought and tired, she knew she wasn't being rational. She could easily lose it. This conversation would go from bad to worse. If she wasn't leaving, she needed Ben gone. To his donga so she could nurse her remorse alone.

"This is nuts."

"Don't you get it?" She was past caring. She wanted out.

Ben's nostrils flared fleetingly. "I thought you might have been more understanding."

"Oh, I've tried, but I'm not sure I could do a week like that ever again. I received one message saying you miss me and nothing else. That hurt."

Ben glared at her. "I didn't want to say anything until I was certain."

"Not one little hint, so I didn't think it was about the guardianship we were discussing?"

"At that time of the morning, no."

Argh! That summed it up for Sally. This conversation was just going around in circles. All she'd done was give and give. She was done. Now it was time to continue doing things her way. Alone. "Just go," she pleaded before she broke down because that was not happening in front of Ben.

Ben dropped his arms by his side, his back straightening as he locked gazes with her, the intensity of the moment palpable in the room. "Maybe I will. And hopefully, you'll make more of an effort to listen in the morning because I have every intention of finishing this discussion."

She shrunk back as an awkward silence filled the room, uncertainty overwhelming her when Ben spun on his heels and stormed out of the room. A moment later, the front door slammed shut.

Uncertain of everything, she stood stock still, heart punching her ribs. The chime of the grandfather clock echoed around the room. She lost count and looked across. Eleven o'clock.

It was so past her bedtime. Now what? There was no way she would sleep a wink. Not worked up like she was. Regrets piled upon themselves until she could barely breathe. How had she turned into such a miserable human in the space of a week? She never gave him a chance to tell her much. Where was the Sally of old? Strong, independent, an all-round woman capable of taking care of herself, and above all, compassionate. What happened to not being that needy person?

And what the heck? What was the verdict? Was his grandfather being poisoned by Gwen?

She released a pain-filled groan as she ran her hands down her face, wishing she could start the conversation again. Except she wasn't ready to forgive yet.

There was only one thing to do. With temples throbbing, wretchedness taking over her heart, an aching and needy body making demands of its own, she walked out of the homestead barefoot, following the same dusty path Ben had taken.

She would either return from this mission having built a new bridge or find it burnt to the ground.

# Chapter 31

Ben sat on the edge of the bed and scrolled through his feed, not seeing anything as text and images blurred past. A mindless task designed to dull everything. Hoping for a miracle. That his mind would somehow switch off; otherwise, he'd have another crap sleep. Lately, his sleep had been unpredictable, which was to be expected with everything on his plate.

The smallish dwelling, a little larger and set aside from the other block that staff used, closed in around him, providing protection. With a basic layout of an open-plan kitchen and living room, a single bedroom and an ensuite through a small doorway, it was a far cry from the space of the main homestead, but it served its purpose after moving out of Grandad's old home after Rhylee died.

It gave him privacy, and he was holding onto that. He wouldn't let his mind go elsewhere to the places he preferred—wide open spaces, fresh breeze kissing his cheeks, slow-flowing rivers, star-studded night skies. It was probably better he was tucked up inside tonight because he was too wrought out to appreciate anything else.

No way was he going to dissect what had just happened. Not tonight. After a day like today, it would be way beyond his capabilities.

Knocking on his door startled him, and his phone slipped to the floor. He bent to retrieve it, hoping whoever was there would go away. He grimaced when it continued. *Shit!* After what just went down, having to deal with a problem on the station would be the final straw.

"Okay, okay, I'm coming." Wearily, he rose, strolling from the bedroom to the other side of the dwelling to open the door. His heart jump-started when Sally stared back at him, full of determination and fight.

The only light came from the bedside lamp he'd switched on in the bedroom. It shone a strip from the bedroom all the way to the front door and over her face. When neither spoke, he tilted his exhausted face. "What?" he said a little gruffly.

"I doubt I'll sleep a wink, so I—"

Ben cut in. "I'm done with talking tonight. We're both in the wrong place, and we'll only make matters worse."

"Great, because I didn't come here to talk."

"Huh?"

"Take your clothes off."

His eyes widened. "Are you nuts? We'll kill each other."

"Great! It'll make me feel better."

Ben raised his hands, palms up and stalled her coming in. "No way am I going to be accused again of expecting you to be that dutiful woman keeping my bed warm. You need to turn around and walk back to the homestead and go to bed."

She had the decency to wince before straightening her shoulders and standing firm. "Not in this lifetime, cowboy. All I've done is give and give some more. Now I'm going to take some back, thank you very much. Now move aside and start by taking off your shirt."

He was too tired to argue and stepped aside regardless. "It won't work. I'm beat."

"I'll give you less than two minutes, and I bet it'll be working." Sally strode in, shutting the door firmly behind her.

"You think?" In the stand-off, her eyes blazed like she wanted to eat him alive. Only the whir of the air conditioner competed with the sound of their breathing. Ben knew he would lose this bet. He saved himself the trouble and stretched his shirt over his head, his erection inside his boxers deciding all on its own what *it* wanted to do.

She took her soft pink tee off too and stood there with a naked top half. His breath hitched. God, he'd missed her.

She looked past him towards the bedroom which glowed on the other side of the donga. She marched past him. "Get your backside in here," she continued, her face a serious canvas as she passed him with a small nudge against his shoulder in the confined space.

He let slip a wry grimace. "We could make this pleasant."

"No, we can't. Not this round." She pushed her pyjama shorts down her thighs and kicked them out of the way once they dropped to her ankles.

"So, there will be another time?" Ben followed through with his boxers, a crazy chemistry beginning to pulse along his skin.

"Damn straight there will be."

Beside the bed, both totally naked, Ben worked hard to even his breathing. Sally wasn't doing a brave job of staying strong and unaffected either. Her fingers curled inside her palms, and her gaze dropped and rose a couple of times, not meeting his. He wasn't fooled. Neither could he claim to be in command here. Especially of his throbbing erection which was currently holding all his power. He took the gamble and cupped her soft, round breast. She hissed before biting down on her lip. This was his cue to take some control back. In a flash, he scooped her into his arms, the warmth of his body radiating against hers, and placed her in the middle of the bed, his weight sinking into the mattress beside her.

She lamely fought against his dominance, giving a half-hearted squirm, until he took her mouth and kissed her with an intensity that unravelled him completely. Within seconds, she was returning his ferocity, his body coming to life with a vicious roar.

She'd demanded this, and God help him, tonight would be anything but tender. The heat was oppressive, and he was so turned on it was bringing a new level of adrenaline, unlike anything he'd ever experienced.

Sally pushed Ben away, needing to fill her lungs. Their gazes locked, while her heart pounded against her ribs, echoing in her ears. Ben squeezed her tight against his hardness, throbbing against her stomach.

She liked it way too much, and since this was her show, she would enjoy every minute. She took his mouth again, the taste of him, the feel of his lips, a memory she wanted to savour forever.

His hands, oh good Lord, his hands, released from his tight grip, pressed and moulded against her soft skin. Along her back, down her thighs, her body screaming for him to hurry up and get to that special place between her legs.

She raked her nails down the contoured muscles on his back, not caring if she left marks along his skin. She wanted him to know there were consequences for disappearing, even if he had apologised.

Her tongue darted in and out of his mouth relentlessly. When Ben moaned, she abandoned his mouth, travelling south. Sucking, nipping, taking over again until she wrestled complete dominance. Found his penis and took it inside. Moulded it between her tongue and lips. Sucking long and hard.

"Stop," he ground out. "I need to get ready."

Sally raised her face, her chest rising and falling over his thighs. Ben's hands remained gripped to the rounded slats of the bedhead, his body rigid beneath her.

She crawled her way back up his slick body, grinding against his crotch, making this slither towards his chest as excruciating as possible. The sounds he emitted were enough for a wide grin to break out on her face. The satisfaction of controlling him filled her with a strange sense of triumph. When she was lying over him, she wound her arms around his neck, tucking her face against him and kissing him there.

"I need to get up ... condom," Ben choked out, almost panting.

Oh boy, the desire for him to enter her now, skin on skin, was so tempting. He was positioned perfectly with his tip nudging her wet and moist entry. "Well, hurry up. I don't have all night."

Ben grabbed both her shoulders, lifting her enough so they stared at each other. He hooked her with his glare. "Yes, you do. I'm going to make it take all night."

Sally groaned, rolling to her side, allowing Ben to rise from the bed. He rummaged in the top drawer of the bedside cupboard, allowing her to ogle his damn impressive backside. God, she hoped this was where he kept his condoms. *Hurry up, Ben.*

With her naked skin tingling in the cool, air-conditioned room, she grabbed his pillow and shoved it over her face, inhaling everything she loved about this man. She wiggled her toes and stretched her legs, igniting more moisture to pool down low. She was so ready for this. One drawer closed and another opened. As she rolled to her side, the pillow fell onto the mattress. "Is Gwen poisoning your grandfather?"

Ben froze, every muscle tense, hands hovering above the open drawer.

"Well, you haven't actually told me," she reminded him.

Ben returned to his search. Once he found a condom, he slammed the drawer shut with more force than was necessary. "Yes, she is."

"Are the police involved?"

"Damn straight they are. The police were organising search warrants today for an arrest." Ben's tone was clipped, and rightly so. This was huge for his family. Life altering.

"Holy shoot." Sally sat up to better listen. "Who does such a thing?"

"A greedy old woman when a man has sizeable cash deposits."

She noted with concern that Ben's erection was deflating. He looked down and groaned. "Can we discuss this tomorrow? Talking about Gwen isn't helping here."

She had every intention of finishing what she'd started and regretted asking the question. "Oh, that's right, you're here to please me."

Ben stared at her from his lofty height beside the bed. "Oh, am I?" he said, face tilted and eyebrows raised. "Not a bit brazen?"

"Nope." She reached for his hips but halted him from joining her on the bed. She took great satisfaction as Ben growled in agony when she took him in her mouth again, working him to full hardness. Strong and throbbing again, he withdrew. This time, it was Sally who wailed her disappointment while he took the time to roll on his condom.

When he joined her on the bed, their mouths fused again. Hard and ruthless, where her body took another battering from his hands. She wouldn't have it any other way.

Finally on top and laying along his length, he nudged her moist entry, entering with a push so hard she cried out.

Ben immediately froze. "I'm sorry."

"Don't be," she gasped, "and please, don't stop."

Ben's laughter echoed around the room, bringing a smile to her face. But it stopped immediately when their gazes caught. Her heart tripped. What was this man doing to her?

They fell into a rhythm that was becoming their way. A little less rough, a lot more emotional, sending her higher and higher to their special place. Just as she was on the cusp of coming, Ben rolled them over so he was on top. With full concentration, he took great delight in sliding in and out for what felt like an eternity. Each push harder while her fingers bit into his backside and encouraged it.

God help her, she never wanted it to end. It only took a couple more pushes, and there was no stopping her as she shattered into a million pieces. Ben joined her chorus of moans, his shuddering body blanketing her with the euphoria that came with release.

She took his weight as he flopped over her, allowing calm to descend. Her happy place. It'd been one frustrating week, and she was so going to hell for her brazen behaviour.

But she'd do it all again in a heartbeat.

# Chapter 32

Sally stretched her legs under the cotton sheet, enjoying the soreness that came with a night of intimacy. She'd woken at four am, used Ben's bathroom, and came back to the bed with one thing in mind.

Opening her eyes a whisker, she spied a thin strip of daylight seeping past the edges of the curtains. She smiled, reliving how she'd nudged Ben awake, demanding they repeat their earlier performance. And boy, what a star-studded show it'd been. It hadn't taken them long. In tune with the tempo of the night, they'd gone hard and furious. She liked it this way.

She slipped out from under the covers and rose quietly. In the dim light, she could see the rise and fall of Ben's chest as he slept. Her heart hammered. Bold, nighttime Sally wasn't so sure how one coped in daylight after her shameless ways. Would Ben see her differently? *She* felt like a changed woman.

Searching the floor, she located her pyjama shorts near the bedroom door. Had she really shucked everything off when she'd stormed in last night, revealing a different Sally behind closed doors?

Donning them, she went searching for her pyjama shirt. She tiptoed towards the front door, finding it on the floor. She pulled it over her head and arms. Maybe a shower would give her the confidence she needed to face Ben in daylight.

Unlike how the poor door was treated last night, she silently turned the knob and opened it a fraction, squeezing past. She closed it with equal care. Squinting into the early morning sun, she turned away from its crisp rays, hastening towards the main homestead. There was some noise and action from the lodgings behind Ben's, but Sally didn't stop to look and didn't come across anyone. For this, she was relieved. A shower and some breakfast would prepare her for the drive back to the digging site.

The reminder that she would be confined in a vehicle with Ben made her inwardly groan. Would daytime Sally be able to keep her hands off him? Or would she be hiding behind them in shame? Last night came rushing back. Who was she? She rubbed the back of her neck as heat steadily climbed up to her cheeks. She needed a freezing shower to douse it. This walk back to the homestead was on par with a walk of shame. Despite her embarrassment, she smiled. In her previous life, she'd never done anything so bold.

Half an hour later, dressed in jeans and a tee, Sally towel-dried her hair one last time before hanging the towel in the bathroom. Last night, she'd spied some bread in the fridge, so toast for breakfast it would be to ease her grumbling stomach, which was adamant about reminding her how famished she was.

At the sound of a vehicle driving into the yard of the homestead, her ears pricked. She detoured away from the kitchen and went out to the front verandah to investigate.

Leading a trail of dust was one of the 4WD troop carriers they used between Richmond and the digging site, complete with a trailer loaded with fresh supplies. And Dean! How had she forgotten about Dean's arrival? She was losing it!

Today was supposed to be like any ordinary day. At the old homestead, in charge of her boys and excited about Dean's arrival for morning tea.

Before Daniel's accident.

Before Ben's unexpected return.

Before last night.

"Sally!" Dean's infectious grin spread across his face as he got out of the vehicle. "I didn't know you'd be here. You told me you'd be waiting for me with some delicious chocolate cake and a hot cup of tea."

Sally laughed, pulling Dean into her arms for a hug. His innocence was exactly what she needed. She'd forgotten how the drivers sometimes stopped at the main homestead for a quick toilet break before finishing the last leg to the old homestead. There was a toilet accessible from the outside of the building. Already, the troop carrier driver was on his way to using it.

"One of the boys broke his arm when he fell out of a tree yesterday. Ben and I drove him here to meet the Royal Flying Doctor. We're heading back after breakfast."

Dean flinched. "Hope he's okay."

"He will be. I think being able to fly in a plane took his mind off the worst of it."

"Want to come back with us now?" Dean asked. "We've got a spare seat."

Sally's breath caught in her throat. This would alleviate having to sit beside Ben for the drive out. Oh, she was being such a chicken, but the temptation to leave now, hungry and all, was too great.

"Thank you. I think I might just do that," Sally replied, her spirits lifting. "I'll go grab my bag."

The driver returned from the toilet and directed Dean towards it, so she turned to go back inside, the screen door flapping closed behind her. Her duffle bag was already waiting in the hall. She yanked out a comb and tidied her hair. Oh, she was so running away from a situation she didn't know how to handle.

With her bag in hand, she walked down the hallway, stopping at the open doorway to the kitchen. Reminded of how Ben wanted to talk first, her heart did a nervous flutter. What if their discussion changed everything? She gulped back nerves and closed her eyes for a moment. She could do this. This talk should've happened weeks ago.

When her stomach grumbled again, she opened her eyes, looking longingly at the fridge. Could she rustle up some quick toast? Considering it for about three seconds, she shook her head. She wouldn't die of starvation and remembered Flora's chocolate cake awaited her at the other end.

Swinging the bag over her shoulder, she made for the verandah, ignoring the nerves roiling in her stomach. She was doing exactly what Ben had.

Disappearing without a word.

She bent down to slip on her outdoor boots. Rising, she pushed the screen door open on fast-forward. With her legs too quick for her brain to catch up, she pummelled into something hard as the screen door shut behind her, her breath whooshing out. When she could fill her lungs again, she sniffed apple-scented soap and breathed it in like an addict.

"Going somewhere?"

She hid her face against his chest. With Ben freshly showered, she inhaled the delicious, clean smell she loved so much. Oh, to stay in this spot forever.

Instead, she took a step back, stumbling over her boots. Ben grabbed her arm to steady her and their gazes locked. His smile slipped as a kaleidoscope of emotions played across his face. Was that hurt she spied because it was obvious she was leaving without saying goodbye? Or maybe indecision? Was he blindsided by what they'd done last night and was the new version of Sally a little unnerving? Or was it indifference? Did he really care that she was leaving?

What was going through his head? She swallowed back the need to throw up on an empty stomach—until she spotted humour looking back at her and relaxed a smidgen.

"Have you decided to hitch a lift with this crew?" He bobbed his head towards the troop carrier.

She bit her bottom lip and nodded, still unsure of how to face Ben after last night. As for her tongue—well, good luck with finding it this morning.

"I'll come and say hello to Dean. It's probably a good idea you're driving away with him because I know of another creek between here and the digging site, and I can't promise I wouldn't stop for a break. A nice long break beside the river."

His soft-spoken words sent a shiver along her skin. She was so up for that. He moved closer, slowly torturing her with his mouth along her cheek. Kissing, nipping gently, his warm breath fanning the side of her face. "I guess it's a good morning to you, Sally," he whispered for her ears only. "Can you make time for me tonight to finish what I was trying to say last night? I know it's long overdue and thank you for waiting patiently."

She pushed back enough to look into his eyes. This time, she didn't miss the longing, the regrets, the apologies. The muscles around her chest tugged inwards, wrapping themselves around her heart. She nodded, prepared to agree to anything, just as he dropped his face and rested his forehead against hers.

"Mum just messaged." His warm breath feathered across her face. "They'll arrive here late tonight with Daniel and Grandad. I'll drive over again in the morning for Daniel and to help settle Grandad in. I don't want to miss an entire day and night without you." His gaze lifted to hers, intense and unwavering. "Okay?"

Sally gulped some more, doing her best not to collapse against him. Her knees wobbled, and her pulse rippled over her skin wherever he touched. What a predicament. If Dean wasn't around, she'd demand he take her back to his room.

"Will you be ready to listen this time? Without breaking into some irrational and cranky woman, who then breaks out into some she-devil in the bedroom."

Sally snorted a laugh, breaking out of her stupor. She stood straighter, touching her mouth to his for a delicious, heated kiss. What an avid description. She would succumb to her needs when it came to Ben, there was no doubt, but in this moment, she needed to be that strong woman who was ready to shoulder life like an adult.

"Good morning, Ben," she garbled, her tongue losing itself in another heated kiss. There would be no running away. Thank God Ben had surfaced in time; otherwise, she'd regret disappearing without seeing him. But Dean was here, and he was a priority too.

She chuckled as they came apart. Oh, how the morning was falling perfectly into place.

"Are you ready, Sally?" Dean called from beside the troop carrier.

She raised her hand to acknowledge Dean. "I guess I'll see you soon," she whispered.

"I'll be right on your tail, literally."

A touch of apprehension coloured this statement. Was Ben nervous about what he had to tell her? If this was a possibility, she would be supportive, however alarming the news was. There seemed so much for her to carry some days. Was she up to bearing someone else's burdens too? What if it broke her?

For now, she pushed aside her concerns. That included the guardianship woes and her determination to go it alone if Ben wasn't interested.

Sally still didn't know how they would get past this hurdle as a couple. She could already see her needing to choose between Ben and the children.

Ben squeezed her fingers entwined with his, giving her pause as they walked towards Dean's smiling face. His take on life was infectious. Since she kept in touch with him, she'd already shared the news of how the mysterious owner of the cat was also the same man who was helping her run the program. She hadn't told Dean yet that they were a thing, but no doubt he would work it out.

Sally peeled her hand away from Ben's so she could climb inside the troop carrier. People like Dean ensured there was always enough good in the world to cancel out the bad. A great example that, no matter how rough a start to life you received, there was always a lot to appreciate. On the flip side, there were people like Jacob's dad and Gwen. Nasty, vindictive, selfish and greedy. Karma was now kicking their butts.

Dean and Ben shared a firm handshake before Dean joined her in the back of the troop carrier, leaving the front passenger seat free. They would chat and catch up the entire way. Sally wound the window down, and Ben reached in to place a quick peck on her cheek.

"See you soon," she said with a small wave.

Ben smiled, holding her gaze for as long as possible as the driver headed away from the homestead.

When the time came, she would listen to what Ben had to say. The good and the bad, whatever it was. It was up to her to ensure the scales tipped in the right direction. Be the strong one, if needed.

She would start by listening without judgement. Then she would decide how to move forward. Even if it was at the expense of her happiness.

# Chapter 33

Acolumn of dust trailed their vehicle as the driver turned off the main road onto the long driveway to the old homestead. Turning back to face the front again, Sally couldn't wait to see the boys and tell them how Daniel was coming along. There'd also be a heap of work and emails waiting for her to catch up on, but adrenaline pumped around her body. She was so ready for this and all that awaited her.

She'd enjoyed the opportunity to catch up with Dean face to face, not regretting her decision to hitch a ride. He continued to volunteer at the council animal pound, so they shared a common bond with the people who worked there. She'd also picked his brains. As an employed gardener with the local council, she was keen to hear his input on improving the start they'd made to the lawn and gardens.

A smile hovered over her mouth as the troop carrier neared the homestead. Ben's promise to stop along the way at another creek was her only tiny regret. She wriggled on her seat, heat coursing down her body to pool between her legs. Last night was hands down the wildest experience of her life. When she took a moment to recall it, her body went all haywire. Thankfully, Ben wasn't nearby; otherwise, she'd struggle to keep her hands off him.

A harried-looking Flora came flying off the verandah and onto the lawn with her arms waving.

Sally frowned. She unclipped her seatbelt and sat forward in her seat, every scenario running through her head.

"Is that Flora? She looks worried," Dean said, peering out of the vehicle from her side.

"Yes, that's her. I wonder what's up?"

As soon as the driver parked the troop carrier, Sally flung the door open. Dean got out of the vehicle too, hot on her tail.

"What's up?" Sally asked, putting an arm around Flora's shoulders and giving her a squeeze.

"I can't find the damn cat." Anguish was written all over Flora's face.

"What cat?" Dean asked, coming to a stop beside Sally.

"Ben dropped off a cat cage when he arrived yesterday. I told him about the accident with Daniel; he handed it over, asking if I could take care of the cat. Two hours ago it took off out the back door."

"Oh, Sally, could it be Moby?" Dean looked between Sally and Flora. "Didn't you say Ben drove his grandfather out to Richmond?"

"It might be," Sally said, concern for the cat beginning to take up space in her head.

"Wait. What's Lincoln doing out this way?" Flora asked. "He hasn't been back this way since Lottie passed on."

*Shoot!* Sally wanted to groan out loud at her blunder. Clamping down on her jaw, she needed to come up with something fast. She'd only vaguely mentioned to Dean that Ben had driven back to Richmond with his grandfather, but Flora's antennae would be flapping in every direction. What was happening with Lincoln was confidential information. She should've kept her mouth shut until Ben's family made it public knowledge.

"Ben's not too far behind us, Flora," Sally said by way of distraction. "How about Dean and I start searching for Moby?"

Flora harrumphed. "A name would have helped. The poor thing has been frightened and nervous the whole time. Now I can't find him anywhere."

"Is everyone at the digging site?"

Flora nodded. "I better get started unloading the trailer; otherwise, there won't be enough morning tea. One chocolate cake won't go far."

Sally heaved an enormous sigh of relief. Fingers crossed nothing got back to Ben about her accidental blunder.

Switching off that concern, Sally turned to Dean. "Where do you think we start looking?"

"You check inside the homestead; I'll look outside around the building."

"Okay, let's go."

Twenty minutes later, and exhausted with all possible hiding spots inside the homestead, Sally walked out the back door into the yard and scanned the area. She spotted Dean sitting cross-legged on the scratchy lawn, not far from the pile of old ironbark fence posts. He was hunched over something.

The sun's warm rays showered over her as she swiped a hand over her sweaty brow. Drying her hand on her jeans, she walked towards him. "Did you find him?"

Dean looked up with a smile that outshone the strong sun. Nestled in his arms and hidden in his lap was a very contented cat. She could hear his purring as Dean stroked the ragdoll's fur.

"Oh, thank goodness." Sally relaxed, her limbs going all loose as the knot of anxiety trapped inside her slowly vanished. She crouched beside Dean and patted the top of Moby's head, glad this was one less headache they had to deal with. "Hello, Moby. I didn't expect to see you here today." Sally looked up and smiled at a contented Dean before looking down at Moby again and chuckling, "Trust me, Moby, you'll be well taken care of while Dean is here."

"Oh, this is going to be such a great stay, Sal. I can't believe Moby is here."

"Well, I'm not exactly sure what the plan is, but I'll try to convince Ben to keep him here a little while."

Dean grinned, lifting Moby to nestle him against his cheek. "I'm not letting him out of my sight."

"Sally!"

She sprung up and spun around to find Ben approaching with a frown that matched his harsh tone.

True to his word, and not ready to relinquish Moby to anyone, Dean rose and walked past Ben with a curt nod. "I'll get him some milk and food." He was back inside the homestead in seconds.

This left her alone with Ben. The sun was still an hour away from reaching its midmorning position, but already, it burnt into her skin with her hat nowhere in sight. Ben's scowl made her uncomfortable. Flora must have said something. *Bugger!* She rubbed at her temple as a headache silently threatened.

Ben glared at her, hands on his hips, intimidating as all heck. *Damn it!* One slip, when she clearly remembered how confidential the news about his grandfather was.

Keeping her mouth shut, she waited for him to say something first.

The longer he glared at her, the tighter her mouth remained. Until his scowl lost its intensity, transforming into one of resignation as tension dropped from his shoulders.

"Was it only last night we were discussing trust? And now I have Flora asking me why Grandad is in Richmond?" he ground out bitterly. "You didn't get that what I told you was sensitive information?" he added with anguish.

The muscles of her jaw tightened further as the agony in his voice ripped her chest in two. She prised her lips open, ready to apologise, but Ben shook his head and stalked off. Like he was leaving for good and wiping his hands of her.

Her jaw slackened as he strode away, making for the track leading to the digging site. Within seconds, he was around a bend and out of view. She shivered as the pent-up air in her lungs struggled to get out. Gasping for air, she realised she couldn't continue without a moment to collect herself.

Her heart raced out of control; she needed to apologise fast. Ben was right. She couldn't be trusted. How had her day morphed into this mess?

She took off towards the track with every intention of catching up with Ben. The muscles in her legs cramped the further she got, making her sluggish. They refused to move any faster. She glimpsed Ben for a second before he disappeared around another bend.

*Hurry up!* Tears welled in her eyes, giving the track and the trees on either side of it a blurry edge. The urgency to reach Ben, to apologise, was all she could process. Around the next bend, she spotted him nearing the junction where you chose right for the digging site or left for the shallower section of the river.

"Ben!"

He chose left.

"Ben!" she called again, but he neither stopped nor acknowledged her.

She wasn't giving up on them. Yes, she'd made a monumental blunder, and it was time to own it. Tears gushed down her cheeks as she sped up, hobbling from an awkward walk to a semblance of a jog. Sweat trickled down her back in rivulets as her cheeks heated. She didn't need to touch the top of her head to know her hair would be hot from the direct sun beating down over her. But there would be shade at the creek and river water to splash over her face. She just had to reach Ben.

When the river came into view, she slowed to a walk and stretched her tee up to wipe her face. She couldn't seem to halt her tears. After everything she and Ben had been through, especially the past twenty-four hours, she wanted to make this right. Sort *them* out once and for all.

"Ben!" she called again, her voice blubbery. The sun's intensity vanished as she reached the tree line near the water's edge and walked into the blessed shade.

Ben stilled, his shoulders sagging as he slowly turned around. She held in a gasp when she noticed his blotched and red face.

*Oh, my God, have I broken this man?* The muscles around her heart clenched and tightened, hurting. All the while, she couldn't look away from the anguish staring back at her.

"Rhylee was sixteen weeks pregnant with our first child, and she never told me."

Sally's heart pounded. For the first time, he'd said his late wife's name.

Ben fell to his backside onto the flat surface of a rock, scrubbing his hands over his face.

"We'd had a brutal argument that night. She hated the outback. Didn't want to live so isolated from everything. I never saw it coming. How—"

The raw, desperate wail coming from Ben's mouth sent a shiver along her heated skin.

"How did I not know my wife didn't want to stay with me? Can you answer that?"

Sally froze, her breath hitched in her throat. Not sure what to say. How to proceed.

"You think you know a person. You're in each other's pockets. Except for mustering, we were together every day. How could I have been so blind? And she was pregnant and didn't tell me!"

"Oh, Ben." So much anguish. She wasn't sure how to proceed but she wanted this to be the place where they talked. Their future together hinged on what happened here. Beside this beautiful section of the river. Under gum trees slanting towards precious water giving so much life. The shallow section of the creek was barely metres away, with only a narrow strip of soft sand separating them and the edge of the cool water. It reminded Sally of another creek where she and this man had made many happy memories.

Hesitant at first, Sally took tentative steps towards the water. Needing to bring her body temperature down, she'd begin by soaking her feet. She toed off her boots and pulled off her socks, tucking them inside. She rolled up her jeans as far as her knees before standing in the blessed coolness. With possible privacy for a couple of hours, there was no need to rush this.

Her tears had stopped flowing once Ben started talking. The few words already shared by Ben spoke volumes about the pain he carried. How they were going to move forward, she had no idea. For now, she would step aside from her ambitions and let him unburden himself.

She was here for the long haul, and if she loved this man—

With a thumping heart, she stole a glance at Ben. She did love this man. How had it never crossed her mind before? Had lust taken over everything?

Enjoying the immediate coolness on her skin, she splashed water over her face and hair, cupping another handful of water and doing it again before walking out of the creek. She sat nestled at Ben's feet, her back resting against his legs. After a moment of silence, Ben spread his legs and wrapped his arms around her shoulders, pulling her closer to his chest, tightening his hold.

"I'm sorry, Sally."

She twisted around and looked up into his tear-streaked face. "Don't be, Ben. I'm here now. Will you tell me everything I need to know?" How many nights ago was it she'd come up with the idea to be bold and ask the questions? Encourage Ben to talk. Start the conversation.

The time had arrived.

He rubbed a hand over his blotchy face before dropping a quick, heated kiss on her mouth. "What if you walk away?"

"Come and find me if I do, okay? But first, let's start with this." Sally pulled out of Ben's embrace and grabbed one of his boots, trying to tug it off.

"What are you doing?"

"We're going to sit in the creek where it's cooler. Come on, help me here," she said, doing her best to lighten the sombre mood that had descended over them. She yanked on his boot until it slipped off his foot. Ben gave her a choked-up, stifled laugh, which was a good start, and pulled off his sock.

Moving to the other boot, they repeated the process. She knew Ben was looking at her without having to glance at him. Could feel his serious gaze piercing her face. With her eyes on the job, she didn't look up.

She would ask the questions and hope she got the answers.

This was not about her.

This was about *them*.

# Chapter 34

"If I'm sitting in the creek, I'm taking these off."

Sally didn't argue since his wallet and phone were in the back pocket of his jeans. Once unzipped, Ben kicked his legs out of his jeans and they dropped onto the sand.

"You should do the same."

She baulked for a moment. "Oh, what the heck," and removed hers, leaving them folded on the flat rock Ben had just risen from.

"Okay, let's do this." She walked to the edge of the creek, finding the shadiest spot a couple of metres away. "This should do." She waded in, sinking into the sandy creek bed. The refreshing water lapped against her waist. For a split second, she considered taking off her shirt and bra too, but that would be a distraction.

Ben followed, cradling her in his arms from behind. They rocked with the gentle flow of water, hands held together around her waist, fingers entwined and her head nestled against his neck. They stayed this way while she relished his closeness, the immediate relief from the cool water going a long way in helping her unwind.

After a few minutes of calm, she slid down some more so the water lapped her chest. She tilted her head back, looking at Ben upside down. "I remember you telling Dean the first day we met that your wife drove off. What happened, Ben?"

His breath hitched, a ragged intake that sent little ripples across the surface. It was like remembering that day still came as a shock. She waited patiently, not going anywhere because she had to hear this.

Ben sunk lower into the water and shuffled back a little so he could lean against a smooth rock jutting out of the water. The water lapped just below her neck as Ben's grip tightened around her waist.

"We'd been arguing over stupid stuff for a couple of months. I can't believe I didn't see the signs from those early days. She was obviously pregnant, but since I didn't know, I didn't question her irrationality too much at the time. She never once hinted she was unwell in the mornings. I never saw her throw up. Nothing. We'd been married for nearly two years. The odd blowup didn't alarm me, but they *were* becoming more regular."

Sally used the gentle current to roll to her side to better watch Ben. His eyes were closed, his face grim. Ben must have sensed her gaze because his eyes fluttered open before closing again. His sombre expression twisted her insides.

"I still thought things were going along just fine. She worked from the station with the school of distance education, coordinating the students, teachers and program. More than once she'd told me she loved her job, so I didn't question it at all. If she was happy with her work, so was I."

Sally stretched her legs so they floated with the gentle tug of water.

"Just goes to show how blind I was."

"Hey ..." She cupped his cheek. His eyes flickered open as he turned towards her, giving her a view of his pain-filled, vivid green eyes. "Were you planning a pregnancy?"

"No. We'd discussed it but wanted some more time. There was no rush, and we were still young. She agreed to use the pill, but something must have gone wrong. Whether she forgot to take some, missed a few days or threw them away, I don't know. I went looking for them afterwards and couldn't find them."

Ben looked away, towards the creek flowing downstream. Sally didn't rush him. Gave him time to gather his thoughts. She took this moment to study him. High cheekbones, a hint of stubble from not shaving the night before. The shape of his mouth that had already given her so much.

A blanket of sadness passed over her. For someone so young, he had suffered a lot. Been forced to jump through hoops many have never experienced in a lifetime. He had qualities she loved. He was driven and passionate. She'd seen it in his fascination with bones and fossils alone.

Here was proof that choosing the wrong person could derail you for many years. Hope that if you matched up with the right person, life might turn out to be a joyous journey.

"She said some weird stuff that night. She was angry I hadn't returned home earlier. I'd been out checking animals and fences because we'd had quite a bit of rain. She reminded me again of how much she hated the isolation of the outback. The wet season has a habit of isolating you even further. Sometimes for months. She didn't want to live out there anymore. Missed her family and friends." He shook his head. "I really believed we could work it out."

Sally tried to picture the troubled woman but had nothing to start from. "Your mum doesn't have any photos of her in the homestead."

Ben emitted a miserable groan. "I found that if I walked into a room with a photo of her, it triggered a flood of hurt. After a particular meltdown, Mum sat me down and told me she would remove them all and put them in a safe place for when I could deal with it better."

Sally nodded, tightening her hold on his hand. The distinct call of a bunch of cockatoos washed over her. She'd spotted them earlier on the highest branches of the gum trees, partially hidden amongst the foliage. She could just see their bright yellow crests from where she floated. With the gentle hum of a cooling breeze, it made for a peaceful setting. Sally hoped it provided the calm Ben needed to keep talking.

"Her final parting words were of leaving for good. That she was never returning to live out here. Did I really do that to her? Just the way she said it, the look she gave me, scared me stupid. She was messed up. Even a little unstable. *Fuck!* Hard to erase and unsee, even after all this time. And—and then she drove off."

Sally didn't have to ask any more questions as Ben continued to talk. About Rhylee leaving in a rush. Finding her in the car barely an hour later. Did she drive off the causeway on purpose, or was it an accident? The guilt that somehow it was his fault. Never able to put it to rest.

While he talked, Sally anchored her feet to the sandy bottom and wiped away the slow trickle of tears down his cheeks. Watching a grown man cry could break you.

"I thought that was going to be the worst of it. When the autopsy revealed she was pregnant, there was no stopping the downward spiral."

Ben loosened his hold and splashed his face. "Sorry about this," he said with a wry grimace.

"Hey, I'm here for you. Okay?"

His watery, bloodshot eyes latched onto hers, and he dropped his face to give her a heated kiss. "Thank you," he said before gathering her close again, with her back against his chest and his arms around her waist.

Ben continued to talk of not being able to see a way forward. Counselling sessions, the dark days he'd considered the unthinkable. More than once.

"That's why my grandfather is everything to me. He saw the desperate mess I was in when I was at my worst. Took me in his arms and told me to stay with him. Nurtured me back to some semblance of normality. Got me doing small things. Repairs, maintenance and gardening. Walks in the rainforest. Eating because I'd forgotten I needed to. I'm not saying the rest of the family didn't care. I think they were giving me space to heal, but Grandad saw I needed more."

Still, he talked. His concerns for his grandfather. The niggle that wouldn't go away about Gwen.

When he paused, Sally straightened. How long had they sat in the creek? An hour? She looked at her skin, which resembled a dried prune. She twisted around to face him. His tears had stopped, and a smidgen of relief flickered in his eyes.

"Then you came along. The best thing to happen to me in a long time. How Jacob's report triggered a warning, which led to everything that has happened over the past week."

"It's been one hell of a crazy ride, hasn't it?"

Ben dropped his face. "I'm sorry for my angry outburst earlier."

"I honestly didn't say anything to Flora. I only told Dean you'd driven your grandfather to Richmond. But Dean's a clever young man, and when Flora told us your cat was lost, well, I guess Dean just assumed it could be Moby."

"Shh." Ben placed his fingers over her mouth. "It's okay. I think we're past the danger point. Gwen should be in police hands by now. I didn't realise how uptight and stressed I was."

"Oh, Ben. What a mess for your family."

"I know. But I owe you everything. If it wasn't for you, I'd still be worrying about Grandad and not knowing why. Until it was too late."

Sally shivered, the water suddenly chilly against her skin. "I think I need to get out and warm up."

She went to rise, but Ben grabbed her arm before she had a chance.

"There's one more thing, Sally. I need to say it now before I lose my nerve."

Sally froze, sensing this was crunch time. Her teeth chattered, and she clamped down on her jaw.

"Sally, I have a very thick folder with my name on it. The government department in charge of guardianships will never grant me that privilege, no matter how much we want it. I was not in a good way and I told the counsellor this numerous times. It'll all be written down. If we go down this path, it'll only set us up for failure."

The disappointment cut deep, even though she understood why. She pulled out of his hold and rose. Her legs were a little shaky as she walked to the sandy edge. "It's fine, Ben. I'll deal with it."

Water splashed behind her as Ben followed. "Don't, Sally. We both know it won't make you *fine*. It won't make *us* fine if we don't find a solution."

She spun around as small grains of sand rubbed against the soft skin of her foot arch. Water dripped off their clothes and skin. She bit into the soft skin of her lip, needing to rein in her emotions. Protecting Jacob and Maddy was a paramount concern of hers. She also wanted to take care of Ben and his fragile mental health because, damn it, she loved him too. The full realisation that she was put on this earth to take care of these three people struck her anew.

But how did she proceed without hurting someone along the way and breaking her forever? How had her life gotten so much tougher?

"I can't choose, Ben. Not today. I'm not sure if I can do it tomorrow either."

"What if you don't have to?"

Anger drove a spear through her chest, burying itself in the sand behind her, pinning her to that spot. "What do you mean? Didn't you just finish telling me how your history won't give us a chance?"

"Yes, but—"

"But what? Why are you doing this to me? It's already going to be hard enough when I have to choose. Damn it! Just leave it be, okay? I'll sort it out."

She turned around, flustered, searching for her jeans and boots, spotting them to her left. Head space was what she needed, and a desire to walk away and think everything over.

"Stop it, Sally."

"No, you stop it." She yanked her arm away when he grabbed it and picked up her jeans.

"There is a way, Sally. Please, hear me out."

"No, there isn't. Not really, is there?" She glared at him, daring him to give her hope when there was none. It was take Ben into her life or take the children. Pretty clear-cut in her books. She'd known this all along. Since the first discussion when he walked out on her and disappeared for a week. Yep, she was back there again. Despite everything she'd learnt since, his disappearance still hurt.

She struggled to pull on her jeans but eventually tugged them up her wet legs, then did up the zipper and button before starting on her socks.

"Will you calm down and listen to me? You're doing it again!"

Sally hissed as she stretched her socks over her feet. "Doing what again?"

"You're turning into that irrational and cranky woman—"

"Oh, that's right," she blurted, on the brink of losing it again if she didn't calm down, "who then breaks out into some she-devil in the bedroom. Is that what you were about to say?" With her boots on, she straightened and glowered at Ben.

Ben ploughed a hand through his partiall wet hair and grimaced. Oh, she wanted him so much. Her heart could easily expand to fit the entire world in. All she was asking for was to accommodate three people, and she'd give it her all. It was her destiny to love these people. She had the drive, the ambition, and the determination to work hard for anything. Why was this proving to be out of reach? *Come on, world. Do something!*

"I've been talking to Mum and Dad. They're prepared to put their life on hold and help us out."

So embroiled in her thoughts, she almost missed a whisper of something good in the air. "Huh?"

"This is what I've been wanting to tell you."

"Tell me what?"

"Mum and Dad will offer to apply for guardianship of Jacob and Maddy. They'll live at the homestead. Be educated like my brothers and I were. Be part of a thriving life in the outback, away from harm and bad influences. There is so much good an outback life can give them. Which means you and I can be part of their lives too. We'll be there for them. They won't lack anything, and they'll have a fulfilling childhood until they're adults and can decide what they want to do. If Grandad decides to stay out here permanently, he'll have an influence on them, too. Trust me, that's a good thing."

Sally swayed on her feet, the surface of the water tilting and the trees bending just that little further before she burst into tears. Hot, salty tears that made no sense. She wasn't unhappy, more the unburdening of relief as it swept over her. Was this the answer to her prayers?

When her knees wobbled, Ben was beside her, holding her up. Supporting her like a drunk after too many drinks. He wrapped his arms around her shoulders, holding her close as she rained tears against his already wet shirt. A safe place she wanted to remain forever.

Eventually, her tears slowed. Disentangling herself from Ben, she took a step back. She would look a mess, but it didn't matter. This was the man she loved, and she needed to tell him. This thoughtful, kind man who was still traversing his own private hell.

When she delved into his waterlogged eyes, whether from crying earlier or soaking in the creek for too long or just the build-up of everything between them, he looked back expectantly. She was yet to respond to his suggestion and was about to say something when he spoke first.

"Do you think it could work?"

*Oh, good Lord.*

"Ben, oh Ben, your suggestion is everything, plus more." Her last few words came out blubbery as the tears trickled down her cheeks again.

"Shh, we've got this, if we have each other." He gently brushed away her tears with his thumb as they rolled down her cheek.

"And I need to apologise. I'm sorry for getting irrational and cranky. You were right; that's exactly the direction I was headed."

Ben smiled, and the entire universe opened with it. Possibilities, opportunities and so much more.

"As long as you follow through with the she-devil I'm getting a taste for."

Despite everything, Sally managed a weak, trembling smile.

"But honestly, Sal, is this a valid plan? Do you think it might work? There's absolutely nothing in Mum and Dad's past that might be an issue, and in Mum's words, 'This will keep me busy until you lot start having grandkids for me to enjoy.' She'll love it, Sal. She's a natural homebody, a mum in every sense, and Dad will always have her back. This means you can continue your passion for the program and still be involved in Jacob's and Maddy's lives. Will you at least consider it as an option?"

Her head was reeling, still in shock there was a solution that didn't involve making a heartbreaking choice.

Ben broke eye contact with her and looked over her into the distance. He swallowed, and his Adam's apple jumped. It was only for a moment before he glanced down again, piercing her gaze with what looked like grim determination. "I'm also determined to leave my past where it is. If I don't have to open that damn folder again, it'll be a good thing." He cupped her cheek in one hand, tilting her face a little. "I *am* much better, Sally. I know it. I can feel it. I'm on the mend in so many ways, thanks to you. With you on my side, by my side, it makes the journey feel less daunting; I'm already well on to the other side."

She drowned that little bit more the longer they delved into each other's eyes. Her heart stirred, sending blood rushing through her veins. Good signs she was at the right place with the one person intended for her.

"It's been a long time since I've uttered these words, but—" Ben coughed to clear his throat and paused a nanosecond, which stretched into infinity. "I love you, Sally, like you have no idea. I need you right here beside me. I don't want to do this life thing alone anymore."

Sally gulped once, holding his gaze. "Me too, Ben. After all we've been through and done, it dawned on me that this thing between us is more than lust, dinosaur bones and saving children. I love you too, and I want to do life with you."

Ben nodded, soaking in her words, probably needing a few seconds to absorb it all. Didn't they both?

Ben glanced at his watch before looking up at the sun. Dappled shadows moved across his face. The whisper of a breeze brushed along her skin in time with the overhead branches and a pleasant coolness stroked against her drying skin. A smile clipped the edges of his mouth before he chuckled.

"What, Ben?"

He rotated his thumb along her cheekbone. "Oh, nothing much."

"I doubt that."

"I'm not even sure why I'm thinking this."

"Thinking what?" Sally persisted, sure she was frowning. What could possibly be the matter now? Hadn't they got over their biggest hurdle? Made it to the other side with a plan in place?

"Well, creeks are our thing. We probably have about forty-two and a half minutes before Flora expects us back for lunch. Sadly, we missed morning tea and her delicious chocolate cake, but I'll survive."

Sally's eyes widened. Surely his mind wasn't going down that track? Not after the emotional upheaval they'd just gone through.

"Yeah, such bad luck." Sally had to admit she was feeling much more relieved about life. They had a way forward now.

He began with feather-light kisses along her brow. Very tame. Sweet. Caring.

Sally was getting the gist of where this conversation was headed, and she was feeling all kinds of wonderful, if not a little nervous. "What if someone comes looking for us?"

"They have no reason to," Ben said, his lips trailing down her cheek. "They'll be starving and wanting lunch, and the boys aren't allowed near the creek without permission from either of us."

"Well, if you say so." Sally met his roving mouth, greedily craving every sensation whirling around her body.

"I only allowed you to get irrational and cranky if you promised me more of the she-devil stuff."

"Oh, is that so?" Sally grazed her lips over the gentle prickle of his stubble, leaving goosebumps on her arms.

"We're mostly undressed anyway." Ben's mouth was near her ear and finding his way ever so slowly down her neck.

"Convenient, I'd say." Even though she'd put her jeans back on.

"Hmm, very." His hands undid the zipper of her jeans, determined, while she toed off her boots.

"In the water or out?" *Silly question, Sally.*

"Definitely in."

As she expected.

She removed the rest of her clothing, dumping them on the sand. Ben followed, removing his boxers and shirt before crouching to rifle in the back pocket of his jeans for his wallet and a condom. When he waved the small foil package, her heart raced the same way it did every time she was confronted with his magnificence.

"How's Penny looking?" he asked, scooping her up and holding her under her legs like a baby.

Sally laughed with delight, unrestrained with pure happiness. She would have mind-blowing sex on the edge of the creek with this complex man, and he would treat her exactly how she wanted. But there was one catch. She would always have to share him with his love of fossils, bones and this second woman dubbed Penny.

"She's looking fabulous, Ben, and I have positive feedback about our plans to house her in Richmond. I can't wait to tell you everything."

"Really?" Ben put her down, pulling her against him where his erection jutted against her pelvis. "I can't wait for the update." He lifted her feet off the sand and walked into the water. "But can I concentrate on this first?" he asked, placing her back down.

"You were the one who asked about Penny!" She laughed and it carried on the gentle breeze, and then she was lost to the man she loved. Fingertips grazed over a muscled torso. An explosive kiss stirred her pulse with the occasional plunge of tongues. His body was hot against hers as they grappled at the water's edge, thankful for the coolness of the water over her ankles, keeping the heat in check.

"You ready to do this fast, Sal?"

The truth was, someone *could* come looking for them, so they couldn't take this slow and easy.

She nodded as a wave of turbulent heat rippled through her as their kiss deepened—long, wet and hard, open mouths, hot and desperate.

Ben stopped a moment and sheathed himself while the water swirled around their ankles. Sally leant a hand to roll the condom along his length, enjoying his moan of pleasure this small act created every time she helped.

She also took a moment to appreciate the familiar growing heaviness between her legs.

Ben guided her backwards into deeper water, body to body, until they stood thigh-high. She wrapped her arms around his neck, her legs around his waist, and forgot about the world as he adjusted her position, found her opening and thrust hard inside.

Instead of kissing, they gazed into each other's eyes, the unspoken emotions hanging in the air. Drowned a little more with each thrust as Ben gripped her backside and created slippery friction as he withdrew and thrust over and over. Building up the age-old tempo that somehow worked for them every time.

Sally's mouth hung open with each one, her breathing getting heavier and heavier. Ben stumbled back towards the shoreline, gently placing her down on the sand. He lay on top as the water ebbed and flowed, tickling her where they joined.

This wouldn't take long. They were already halfway there as her mind shut down, narrowing to this one act.

Later, she would dwell on a life with Ben and all she wanted to achieve. There was so much to fit in, and she wanted to get started straight away. But for now, she pushed harder against his thrusts, enjoyed the gentle massage of soft sand along her back. Moaned freely in the magnificent outdoors and found his mouth again. This special connection they experienced every single time always left her intensely surprised.

Together, they would be unbeatable.

*Watch out, world. Here we come.*

# EPILOGUE

*O*ne Year Later

Sally and Maddison hip-bumped in time with the beat of the music. The little girl's laughter vibrated around the lawn surrounding the main homestead as she shook her shoulder-length dark hair across a smattering of sun-kissed freckles on her pretty face. The DJ was setting up under a makeshift tent and testing its sound system. Sally gave him an encouraging thumbs up and continued with her moves and shakes.

There would be music and dancing under the stars until late. For Sally, it was its own kind of exhilaration. A sense of freedom in a whole new way. Dressed in her favourite jeans and a Kermit-green halter-neck blouse, it sparkled with sequins which matched the earrings dangling from her ears.

Though she didn't know the lyrics, she hummed along and did all the fancy moves while a giggling nine-year-old Maddison copied her every step. With a playful flick of her head, sending her blonde hair flying, she made it look like another dance move.

Sally glanced across at Ben as he took a swig of his beer. His gaze hadn't left her for most of the day. Right now, he was doing his best not to crack a smile, his lips twitching. He was in a funny mood, but she let it rest. Was he brooding? Was something bothering him? Or was he hoping to steal her away to the river for some privacy?

Summer had slipped into autumn. The temperatures dipped too much at this time of the year to be dallying near water after the sunset. In summer, well, that was a whole different story.

The thought of sneaking away sent a jolt of awareness over her skin, raising goosebumps. With her arms in the air, she laughed and twirled Maddison once again. Too much sex was turning her into this insatiable woman who couldn't get enough. How had she lived her previous life with so little?

Jacob sat next to Ben and Grandad on stools set up for the guests. Thick as thieves when together. He, too, refused to crack a smile and shook his head at their shenanigans. Unimpressed as any thirteen-year-old would be.

Hard to believe how a solid family base had transformed these two kids. Jacob would always be serious and thoughtful, but Maddison was a delight in her own spontaneous way. It hadn't happened overnight. There were tough days, but they both forged ahead as they glowed with the love and security they received.

Sally signalled for the boys to join them. Ben took another swig of his beer and stayed put. Probably in solidarity with Jacob, knowing full well he'd never get up and join them. Not at his age, anyway.

With the guardianship finalised months ago, Jacob's and Maddison's lives were focused on allowing them to be kids, ensuring they caught up with their education, and making up for all the little things they'd missed out on.

Jacob had taken to the horses, bonding with them as few humans could, improving his riding skills every day. He'd joined the team on the last mustering camp, surprising everyone with his tenacity and skill. The kid was hooked. He was also pretty darn good with the station's motorbikes and tinkered for hours if one needed fixing.

Maddison loved to cook, which was a good thing because, with Ellen's encouragement, the kitchen was always a busy place. The food coming out of it was a delicious sensation every time Sally and Ben made it back to the main homestead.

Ellen came through the front screen door, hands ladened with a jug of chilled punch and glasses. Balancing them carefully, she came down the three homestead steps and placed the tray on a nearby table. They'd already prepared a feast for the party. The boys were in charge of the two spit roasts, their delicious aroma wafting over them as the sun continued its descent. The women had prepared the salads and desserts. It'd been a hectic couple of days of preparation, and the fun was about to begin.

A marquee set up in the yard housed tables and chairs, not far from where a secure bonfire would be lit later. They'd strung up festive lights and decorated an event board with gold and pink balloons in a fashionably designed display. Lit up on the board were the words *Happy Birthday Sally*.

Beyond the marquee was a collection of tents. While Ellen had some station accommodation available, it wasn't enough for all who'd ventured out for the celebrations. The station accommodation already housed Ben's other brother, Martin, for when he was home. Martin's long-time mate, Theo, had tagged along this weekend and took up another single unit.

Ben and Sally had a designated unit they used whenever they weren't running the program at the old homestead. Then there were the usual station employees and a place for Grandad who permanently lived at the homestead again.

With Gwen's recent conviction and jail time, it was even more important that the family surrounded Grandad. While Grandad missed his Malanda home, Ben's younger brother, Damon, and his girlfriend, Elyse, lived there for now, keeping it in order until they made a decision about its future.

Ellen returned with a platter of nibbles and treats, placing it under a food screen so the pesky flies didn't sample it first. Ellen smiled in Maddison's direction, swaying her hips too and engaging with the girl. This got more giggles from Maddison and the inkling of a possible smile from the boys.

Sally looked up when the homestead screen door clinked shut again. Freshly showered and dressed, it looked like Paul was ready to join the party. She beckoned for him to join the girls. Dressed in his best jeans and button-down shirt, he shook his head with a chuckle. Comfortably settled in his favourite outdoor chair on the verandah, he happily watched Ellen sway her hips, with the occasional smile and eye roll, much to the delight of Maddison.

Today was special for a couple of reasons. The entire close-knit family, invited friends and community had gathered in Richmond that morning for the official turning of the first sod by the mayor. Hard to believe, but the process to approve the construction of a building, its sole purpose being to house a museum for the fabulous Penny, was approved. They'd done it! Nagged, convinced, persisted and argued about how to show Penny to the world now that she was out of the earth in her entirety and waiting patiently for her new home.

It involved multiple trips to Brisbane to argue their case with the Queensland Museum and the State Government. Had taken a lot of convincing that spending their money on this project was worthwhile. They'd won, and the construction of the museum was about to begin.

Family and close friends had travelled great distances to be in Richmond for this event, which would go down as a great day in the town's history. Invited to stay a couple of days at the main homestead, Ellen was in her element. Nothing fazed her, and together with Flora, they had this party totally under control.

Tonight's birthday party was the perfect excuse to keep the entertainment going. It was only fitting the celebrations continued well into the night.

Sally slowed down with the dancing and accepted a chilled glass of delicious fruity punch from Ellen as she passed a tray around.

"Happy birthday, Sally," Ellen said for about the tenth time that day.

Sally laughed and raised her glass as a thank you just as a sleepy-eyed Harper walked towards them. Liz and Connor were only a few steps behind her. Unusual for a nearly three-year-old to want a sleep during the day, Connor and a pregnant Liz, along with Harper, were still suffering from jetlag. Their arrival in Australia barely forty-eight hours ago necessitated a phenomenal effort to get to Richmond in time for the community's celebrations that morning. No wonder they were dead on their feet and needing a sleep to catch up.

"Come over here, Harper, and dance with me." Maddison took charge of the toddler with ease, taking hold of her hands and swinging her around.

A wave of pride washed over Sally as she sipped her cool drink. While Paul and Ellen had taken on the guardianship of the siblings, she and Ben played a huge role in their lives. Her heart burst with so much love, beyond grateful for how filled it was.

Sally sauntered over to Ben and wrapped an arm around his shoulder, giving him a hug. Leaning in so only he could hear, she said, "Have I told you lately that I love you?"

A wide grin spread over his face. "That could be the title of a song."

She groaned at his attempted humour as he cupped her cheek and drew her closer still. "I haven't had a chance to give you your birthday present yet."

Sally chuckled, knowing exactly what he meant. "Lame. So lame. Not something different for my birthday?"

Ben's sparkling green eyes danced with merriment. "What if I did have something different in mind?"

"The night is young, I guess, so we'll see, huh?"

"I guess we will," Ben added, squeezing her hand before she left his side. She spotted Nate and a pregnant Roberta walking over to the marquee. Invited guests were showering and getting dressed for the feast and beginning to drift over. There were so many she wanted to catch up with, and Ben's promise of a gift was relegated to the back of her mind. A gift wasn't important when she had so much already. If they ran out of time tonight, there was always tomorrow.

Spending time with Roberta and Liz was well overdue. As was spending time with her parents. They'd made a special effort to come out this way from Malanda and occupied one of the tents. They, like her, were proud of her past year's achievements.

Her life was one busy schedule. Being able to stop for even five minutes these days seemed impossible. Maybe it was time to do so. The hard work was done, the program was still on track and successful, and her relationship with Ben grew stronger each day. When Roberta waved her over, Sally veered towards her, swallowing back the lump of emotion caught in her throat. If she didn't slow down, life would race away from her at breakneck speed.

Near the makeshift bar, Sally gave Lucy a wave as she and her husband headed for a cool, refreshing beer. Lucy's two daughters skirted past their parents and raced towards Maddison, having already established a friendship months ago.

"Happy birthday, Sally."

Sally spun around. "Oh, hi Lucia."

"Thank you so much for the invitation. I hope it hasn't put you out."

"Absolutely not. The more the merrier." Ellen had prepared for this and erected spare tents just in case. When Liz mentioned Connor's sister, Lucia, was in the north for work, Sally insisted they bring her out to Richmond. Now living in London, the Canadian-born woman with her pale complexion and the same sea-green eyes as her brother had the prettiest complexion on skin yet to be touched by the harsh outback sun.

"Everything has been an eye-opener, that's for sure. Now I understand why Connor fell in love with Australia."

Sally loved the sound of Lucia's interesting mix of accents. "And we love having Connor here."

The bright disc of the sun now rested below the horizon, and the stars began popping out one by one. The numbers at the bar doubled in minutes as guests queued for their first drinks. With the DJ's music in the background and the crowd busiest at this spot, the level of chatter ratcheted up another notch. The party had started.

Sally leant in closer to Lucia as she spoke of her reasons for coming to Australia and the wartime mystery she was researching for her boss. For a split second, she longed for the stargazer's lounge where it would be quiet and peaceful. With the party set up on the homestead's lawn, and all the station employees invited to tonight's event, maybe she and Ben could sneak out there for a minute.

Someone brushed past her shoulder before she could conjure up any naughty thoughts. "Sorry, Sal, just going for my first beer."

"Hey, Theo." Sally grabbed Martin's mate by the arm to halt his progress. "Have you met Lucia yet?"

Theo stopped in his tracks, and his eyes opened wide comically. "Whoa! How did I miss the prettiest face here?"

Lucia burst out laughing. Theo, in his comfortable jeans, a blue button-down shirt with the sleeves rolled up to the elbows, and wearing R.M. Williams boots, was a rugged Aussie.

Dubbed the gruff recluse by Martin, Theo was an intensely private man. Freshly shaved with sun-bronzed skin, he was a sight for sore eyes for the pale Londoner.

"Lovely to meet you, Theo."

"Who are you and how did you get here?"

Sally had met Theo a few times over the past months, and this was a lot of words for a normally quiet man around strangers. Completely out of character, he did a cursory glance at Lucia.

Sally did her best to keep her laughter in check. Here was a single man being confronted by a gorgeous woman. Any hot-blooded male would do the same, even the reserved Theo.

"Lucia is Connor's sister and is in Australia for work."

"Is Connor that Canadian friend of yours?" Theo asked Sally.

"Yep, got it in one," Sally replied.

"So, why do I detect a bit of something else when you speak?" Theo asked Lucia.

"I've been in London for a few years now."

"Ah ... I see. How long did you say you were here for?"

"Not sure, to be honest. I have a project to complete with no real timeframe in place," Lucia said in a prim and proper voice.

"Perfect. Let's see how quickly I can mess up your accent with a touch of Aussie."

Lucia's eyes crinkled at their edges while Sally kept her groan in check. Lucia would learn fast that, behind the shy façade Theo showed the world, to his close friends he had a wicked sense of humour. He would lay on thick the Aussie slang, making it impossible for Lucia to understand the gentle ribbing due her way.

"Go easy on her, okay?" Sally warned.

"Me, Sal?" Theo cracked a half smile but turned back to Lucia. "I was just going to grab a beer and sit in the corner all by myself. Unless you twist my arm, that is."

Sally tutted. "Take care of her and be nice."

"Always on my best behaviour, Sal, you know me." Facing Lucia again with a proper grin, Theo asked, "Would you like a drink?"

Lucia was doing her best to hold a straight face as her lips twitched at their edges. "I would love a wine."

"Huh, wine?" Theo frowned. "We probably don't even have any. Are you up for trying an Aussie beer?"

"Oh, okay," Lucia said, a little hesitant.

Sally laughed, shooing them away. Turning around, she spotted Ben talking to Connor and sharing a beer. Scanning the growing crowd, she searched for Roberta again. Now chatting with Liz, Sally walked in their direction, confident Lucia was in good hands. If Lucia cracked the introverted shell Theo sometimes hid behind, she would find a gentle and caring man and an Aussie larrikin with a sense of humour.

Liz told her Lucia was coming off the back of a failed relationship and had happily fled London to clear her head. Sally knew Theo was still searching for the one.

Maybe an authentic outback party might be just what the doctor ordered.

***

The Nutbush ended with a cheer from the crowd, and Sally thought she'd heard the tinkling sound of a spoon clinking against a glass. With her heart pumping a little more than normal after dancing nonstop for the past half hour, she wrapped her arms loosely around Maddison and Lucy's girls as they crowded close to her side, waiting for the DJ's next choice of song. The little girls giggled and chatted while Sally took a moment to catch her breath. She turned her face towards the fresh breeze, enjoying its gentle brush over her heated skin.

When the clinking continued, she twisted around to find the source of the sound. The music completely stopped as Ben took hold of the DJ's microphone.

"What's happening, Sally?" Maddison asked with a frown.

Just then, Ben spoke. "I hope everyone is enjoying the party. Tonight, we have a birthday cake to cut, and I was hoping Sally would come up here to do the honours."

"Sally is going to blow out her candles," Maddison said to Lucy's girls, a wide grin now filling her face.

Sally inwardly groaned, hating the attention this would require. She tucked a wayward lock of hair behind her ear and looked at Ben pleadingly, hoping he'd change his mind.

"Come on, Sally, come and join us over here," Ben said into the mic, using his free hand to wave her to the makeshift stage.

When she didn't budge, the crowd chanted, "Sally! Sally! Sally!" The loudest noise was coming from Dean and the current half a dozen boys doing her program. Now, she did groan aloud as she looked across at the ragamuffin bunch.

Dean came out to the old homestead once or twice for every new set of boys and quickly became their favourite. The way he interacted with them was a unique gift. A powerful one. He was another special human in her life and now was not the time for her to shy away.

Forcing her legs to move, she walked from where they'd been dancing on the lawn to where Ben waited. Connor and Nate shifted a small table, placing it in front of where the DJ was set up, then Ellen and Flora placed the birthday cake in the centre.

Ben gave her a wink as she sidled up beside him, allowing him to sling an arm around her shoulder and draw her close.

"Ladies and gentlemen, we have one very special lady here. Not only is she beautiful, inside and out, but she's also hardworking as all heck, with her heart in the right place."

A wave of cheers and applause erupted from the guests.

Ben handed her a beautiful old knife with a mother-of-pearl handle. She gripped its smooth surface, which fit perfectly in her palm. Ellen lit the sparklers on top of the cake, and when they burst into light, Sally cut the cake to a hearty chorus of Happy Birthday, always conscious of Ben behind her with his hand on her waist. Her anchor point in all this craziness.

"Would you like to say something?" Ben asked when the singing ended and a hush fell over the crowd.

*Not really.* Public speaking wasn't her forte, but she took the mic from Ben as he left a sweet kiss on her cheek.

"Happy birthday, Sal," he whispered. "You've got this."

Overwhelmed by a rush of intense emotion, Sally's eyes filled with tears, threatening to spill over and stream down her face. How had she got here? There was so much to be thankful for. She swallowed and tried to gather her thoughts. Something rubbed against her ankle, and she looked down. *Oh, Moby.* What was he doing here in amongst all the noise and action? Moby looked up at her with his inquisitive eyes, meowing once before scampering off. Like he'd been sent to boost her confidence, even though he knew very well she'd rather be curled up on the sofa with him tucked under her arm.

She looked back up and faced her friends and family, swallowing once more for good measure. "Ah, thanks, everyone. Thank you for the birthday wishes and for sharing this amazing weekend with us."

A few whistles floated through the air as Ben squeezed her waist again.

"I just want to add how thankful I am that I clumsily stumbled over Penny." Ben snorted behind her, and at the same time, the guests gave another burst of laughter. "Yes, she's the other woman I have to share Ben with, but that's okay." More laughter filled the night air.

"But seriously, Penny is the star of this show. I can't believe how much my life has changed since meeting her. Even if I had to eat dirt to do so."

Those gathered chuckled some more, and Sally was warming up to what she wanted to express.

"I have a feeling the Richmond you know of today will change soon, and I hope it's a positive thing. I'm pretty chuffed that I played a small role and that Penny's presence will continue to give and give some more. She'll be the giving star of this community, even if it's taken her a few million years to get around to it."

Another round of applause and wolf whistles.

"Thank you all again, and I hope you're having fun tonight. Now, before I forget, a big thank you to Ellen, Paul and Flora who have worked nonstop for days to put together this party."

Another round of clapping and whistles as Sally twisted around and passed the mic back to Ben.

"Seriously, Sal, you rock," Ben said into her ear as he took back the mic. A chuffed smile filled her face. Yeah, she did. With that thought, she pinched a square of chocolate off the top of the cake and put it in her mouth. *Hmm.* Sucking on the delicious dark chocolate, she moved aside for Ben to join her.

"Okay, everyone, there's more for me to say. Sorry, but yeah, I want to thank everyone again for making the effort to come this weekend." Ben waited a beat until the chatter died down again. "There's one thing left to do. I know the day is nearly done, but I promised Sally a special birthday present. Of course, this good woman had her head in all the wrong places when I told her this. Made a lot of assumptions about what her present was going to be."

Sally choked on a laugh and turned to face Ben with her mouth wide open. There were wolf whistles from the men and more laughter and cheering from the rest of the crowd. Ben snuck in a kiss and made the most of her dropped jaw by darting inside with his tongue before drawing back with an embarrassed chuckle.

Oh, boy, he would pay—dearly—despite the shiver of delight over her coolish skin. Yep, later that night, or early the next morning, she would demand many things from him.

"Okay, okay, everyone, do you think Sally should get the gift now and open it?"

As Sally expected, the crowd was adamant she received it and opened it now. Ben pulled a rectangle box from behind his back and gave it to her. The box was about the length of a school ruler. Narrow but tall.

Ben passed the mic to the DJ while he wrapped his arms around Sally from behind and whispered in her ear. "Time to open it, Sal."

Her hands shook. They rarely gave gifts to each other. As far as Sally was concerned, her life with Ben was a gift every day. One she never took for granted. But she was curious to know what Ben had bought her.

Under the bright, colourful wrapping was a white cardboard box. This encouraged oohs and aahs from the onlookers. Funny how the crowd could whip up so much excitement for a plain cardboard box. She played along with the game and opened the top of the box. Inside, nestled in plastic bubble wrap, was a package, which she carefully pulled out. Removing the bubble wrap, she uncovered a stainless-steel Yeti mug, complete with her name engraved on the side. One she couldn't break if dropped.

She snorted a laugh as Ben took back the mic. "Does anyone else have to work extra hours just to cover the cost of broken mugs?"

Heat raced up the back of her neck, but thank goodness it was too dark to see anything. They were too busy laughing and cheering to notice. She turned to Ben and received a mischievous smile in return. Okay, so she'd broken a few mugs in her time.

"Uh oh, I think I might be in trouble," Ben said into the mic with a chuckle.

More laughter and even Sally couldn't hold back a giggle.

"Did you know we met over a broken mug?" Ben told the crowd.

Oh, he was good. He had the guests wound up perfectly.

"Should we get her to unscrew the lid and check if there's something inside?"

As expected, the guests agreed with everything Ben said with cheering and banter. Ben took the unbreakable mug from her, left a soft kiss on her forehead, and unscrewed the top of the mug.

Ben pulled out a smaller box. Much smaller. Ring-sized small, and the guests cottoned on quickly. Way faster than her slow brain. Ben's hand trembled as he tucked the mic under his arm and opened the box.

Oh, good Lord, this was the last thing she expected tonight. She touched a hand to her heart when Ben swallowed nervously. This was a big deal for him. He'd done this once before and had paid a hefty price for years. He was no longer laughing or smiling. Neither was she. Her heart raced crazily inside her chest.

He managed to juggle the small box and the mic, which he'd rescued from under his arm. "Family and friends, give me a minute while I get down on one knee. And you'll have to keep the noise down so I can hear what Sally says. Her answer is very important."

The air buzzed for a moment before the guests quietened down. Sally's knees trembled. Ben was such a private person; coming out like this was way out of his comfort zone. No wonder he'd been in a funny mood all day. All week. She'd put it down to the stress of organising this momentous day. She was totally unprepared until she looked down at Ben on one knee and witnessed the strength of his love staring back at her.

"Sally, you are my rock. My everything."

She gulped, incapable of words even if she wanted to say something.

"You are the reason for my existence, and I want you in my life forever. Will you—" Ben hesitated for a fraction of time, his Adam's apple bobbing as though nerves froze his words. Her heart melted. "Will you marry me?"

Any attempt for the guests to remain quiet disappeared into the ether as more wolf whistles echoed into the night, interspersed with other voices insisting they hush and remain quiet.

A bubble of joy built up momentum, and at the same time, a coolish breeze whispered around them, leaves dropping and scattering like confetti over the guests and lawn. One leaf landed on Ben's hair. She reached across to remove it, but the breeze gently lifted it, sending it on its way. Tears trickled down her cheeks as she managed a nod. When Ben placed the mic near her with a slightly shaking hand, it was the prompt she needed to answer.

"Yes!" She stumbled over the word, not sure where she was for a moment as dizziness enveloped her. Until she found herself in Ben's secure hold, his mouth against hers in a hot, searing kiss, the rowdy group of friends and family now making enough noise to alert the neighbours four hundred kilometres away.

She relaxed against him. Her pillar of strength.

Forgot she was at her birthday party with so many people surrounding them.

She kissed Ben back in a way that they should probably find a room, ignoring the cheering and noise.

She mentally shrugged.

It was where she was staying.

Forever.

# AUTHOR NOTE

Thank you for being here again and choosing to read the third book in The Sway of The Stars series. Look out for my fourth book in the series, which will be Lucia and Theo's story.

Think cute, sun-bronzed Aussie and headstrong, pale Canadian (now living in London) who's scared of spiders. Totally unsuited, right? Wrong! Find out how they find their HEA and solve a wartime mystery that Lucia is sent Down Under to investigate.

But back to this book and why I chose to write a story about Richmond and dinosaurs. For those who know me, I have owned a business for many years. Through this business, I've met many interesting people. There was one customer whose story struck a chord with me. He was a young man (probably early thirties) who told me he travelled between Malanda and Richmond because he loved to dig for dinosaur fossils.

This intrigued me, and I began to dig (sorry about the pun) for more information about why a person would spend so much of their spare time doing this. And boy, was this an eye-opener rich in history and intrigue. Who doesn't love a real dinosaur discovery story?

Richmond is one of three outback towns in Western Queensland which makes up Australia's Dinosaur Trail, the other two being Winton and Hughenden. Each town has its own unique dinosaur stories to tell, and for this book, I chose to tell a story against Richmond's background and history.

What's fascinating is that my story aligns with what did happen in Richmond. Back in 1989, an outback grazier (Rob Ievers) and his brothers found the fossil of a prehistoric marine reptile. Little did they know how this discovery would change the course of their lives and make such a huge difference to the township of Richmond. This dinosaur fossil discovered (and named Penny) was a very special polycotylid (family of plesiosaurs). Once unearthed, she was one of the most complete vertebrate fossils in the world.

Once this came to light, Rob realised there was a tourist industry opportunity right there in Richmond. Why keep it in the big cities when it could be displayed in the town where it was discovered? Big dreams for sure because I don't doubt that the Queensland Museum wanted it just as bad.

It would take a lot of hard work. It didn't happen overnight, but it did happen.

It would take until 1995 before a museum would be opened and operational in Richmond, with plenty of hurdles for Rob to clear since this life-changing discovery. Together with the town's mayor, they shared many flights to Brisbane, arguing for the funds to build a museum to keep Penny in Richmond.

If you search Kronosaurus Korner, this modern-day museum built in the heart of Richmond is a testament to a vibrant community, the passion of this one man and a community that supported him all the way.

And what an achievement. Visitors are always surprised to learn that the museum displays real fossils rather than casts. And yes, Penny sits on display, showcased in all her glory. I know. I've seen her. This museum also boasts a full-time curator, doing prep work to the same standard as the Queensland Museum in the state's capital.

See! Anything can be done and achieved in rural and remote outback communities anywhere in Australia, and Richmond is proof.

But that isn't all. Another local discovery by the Ievers family on their Richmond property turned out to be even more valuable and scientifically important. This next fossil discovery was first classified as Minmi paravertebral. But thanks to a very clever palaeontologist, Lucy Leahey, it has since been renamed Kunbarrasaurus ieversi and is one of the most complete ankylosaurs ever found anywhere on the planet. Doesn't get any more special than that in my books. For this amazing fossil, the Queensland Museum won out, and they got to keep it, but a replica is kept on display in Richmond.

Because of all this and the drive and passion of this one man, Richmond is no longer the same place it was before the completion of the museum. No longer do outback travellers pull up at the service station to fuel up, grab something to eat and keep going because once upon a time, there was no reason to stop.

Now, they stay for a few nights or even a week. Families come with children and dig for their own fossils at the free fossicking sites set up by the council. They bring business to the community, like the caravan park, shops and cafés, whilst enjoying Lake Fred Tritton and its facilities—Richmond's very own outback oasis constructed by a very proactive council. Kudos to them all.

And lastly, there are a few people to thank. A big thank you to Kev Petersen of Kronosaurus Korner. He provided me with information when I asked, and he even sent books and material to me in the post. Lucy Leahey, a very clever palaeontologist, for answering my many questions about things I knew nothing about. I take full responsibility for any mistakes I've made. The dinosaur language is very complex, and I hope I have all the names right.

I also want to thank Lee-Anne for answering all my medical questions and the side effects of rat bait poisoning. Even while we waited for our local police officer to leave my store so we could continue the discussion. Lots of laughs that day!

And thank you to Deb, who answered all my guardianship questions. A remarkable woman nurturing many young lives in her own special way.

And lastly, thank you, my readers, for coming back for more and supporting this Australian author.

Frances.

# ALSO BY FRANCES DALL'ALBA

The **Australian at Heart Series** tells the stories of four interconnected siblings.

### <u>Little Blue Box – Book 1</u>

Regrets, lies, and earth-shattering secrets. When Ella learns the identity of her biological father, nothing will stand in her way. Not even his power. When things don't go to plan, can one little blue box put Ella and Zane back on the same path?  This second chance contemporary romance is filled with suspense, emotion and a life-changing sizzling romance.

### <u>The Stone In The Road – Book 2</u>

Emotional, passionate and heart-wrenching. This suspense-filled captivating romance will have you dancing in the rain and smiling through your tears. Set in tropical northern Australia, we don't always get to choose our path.

### The Silk Scarf – Book 3

An unravelling silken scarf ... mysterious gold ... a breathtaking romance.
An emotional and unforgettable contemporary romance set in Australia.

### Rustic Denim Love – Book 4

Forgotten secrets ...  blazing fires ... burning love.
She's busy and diligent, doing the best she can to save her crumbling family.
He's funny and witty, with a solution for every problem.
This one may just beat him.

Link to read more and BUY.

**https://francesdallalba.wixsite.com/francesdallalba/australianathe
artseries**

**Sway of The Stars Series** will share the stories of a group of friends.

### The Shooting Star – Book 1

Hidden treasures ... broken spirits ... tangled love. A modern-day treasure hunt where hidden treasures will tangle their love and break their spirits. Duty or love, or can they have both?

### The Glittering Star –Book 2

Shimmering waters ... towering giants ... buried mysteries. She's the no filters chick. Funny, full of life and always ready for a good laugh. Until her mother drops a bombshell. He's the environmental warrior. Passionate, driven and determined to save the world. Burnt once before, he's moving on and doing things his way. So how did they end up hand cuffed together on day one?

### The Giving Star – Book 3

Endless roads ... timeless discoveries ... unbreakable love. She's packed up her life ready for change, with one regret still hanging over her head. He's working his way back from hell, adamant he's never going there again. But one stumble, one discovery, and one hotbed of attraction ... and the entire game plan changes.

<u>**The Priceless Star – Book 4**</u>
Forgotten treasures ... a perilous ransom ... shattered hopes
She's chasing answers long buried since the war.
He's content with a steady working life. Until he's not...
Sent to Far North Queensland to research a wartime mystery, Lucia
Levorico escapes her privileged life and finds unexpected passion with
reserved local, Theo Mather, under an outback sky – until a sudden
goodbye and a devastating worksite tragedy tear them apart. When a
ruthless ransom plot targets Lucia's wealth, their only reprieve will come
from sharing the unravelling of a wartime mystery and its priceless treasure.
Unless they're willing to fight for what they have.


<u>Link to read more and BUY</u>.
**https://francesdallalba.wixsite.com/francesdallalba/swayof the
stars**

**Eight Seconds**, is a standalone story inspired by Australia's first female open bullrider. She pushed past the barriers and succeeded in a male dominated sport, creating a new legend showcased in two Australian halls of fame.

**Triumph, hardship, true grit … and one crazy dream.**
**An inspirational story about one woman, with one dream, and one almighty driving passion.**

Link to read more and BUY.
**https://francesdallalba.wixsite.com/francesdallalba/eightseconds**

**Jack& Eva,** is a standalone contemporary romance set in tropical North Queensland. It showcases our unique and adorable Lumholtz tree kangaroo and the valuable work done by Dr Karen Coombes in her care and continued research of them.

**Broody meets bubbly … and a bunch of cuddly tree kangaroos.**
When the tempest blows over, will Jack and Eva be able to find a way forward, or are they destined for a train wreck with a bunch of furry animals caught up in the middle?
Fall in love with our adorable tree kangaroo while reading an emotional and passionate contemporary romance set in Australia.
Link to read more and BUY.
**https://francesdallalba.wixsite.com/francesdallalba/jackandeva**

# ABOUT THE AUTHOR

As a contemporary romance author, Frances loves nothing more than losing herself in a good romance. She's all about helping you forget the housework, or the bus to work you're going to miss, if you don't put the book down now!

She's devoted to giving her readers an emotional, passionate, possibly some ugly-cry, fairly steamy love story, that'll melt your heart and have you fighting for the happy ending right until the end.

Frances sets her books in North Queensland. She makes no excuses if some of her settings include amazing lakes and waterfalls, stunning views from tops of mountains, spectacular outback scenes, or crystal-clear creeks shadowed by tropical rainforest.

When she isn't writing, Frances is climbing mountains, searching for waterfalls, and swimming across lakes. She loves to exercise, would prefer it if someone else cooked dinner every night, and never notices dust on the furniture.

She lives with her husband in tropical Far North Queensland, Australia, and uses her great baking skills to tempt her family to visit home as often as they can.

### Say hello to Frances

Visit her website https://francesdallalba.wixsite.com/francesdallalba and subscribe to her newsletter. It will keep you up-to-date with everything happening in her author world.

Follow Frances on Facebook, Instagram, Bookbub, TikTok, and Goodreads. To do so, click on this link: https://linktr.ee/francesdallalba

### Still have a question?

Ask her at https://francesdallalba.wixsite.com/francesdallalba/contact

<u>**Leave a Review**</u>

Did you enjoy this book? The best favour you can do for an author is to leave a **review**. If you'd like to leave a review, go to your place of on-line purchase of the book, or search for the book on **Goodreads** and leave a review. Thank you.